DEBBY AT MR. WOOD'S.

"'My father is a Tory, and a soldier in the British army,' said Deborah."

See page 325.

A LITTLE MAID
of CONCORD TOWN

A ROMANCE of the AMERICAN REVOLUTION ∴ ∴ ∴ ∴ 1775

Lothrop, Harriet ❨❩

By
MARGARET SIDNEY
AUTHOR OF "THE JUDGES'
CAVE," ❧ "FIVE LITTLE
PEPPERS," ETC.

Illustrated by
FRANK T. MERRILL

BOSTON
LOTHROP PUBLISHING COMPANY

Margaret Sidney was the pseudonym of American writer Harriett Mulford Stone Lothrop (June 22, 1844 – August 2, 1924). In addition to writing popular children's stories, she ran her husband Daniel Lothrop's publishing company after his death. After they bought The Wayside country house, they worked hard to make it a center of literary life.

BIOGRAPHY:Harriett Mulford Stone was born in New Haven, Connecticut, in 1844. The daughter of New Haven architect, Sidney Mason Stone, she was "brought up in an atmosphere of culture and learning enhanced by free access to her father's large library."From early girlhood she "delighted in creating imaginary people". She was educated at seminaries near her home and graduated from Miss Dutton's School at Grove Hall in New Haven in 1862. While a student there "she displayed such mental alertness, combined with retentive memory and a great imaginative and poetic talent that she was marked for future success." She traveled extensively in the United States, and began creating literary compositions early in life.According to a Hartford Courant article, "she wrote constantly but destroyed manuscripts".

She published nothing until 1878 when, at the age of 34, she began sending short stories to Wide Awake, a children's magazine in Boston. Two of her stories, "Polly Pepper's Chicken Pie" and "Phronsie Pepper's New Shoes", proved to be very popular with readers. Ella Farman, the editor of the magazine, requested that Stone write more.

The success of Harriett's short stories prompted her to write Five Little Peppers and its 11 sequels. The original novel was first published in 1881, the year that Stone married Daniel Lothrop. Daniel had founded the D. Lothrop Company of Boston, who published Harriett's books under her pseudonym, Margaret Sidney.

Harriett and Daniel may have both had an interest in history and in famous authors. In 1883, they purchased the house in which both Louisa May Alcott and Nathaniel Hawthorne had lived. Nicknamed The Wayside, the house is located in Concord, Massachusetts. The year after Harriett and Daniel moved into the house, Harriett gave birth to their daughter, Margaret, at the age of 40.

Daniel Lothrop died on Friday, March 18, 1892, when Harriett was 48 and their daughter was just 9 years old. There was a gap in the release of the Five Little Peppers books from 1892 to 1897, while Harriett continued to run the publishing company Daniel founded. Eventually, she sold the company, which later became Lothrop, Lee & Shepard Co. It continued to publish Harriett's books under the name Margaret Sidney when Harriett resumed writing the Five Little Peppers series.

THIS VOLUME IS DEDICATED BY
THE AUTHOR.
PREFACE.

SOME dozen years or so ago, the author of this volume planned to write an historic story of Old Concord, dealing with the months and the years prior to 1775, to show the natural sequence of events that gave to the old town her opportunity " to fire the shot heard round the world," and made her so large a factor in shaping the destiny of the American Republic.

It was no mere chance that set apart the Old North Bridge at Concord as the arena where was enacted the opening scene of that struggle for independence that made the Colonies a free nation. Old Concord had long been preparing for what God in his providence was preparing for her; and the brilliant episode on the igth of April, 1775, was but the natural result of that long and faithful preliminary work. Marvellous indeed in the eyes turned backward to that April morning, is the outcome! In the words of the late President Dwight, " In 3

other circumstances, the expedition to Concord, and the interest which ensued, would have been merely little tales of wonder and of woe, chiefly recited by the parents of the neighborhood to their circles at the fireside, commanding a momentary attention of childhood, and calling forth the tear of sorrow from the eyes of these who were intimately connected with the sufferers. Now the same events preface the history of a nation and the beginning of an empire, and are themes of disquisition and astonishment to the civilized world. From the plains of Concord will henceforth be dated a change in human affairs, an alteration in the balance of human power, and a new direction to the course of human improvement. Man, from the events which have occurred here, will, in some respects, assume a new character, and experience, in some respects, a new destiny."

The fact and fiction of the story contained in these pages can be easily separated in the mind of the reader, and yet preserve a harmony of action. Deborah Parlin, the Little Maid of Concord Town, is purely a work of imagination, together with the setting of the picture of the Parlin family in the little cottage on the Lexington Road, whose last tenant was Ephriam W. Bull, the originator of the Concord grape.

Hawthorne's weird tale, the last that was traced by his pen, located Septimius Felton and Aunt Keziah in " the two-story house, gabled before, crowded upon by the hill beyond," now known as Wayside ; and, in deference to that exquisitely fanciful creation, they still wander in and out the pages of this story. Ab-ner Butterfield and good Mother Butterfield are summoned from the realm of fancy to serve the will of the author ; and it is unnecessary to add that Jim Haskins is a figment evolved for like purpose.

Bernard Thornton, the young British officer, belongs to the like shadowy realm, summoned hence at the same behest, to bear his part and lot in the events narrated in these pages.

The picturesque and dramatic episode in the life of beautiful Meliscent Barrett so attracted the author these dozen years ago, that she was impelled to use it as a central force around which to adjust her story. Tradition and fireside tales are, after all, much of the warp and woof of our Colonial and Revolutionary history; such annals inspire and lead, perchance, swifter to the true spirit of those epochs, than the labored art of the historian.

The slow building of this volume, from year to year, often laid aside for less congenial pen-tasks, yet never out of mind, has weighted the author with a debt of

gratitude impossible to individually acknowledge or repay. For numberless courtesies that greatly assisted the development of this book, for valuable information not to be obtained in the ordinary channels, or that proved and strengthened that already found, the author would here tender her most grateful and appreciative acknowledgment to the citizens of the old town, who have thus aided her in her arduous but most congenial task. A list of books on another page is cited as partial authority for the historic basis of this volume, which has aimed in every line to be true to the letter and the spirit of the period of which it treats.

WAYSIDE,

Concord, Massachusetts, May, 1898.

CONTENTS.

CONTENTS.
CHAPTER
PAGE

A LITTLE MAID OF CONCORD TOWN.

THE LITTLE MAID.

DEBBY ran up the Ridge as fast as her clumsy shoes, and the pail of milk with the loaf of brown bread in a clean towel which she was carrying, would allow. At last she brought up panting, as she stumbled to the summit, and paused to take breath.

It was a goodly scene, and one well calculated to soothe the troubled breast. Below her, some fifty or more feet, lay the Old B.iy Road. Across this winding thoroughfare was the Town Meadow, through which ran Mill Brook, purling noisily under Fox Bridge before it lost itself in its rush across the big open meadow. Off in the distance, with its guardian slope of hill-crowned forest, shimmered Walden, whose shining surface had reflected the dusky faces of the first dwellers ip this happy valley before the white men came.

But Debby was far from being at rest in any portion 9
A LITTLE MAW OF CONCORD TOWN.
of her healthy young body. All her soul was filled with bitterness. She set down her milk-pail, and deposited the loaf of bread upon its cover, and stretched her arms restfully. " I wish the Reg'lars would come this blessed minute ! " she exclaimed with sudden impulse, blind to the beauty of the scene before her, " and have done with all this watching and waiting for them. Let King George do his worst; he will see what we are made of."

She sent a swift glance on every hand, as if the landscape were distorted with redcoats flashing behind every bush, and torturing the morning glow with their detested brilliancy of coloring. " Oh, I hate old King George!" and she stamped her foot on the pine-needles.

A crackling in the bushes struck upon her ear. Debby turned with the swiftness of a young fawn, and peered in its direction, to meet a sharp pair of eyes fastened upon her round face, the person to whom they belonged halting leisurely for that purpose just within the nearest thicket. It was an old woman of most unpleasant aspect, of a dark yellow face; and as her head was tied up in a handkerchief, and her body bent as if with many grips and twitchings of rheumatism, she gave more the appearance of an anciert witch, than a good New England resident of the old

town. And Debby would have given preference to a meeting with the witch.

"O Miss Keziah!" she exclaimed, as she backed off, and began to pick up her pail and bread, " how do you do to-day, and how is Mr. Felton ?" for she thought it incumbent on her to say something pleasant to this old personage whom, notwithstanding she was her nearest neighbor, she would never choose to meet in a wood alone.

Miss Keziah cackled and showed her toothless gums.

"Septimus is well enough," she said, her voice not lacking a tone of contempt. "As long as he can sit with his nose in a book, he will do from day's in to day's out. But well, well, as he is to be a minister, we must let him be, and thank the Lord it's no worse. But hark ye, my pretty, don't deceive me with your fine speeches and neighboring ways. T heard what you said about our good king. Don't think an old woman's ears are heavy. Besides, the birds will tell it; the birds will tell it." She waved her long, skinny hands, much soiled with digging in the ground after her favorite roots and herbs. "And every leaf will whisper it." Here her voice sank to a sepulchral whisper that sent "the creeps" down Debby's back. "Keep your tongue safe locked in your head, child, where every woman's should be, for the times are

12 A LITTLE MAID OF CONCOKD TOWN.

troublous, an' may the Lord bless us all!" She advanced with a long step and a hitch out of her thicket, and laid her skinny hand on Debby's young arm.

The young girl trembled under the piercing gaze from the black eyes. She strove to shake herself free; but instead she stood still, partly from her fear of rousing the anger which she felt always smouldered near the surface of her neighbor's face, and partly because a certain fascination, like that holding the ancient mariner, overcame her against her will.

But if her feet tarried, it was no time to be halting with her principles; so she burst out, "But I do hate old King George, Miss Keziah, and I should be a sinful girl not to say the truth. Oh ! he's a bad, wicked man, I can't help it if he is a king, torturing us poor people and starving us, and sending soldiers to fight us. You know he's bad; and you ought to hate him too!" she brought up, her blue eyes blazing.

"Tush, tush, child!" commanded the old woman, not relinquishing her hold, but gazing warily around the wood. "Never let a word escape you like that again. Why, the Reg'lars would burn your house about your ears, an' kill you. Oh, lack-a-day!" Here her old arm dropped powerless to her side. "An' that's to be our fate — all of us, mayhap."

"No, it isn't, Miss Keziah," cried Debby stoutly, her heart panting under her blue kerchief; "I tell you we'll fight 'em to skin and bone." She clinched her small brown hands tightly, and her breath came hard, "And we'll make those redcoats run. Every single one in Old Concord will fight, and we'll show them we're not afraid of 'em a bit."

The old woman hitched back against a tree, and cackled contemptuously.

Pretty child," she exclaimed, in a gust between her fits of laughter. "Oh, what a paltry thing for safety we have! You'll see, when the Reg'lars really come ! Ah, like an infant in the mother's arms you babble and coo of safety, when the skies are red with blood that is to drop on this path before us like dew from the wings of the morning;" and she pointed to the road beneath.

Debby shivered under her homespun gown like an aspen leaf; but she spoke up stoutly,—

"And there will be two kinds of blood to run, Miss Keziah ; and the old Britishers will get the worst of it." And here the fire within made her cry out, as she hastily seized her pail and bread-loaf, "And I despise people who talk as you do; you're most as bad as Tory Lee ! "

With this parting shot she skimmed along the pla-

teau, across the top of the Ridge, until she struck the eater-cornered trail that straggled down its western slope.

Clear across the Great Field she plunged, regardless of distance and of her burden, until she was over on the old Bedford Road. Running down a good piece, she came upon a little red farmhouse, with its lean-to and its barn all under one roof. Into the kitchen in the ell she ran on indignant young feet, and set down the pail and bread-loaf on the pine table.

" Mother sent these," she said breathlessly.

"Why, Debby!" exclaimed her aunt Sophia, "what's the matter, child? Dear, dear, you are clean tired out ! And how is Sister Ruhama? " all in one breath.

"I'm not tired," said Debby shortly, and pushing back her sunbonnet from her hot face; "but I've had things said to me that are hard to bear;" withholding through habit all unpleasant explanations from Aunt Sophia, whose feeble frame was slowly but surely succumbing to the dread New England disease, consumption. "Where are the boys? " she asked hastily.

" Had things hard to bear said to you ? And what are they, Debby, child?" cried Aunt Sophia, her thin lips twitching at the prospect of hearing news, even if unpleasant.

"Oh, dreadful things!" exclaimed Debby. Then she stopped abruptly. " Where are the boys, aunt ? " she asked again, quickly.

"I don't know. Simon went out after bringing in the wood, and I doubt not that Jabez is with him busy about something. Sit down an' rest yourself, Debby, an' tell me how things are at home."

But Debby had rushed from the kitchen, and was now skirting the old barn and woodshed. There, behind the woodpile, she heard a noise that suggested "boy;" and she speedily stood before Simon, whose sheepish face proclaimed immediately that he had hidden something behind his back.

"Oh! it's you, Debby," he cried in great relief, bringing it out before him. He was engaged in cleaning an old musket, when her footsteps startled him. "I thought it was mother, an' I don't want to scare her."

"You're getting ready to fight, Simon," cried Debby, with sparkling eyes, all her evil time with Miss Keziah flown to the winds. She seated herself on a projection of the woodpile, and cast her sunbonnet away from her, while she gave all her attention to the implement of warfare in his hand. " Oh, how perfectly splendid!" she cried.

"Yes, I am," said Simon with energy, and bobbing his tow head. "An' I don't care how soon it comes,

either, after I get this old gun ready. And Jabez is up in the barn-loft cleaning his."

"Has Jabez got a musket too?" cried Debby. "Where did you get 'em, Simon?" her mouth watering, so to speak, at the sight. "O Simon, if I were only a boy! Do let me take it in my hand just a minute," she pleaded.

"Well, you ain't a boy," replied Simon, holding fast to the musket; " an' you never will be," he added, with that matter-of-fact acceptance of the honor with which men at that period carried their leadership. Then, scrubbing away for dear life on the gun-stock with a bit of old flannel, and oblivious to her question, "There's goin' to be an awful time, Debby; i'ts a-comin', sure," he declared, setting his teeth together hard.

" I know it," said Debby, folding her hands in her lap, " and that's what I want to help for. O Simon! don't you suppose they'll let us girls do something ?" she gazed at him imploringly.

" Not to fight," said Simon, straightening up. " Old Concord won't be pushed so hard that she'll let the women and girls fight. We'll take care of you all, Debby."

"I don't want to be taken care of," said Debby petulantly. "I want to fight the Britishers and old

King George myself. Oh! it's mean I'm nothing but a girl." She fell back on her old plaint.

" There's to be a town meetin' to-day, I s'pose you know, Debby," said Simon, with the air of imparting fresh news.

" Don't I know it," cried Debby with scorn. To tell the truth, very little escaped her, a fact which her cousin well understood.

"Uncle John is goin' to town meetin', of course ? "

"Of course," assented Debby; "he was up to Mr. Wood's last night talking it all over."

" It's time for us to strike if we're ever goin' to stand up for ourselves," exclaimed Simon with great energy, bringing the butt of the musket down on the ground with a crack. Then he brought it up to his shoulder, and sighted along its barrel, in a way to make Debby's eyes sparkle with envy.

" I should think our country would want the girls to do something for her," she exploded, with very red cheeks.

"Well, she doesn't," said Simon coolly; "for we men can take care of you."

"You are always talking of our being taken care of, Simon," cried Debby, getting off from the woodpile in irritation; "that isn't in the least what I want. I just long to do something myself for my own country, and

18 A LITTLE MAID OF CONCORD TOWN.

to fight for her. It isn't fair to give it all to the boys. Our country belongs to everybody, the women and girls, the same as to the men."

Simon, not being able to controvert this, wisely kept silence, and took satisfaction in flourishing the musket, and putting her through her paces, so to speak, as if she had been a thoroughbred.

"And the time will come when it'll be nice and respectable for us to help," cried Debby excitedly, "just the same's if we were boys ; so there! I'm going to fight for my country the very first chance I get"

"Well, you'd be drummed out of service," said Simon derisively, "as soon as you got in. We don't have petticoats in Old Concord Town for soldiers, I can tell you, Debby Parlin."

Debby looked down at her homespun gown, and kicked it in disdain. "Well, I'm going up to Perces Wood's," she said at length, thinking it wise to change the subject; " I've got to spin with her. So I shall hear all about town meeting and everything else before you do, Mr. Simon."

The color came into Simon's cheek like a girl's. "Say, Debby," he said, as she turned to go, "if you see Joe Burrell up there, you just see how the land lays, about Perces, you know. He'll most likely be

nosin' round there to-day, pretendin' he wants to know about-town meetin'."

"I don't know as I will," she called back with a tantalizing laugh. Her sunbonnet had slipped to her shoulder, disclosing a round face with a pink flush overspreading either cheek, where the dimples played with the light and shade of her face. " I get no satisfaction out of you at all this morning, Simon. You won't even tell me where you got your guns. You're a very poor cousin to have; and yet you want me to do all sorts of things for you," she added, laughing at the sight of his face.

" Oh! didn't I tell you ?" exclaimed Simon. " Well, that's because I was so full of business getting the old thing ready. I'd just as lieves you knew, Debby. Abner Butterfield got 'em for us."

"Abner Butterfield!" exclaimed Debby, unable to control her start of surprise. " Goodness me, Simon, what are you talking of ? The idea of Abner Butter-field having anything to do with guns and fighting. Why, he wouldn't know nor care if there were to be ten thousand wars; he'd stand stock still and not know till it was all over," she ended with a short laugh.

"That's where you wrong Abner," declared Simon stoutly, and pausing a minute to regard her with

disfavor; "because he's quiet like, an" doesn't talk about how he feels, folks don't see him as he is. But you ought to know better, Debby Parlin."

" And why ought I to know, pray tell, Mr. Simon Brown ? " cried Debby airily, and hopping lightly from one foot to the other as if she quite disdained the whole subject. " I'm sure I don't Anow nor care how Abner Butterfield feels."

"Because Abner lets you see how he feels, an' you know just what stuff he's made of," answered Simon, ignoring her airs.

" I don't know as I know much more about Abner Butterfield's feelings than you do," retorted Debby with a fling to her checked apron. " I'm sure I don't see why I should; for I'm tired to death hearing you talk of him, and I never listen if I can help it."

Simon brought his thin lips together firmly, and turned back to his gun-cleaning with redoubled vigor. " And I haven't any patience with you tor everlastingly bringing him up," said Debby, shaking the light waves of hair away from her brow, " none at all, Simon."

Simon kept a cold shoulder for her, and even began to whistle the last bar of " The White Cockade. 1 '

" You always make me run, Simon," said Debby, showing not the smallest disposition to stir from her tracks, "whenever you begin to talk of him."

Simon, an imaginary fifer, tooted merrily on, without the smallest heed to his cousin.

"And 'tisn't because I take the slightest interest in what Abner Butterfield does," went on Debby, drawing near in order to get her words in between the martial strains — "oh, dear me, no ! He does vex me so, Simon; he's so big and slow. But I'm so astonished that he'd do anything like the rest of us Concord folks, to show that we can't be ground down to the dust at the bidding of a foolish and wicked old king."

"When the time comes, Debby Parlin," said Simon, unpuckering his mouth to utter the words forcibly, " Abner Butterfield'll fight as well an' as long as anybody else. You'll find that out. He won't give up till he's dead."

Debby shivered dreadfully under her blue homespun; but she gave a toss to her pretty head, and said lightly, " Fiddle-strings, Simon. Oh, dear me ! — well, I mustn't stay any longer. I ought to be up at Mrs. Wood's this blessed minute. The idea of wasting my time over Abner

Butterfield I"

"I don't see why you don't start," observed Simon* looking at her. " Well, remember what I said about Perces an' Joe Burrell, Debby."

"And you remember all I've said about Abner But-

22 A LITTLE MAID OF CONCORD TOWN.

terfield," said Debby, making a great show of haste as she turned off. "The idea of your keeping me here talking of nothing but Abner Butterfield."

Suddenly she turned and came back with one of those swift characteristic movements that to one who knew Debby, were never surprising.

"Simon," she said, and the color died out of her cheek, "you're right. There's an awful time a-coming."

Simon nodded, his lips drawn tightly over his teeth.

" And I 'm glad of it; for it's best to get it over with," went on Debby in a low voice. "At any rate, Simon, if we girls can't fight, we can talk and pray."

"Yes," said Simon, "there's an awful lot o' prayin' been goin' on in this town." He glanced up involuntarily, as if he expected to see the supplications on the way over his head. "An' they all ain't for nothin', now, I tell you."

" Simon," said Debby, and her face grew suddenly very grave, " I b'lieve we can V be beaten. You see, God couldn't allow it very well, after getting us over here and promising to take care of us, and keeping us along till this time. So I know we shall be free and independent. Just think of it, free and independent! " She clasped her hands. " O Simon! after all we have suffered in this town, and in all the other towns, to

think of relief coming." Her blue eyes glowed with fire, and her bosom heaved.

Simon could find no words, so he silently redoubled his work on the old musket.

" It has been so long now," went on Debby. "Our one thought from morning till night has been, what shall we do—what can we do — to bring things right? " We cannot give up like slaves; we can only die. Simon, why don't you say something?" she broke off impatiently.

"Because I can't," replied Simon. "It gets too full up here, when I try to speak about it." He touched his throat with his brawny hand. "Seems if I sh'd choke."

"It's been so many years now," went on Debby mournfully, shaking the soft waves across her brow, "since I've heard nothing else. Why, I was such a little girl, Simon, that I don't remember when I didn't hear it all day long, most."

"I guess we all can say the same thing," said Simon grimly.

"I know it," said Debby, delighted to get him to talking. "Of course we've all grown up on it. And do you suppose that the talking and praying of all these years is going to be wasted, Simon?" She brought her clear eyes full to bear upon him.

24 A LITTLE MAID OF CONCORD TOWN.

"No, I don't, said Simon shortly. He had a habit when much moved, of bringing his thin lips togethei with a snap, as if to shut out superfluous words. So now he barely allowed his answer to shoot from his mouth ere he was silent once more.

"No, no, no," said Debby, with sweet cadence, yet decisively. "All the prayers are not to be wasted. Poverty and suffering," her voice sank mournfully — "O Simon! what haven't we suffered holding on to our principles ? "

Simon thrust the musket from him with a sudden gesture, and faced her. Then he picked it up again, clinching it fast.

"If you talk like that, I'll forget my principles, an' go an' fight those infernal redcoats before it's time. Do I forget her, Debby Parlin?" He pointed his other fist in the direction of the kitchen. "An' her dyin' by inches because she can't get good food to sustain her? An' how the worry to keep out o' debt killed father, an' left Jabez an' me with a load on our shoulders of interest on th' mortgage that we can't pay, an' that is eatin' us up? Remember? O God! can I ever forget ? "

He was dreadful to look at. Even his shock of tow hair seemed to erect itself in defiance as he blazed away. Debby was almost frightened to death

at the storm she had raised, and she hastened to say,—

"Well, so long as we have got such good men to take care of matters as there are in this town, I think everything will be right. We are law-abiding people, you know, Simon," she added, repeating one of the many phrases she had grown up on.

Simon's face still worked fearfully. But he returned to his work, as, knowing himself well, he could be held in check only in that way.

"And we can't be beaten if we don't run," said Debby at last, and the light returned to her eyes. "And it's something to be proud of that we've never been afraid yet, but we've said what we thought we ought to. So Concord has been heard from."

"She's always been heard from," cried Simon, with sudden fury; "and she'll be listened to, I tell you, when she speaks finally," as Debby went slowly down the road.

26 A LITTLE MAID OF CONCORD TOWN

II.

TORY LEE.

AS Debby went slowly on her way, her head drooped XjL till her soft chin nestled in the blue kerchief, giving her so little the appearance of the usually blithe maiden, that the townspeople meeting her would have turned to watch the sad little figure, had it not been that all the citizens, young as well as old, bore about them the same depressed atmosphere. The whole air seemed charged with the gloom of the present suffering and distress, and the foreboding, that yet was unlike fear, of the deeper gloom of coming events. It was as if a great crisis were approaching; and while each countenance and movement expressed this, it was dominated by a determination and high resolve, that gave to the provincial face a striking beauty of expression.

The men were gathered on the Milldam in little knots, engaged in conversation of a serious and weighty character that breathed an over-ruling excitement to thrill each new-comer. Evidently some fresh cause

for alarm had seized the village in the early morning, to judge from the scraps of talk that fell upon the ear of the chance passer-by. It was noticeable that several farmers carried muskets, and that the impulse to get the instant opinions of their fellow-townsmen was a general incitant that possessed all classes of citizens. There was the revered parson who was daily stopped in his walk through the town's centre by the earnest seeker after the latest news from Boston, or for the clerical opinion, now with a large group surrounding him. It was easy to understand by his kindling eye, the nature of the words flowing from his burning lips, and that something unusual had inspired them.

Debby raised her head from her deep dejection as she passed the group, longing to stop and listen. But for a woman or a girl to gather patriotism in this way was considered unseemly; so she went by with added bitterness in her breast at the fate that had denied her a lusty boyhood.

Occasionally a face would gleam upon her as she went along, that held something more than the determination and high resolution kept in check. Fierce and bitter would be the flash of the eye, and a suggestive handling of the musket, or the brandishing of the stout stick, while muttered words of immediate

military action caught her ear. But it was noticeable that some citizen would quietly approach such a man, and, laying a hand upon his shoulder, would, in low tones, talk until he was calmed down, not so much perhaps by the words uttered, as by the weight of the name and influence of the man who was speaking.

One going through Old Concord Town on that hot July morning needed no words to be told that its citizens were banded together as one family, and that the desire for Liberty was the band that united them. Each man seemed a veritable "Son of Liberty," a mighty host himself, dependent, as the Israelite of old, upon the God of his fathers. To an onlooker it would have been impossible to misunderstand the signs of the times; and every participant in the life of the village on that day, man, woman, or child, felt in his and her very soul that an important step had been taken in the sequence of events urging forward the crisis.

Debby could endure it no longer; but rushing past a knot of farmers whose stern faces and set jaws filled her with the fire of an unspeakable hope that now really the war was about to begin, she ran up the road a good piece, to a matron, standing, as befitted a woman, at a long remove from the crowd on the Milldam. •'Oh! tell me, what is it?" cried Debby, clasping her hands, her sunbonnet slipping back to her shoulder, allowing the soft waves of hair to escape.

" The Lord help us, Debby 1" ejaculated the woman, turning a solemn face to the girl; yet the thin nostrils quivered, and there was a light in the black eyes; "it's coming; I've known it long, and now it's here."

" Is the war actually to begin ?" cried Debby with sparkling eyes; "tell me, Mrs. Hosmer; oh, do tell me!"

"We shall not bear much longer such stress and strain," said Mrs. Hosmer, her black eyes flashing; "it is not in human nature. Listen, Debby; some news reached us this morning, only an hour since, and look at the number of men gathered to discuss it." She pointed to the rapidly augmenting groups below on the Milldam.

Debby quivered in every limb. "But tell me," she implored, "what is the news?"

"I only know it is fresh oppression. The king thinks we need more discipline ; and the news comes that he has sent over to Boston such a command. I fear that the excitement will break down our determination not to strike unless attacked."

" And what do you call an attack ?" cried Debby, pale with anger. She clinched her young right fist till the nails struck into the palm. "Shall we be ground

down so that we cannot possibly be able to defend ourselves before we fight ? Oh, oh !"

" Nay, child," said Mrs. Hosmer, controlling herseli by a violent effort ; "but we shall injure our cause if we give way to excitement. When we strike, we must do it in the right way. Never fear, Debby, the day is coming in the Lord's own time when we shall fight."

She turned off; and Debby, wild with distress, in which anger and hope for the immediate battle waged equally in her breast, sped off up the road to Mr. Ephraim Wood's, her destination, where she should have been at the spinning-wheel an hour ago. He would know, for Mr. Wood knew everything, she said to herself as she hurried along ; and Mrs. Wood would tell her what all this dreadful news was, and just how King George was to persecute them afresh. She resolutely sped on, turning her face neither to the right nor to the left, and presently she ran up to the comfortable Wood mansion, fronting the shining and peaceful river.

"Perces," she called, hurrying over the big stone steps that guarded the entrance to the dooryard, and running around the side of the house to the kitchen door, " where's Mrs. Wood ?"

" In here," called Perces from the kitchen. " My senses, Debby Parlin!" at sight of her scarlet face,

" you've run every step of the way, I'll be bound," as she met her at the door. She was much younger than Debby, but big and strong for her age.

Perces's mother looked pale ; but there was a strange light in her eyes, although her hands were busy as usual over menial tasks. " What is it — oh, do tell me, Mrs. Wood ?" gasped Debby, holding her with insistent blue eyes.

" News has come but a short time since," said Mrs. Wood, "that an 'Act for the better regulation of the government of Massachusetts Bay' has been received in Boston, and a Mandamus Council and many other officers are being appointed over us to make us obey the king and Parliament. Now you know it all, Deborah, just as much as we know ourselves."

" Oh, the wicked, wicked king! " cried Debby, feeling some of the glow depart. Clearly the war had not actually begun ; it was only the old story of more oppression.

" Hush, hush, child ! Calm yourself," said Mrs. Wood. " Now I have been hindered this morning with all this excitement, and I am not ready to set you to work. Go out and sit down in the air, and cool off. I will call you when I need you."

" Isn't Mr. Wood going to do anything ?" asked Debby anxiously.

"Yes; all he or anv one can," answered his wife.

32 A LITTLE MAID OF CONCORD TOWN.

"He is in the keeping-room with Mr. Flint and Mr. Merriam. Don't worry, child," Mrs. Wood's voice fell to a gentle cadence; " God will take care of us."

Debby went out to the old flat door-stone, thankful, since God would take care of them all, that he had appointed Mr. Ephraim Wood to see to things, and heaving a sigh of relief as she thought of such a strong hand at the helm. She sank down and, twitching off her sunbonnet, began to fan her hot face.

" My, but ain't you hot 1" exclaimed Perces, looking at the drops of perspiration that ran away from the damp rings of hair on Debby's brow; and she stepped into the kitchen and brought out a great turkey wing. " You set still, an' I'll fan you," she said, waving it back and forth.

Debby caught it out of her hand. "You go back to your work, Perces. Mrs. Wood's all tired out. Oh, dear me, how I do wish the fight would begin this very day!" She let the fan slip to the ground while she clasped her hands together, nursing her knee with them.

Perces made big eyes at her. "Well, I'm sure I don't wish so," she said. " There'll be a terrible time, Debby Parlin, when the fight really does come."

Debby lifted a hot, distressed face up to the younger one above her.

"It is'only putting off the dreadful time," she said brokenly. " O Perces 1 what shall we — shall we do?"

Perces gazed steadily with large and quiet eyes, like a ruminating animal, over the landscape before her; then she brought her regard back to Debby's face. " I don't know," she said. " No one knows. But God is going to take care of us, I guess. My father says that our rights have got to be respected, and that it behooves the town to take a firm stand. Those are just his very words, Debby. I heard him tell Mr. Flint so before he shut the door."

"Are they?" cried Debby, leaning against the door-jamb to look up at her and drink in every word. Somehow that "behooves," uttered as she knew Mr. Ephraim Wood had brought it out, gave her solid comfort, being like a granite rock for support. She heaved a long and restful sigh.

"Perces, I verily believe your father will fix it up," she said out of the depths of a heart devoted to the big stanch patriot who held so much of the town affairs in his grasp.

"Yes," said Perces stolidly; "he and the other men. Well, you better go round to the other side of the house, Debby, you'll get cool quicker." Somehow Perces always struck one as being a woman grown, with her

large ways to match. And repeating this injunction, she went back into the kitchen.

Debby crept off her step; and forgetting the turkey wing, she passed around to the front of the house, where the shadows under the " laylock " bushes looked tempting. Here within their cool recess she cuddled up, intending to stay but a few moments, and then, not waiting for Mrs. Wood's summons, to present herself ready to achieve some household work, even if the spinning-work was "off the carpet." Whether the droning of the insects soothed her, or the soft breeze that now sprung up and played around the damp rings on her forehead fanned her into repose, no one can tell. Certain it is that poor tired little Debby was soon in the land of dreams, her head drooped on her bosom as she leaned against the house-side under the lilac-bushes.

In her dreams she was seeing innumerable companies of redcoats marching down through Concord Town, to be always met and chased by the Provincials, who drove and beat them stanchly back. To Debby, revelling in these victories, it seemed as if the Reg'lars melted into thin air, so completely did they vanish, only to reappear, when the same performance was repeated, always to end with victory for Concord.

It was naturally to be expected, therefore, that with

such delightful visions her sleep should be restful. It was so much so, that she was smiling, dewy-eyed, rosy from slumber-land, when she at last stretched her young limbs, now no longer tired, and unclosed her eyes. She was conscious of voices in the room whose windows were above her head. But before she could rouse herself out of her dreamy state enough to take in the sense of the words, she was made aware of some one looking steadily at her around the corner of the house; and quick as lightning she saw the face of Tory Lee, the neighbor of Mr. Wood, as he vainly endeavored to draw back before he was discovered. In a flash it swept over Uebby's brain. "You've been listening," she cried, springing to her feet, "Old Tory Lee! " pointing her finger at him, "to what Mr. Wood and the others are saying;" for now she heard the deep tones of the master of the house engaged in earnest conversation with those citizens who, she felt sure, were to be the leaders of the town in this fresh trouble and oppression. Without a minute's reflection, as Tory Lee stole off across the field in the direction of his mansion, she ran after him. "Old Tory Lee!" she cried in scorn and anger.

"Girl!" he turned on her, tall and stalwart he was; "how dare you call me that! " he blazed at her.

"Because you are!" cried Debby, standing her

ground, very pale and determined. " Oh ! we are suf fering and poor and distressed, God knows. You can have your fine mansion and fine clothes; but I'd rather suffer everything than to carry around your black heart. And now you've been listening, I feel sure, Tory Lee."

She was not conscious how much she had raised her voice. Had not the men with Mr. Wood in the room a short distance off been deep in an agony of thought and consultation, they must have heard the fine, shrill call. Some passers-by on the main road caught it, especially two young farmers coming along with swift footsteps. Their muskets were in their hands, and they were stepping off as if actually marching to battle.

"Tory Lee ! Tory Lee! " No sooner did they hear the words than their march changed to a quick run. "Tory Lee! Tory Lee! " They took up the cry, and passed it along; and presently, there being an unusual amount of travel produced by the exciting news of the morning that was bringing many farmers to the centre of the town, there were about half a score assembling from different points, and all closing around Debby and the unfortunate man.

In a flash she saw the mischief she had made; and though indignant at sight of the man, the stories of

whose connivance with the foe against his own townsmen had made him revolting to her, yet she trembled in pity for him; she was in dread, too, lest the young, excited farmers might do something to plunge the town into shame and sorrow. She held up her hand to them imperatively, and they instantly paused. All of them knew her. Who in the town did not? Farmer Parlin's winsome maid, sitting so demure between father and mother in the square pew in the old meeting-house every Sabbath day, her face like a wild rose peeping out from her big bonnet; and in the breast of more than one who thus knew her dwelt a marvellously clear reflection of her cheeks and eyes and hair, to last six other days of the week, till the next Lord's day should arrive, when the reflection could be renewed. So now they one and all obeyed.

"Run for your life," commanded Debby in a low voice, while all the color fled from her face to "Tory Lee," who needed no second bidding. And, although a fine and somewhat stately man, he was not above a nimble run, with more thought for speed than for grace; so that his long limbs soon carried him within his own confines, and to the safe retreat of his big mansion.

"The times do not warrant anything like this," exclaimed one young farmer, who, as Debby had re-

38 A LITTLE MAID OF CONCORD TOWN.

ceived his advances with cold disapproval, had not so much to lose by her present displeasure.

"And why am I not warranted, Mr. Haskins ?" replied Debby in a high, cool key, " pray tell. When by my cry you were summoned, clearly I have the right to settle the matter."

The young fellow looked chagrined; but another, swallowing his wrath at sight of "Tory Lee," and his disappointment at failing to mete out some sort of punishment to him, broke in, " Debby speaks well, and of course we'll let the villain go."

" Yes, of course," assented still another, though with difficulty; " but after this he must look out, or we'll invite him to a ride with a tar-and-feather coat."

And they were about to pass on, when Abner But-terfield came down the road, his first intimation of the news from Boston being late, as his farm was in one of the out-lying districts. When Haskins, the first speaker, caught sight of his big, sturdy figure, it seemed to arouse all his animosity, that, fired by the excitement of the morning, was burning fiercely.

" I d'no about that," he declared obstinately. " I believe that we owe Tory Lee more'n we can ever pay him up ef he lived a hundred years. Who knows but what his finger has been in the trouble stirred up fresh for us to bear now ? Boys, what d'ye say to 'hat coaf

o' tar-an'-feathers now, an' after that a dp in the river. Come on, I'm for it! "

He sprang off in the direction of the Lee mansion; and a half-dozen young fellows with hot blood, fired by the news of the fresh persecution brought that morning, dashed after him. Debby uttered a low cry, and clasped her hands in terror. Every drop of blood seemed to desert her body as she stood there a frozen little thing.

Abner Butterfield strode to her side between the group of young men still obeying her. •'

What is't, Debby ?" he demanded, reaching her side.

" O Abner!" she sprang out into life and action again. " Make them stop," she entreated, the color now spreading over her face; " they are going to harm Tory Lee. It is all my fault ; I was upbraiding him, and they heard me. Abner, stop them! "

At this juncture Haskins gave a jeering laugh. It was madness to him to see Abner Butterfield appealed to by Debby; and now he determined that Tory Lee should suffer for it, if the skies fell. He nourished his musket high above his head, and called upon all good patriots to fall in to this righteous work, "unless you want to be reckoned along with the old traitor."

That was enough after the news of the morning; and every soul of them except Abner ran, with all the

40 A LITTLE MAID OF C01VCOXD TOWN.

ardor of youth on fire with love of country, across the road, and swarmed over the broad Lee acres. Debby could see a long, pale face at one of the large windows, and then it was withdrawn. She wrung her hands in anguish. "They will kill him!" she cried, "and his blood will be on my head."

"Debby," said Abner, laying his big hand on her arm, "don't feel badly. They won't darst do anything but give him a scare."

"I've killed him!" cried Debby, with wild eyes. "0 Abner!" She crept up closer to his big side, and shivered like a hurt little thing.

"They will not darst," he began again; and his hand smoothed her bright hair as softly as her mother could have done. Just then a shout, discordant and angry, smote the air. It came from the house-place of the Lee mansion.

Debby broke away from Abner's hand. "I shall tell Mr. Wood!" she screamed. And speeding down the road to the house, while Abner strode off to do his best to quell the incipient riot, she burst on unsteady feet into the august presence of the three councillors. "Oh, sir!" she cried through white lips, "and Mr Flint and Mr. Merriam, save Tory Lee! "

III.

WITHIN THE LEE MANSION.

"TT7HAT does the child mean?" exclaimed Mr.

V V Wood, pushing the papers on the big mahogany table around which they were seated away from him. He got out of his chair, and took hold of Debby's trembling arm. He was a large, powerful man, weighing two hundred and fifty pounds or thereabout, and very tall and straight; and he towered so high above the little maid that she breathed gratefully, "O Mr. Wood I you can stop them," she cried.

"What does the child mean?" exclaimed the good man again in perplexity; then he started to the door, still holding Debby's arm. " Mother," he called, " the little Parlin maid seems to be ill; you had better come and care for her."

"Oh, I'm not ill!" protested Debby, wringing her hands at all this delay; "I'm afraid for Tory Lee; don't you hear them, sir? And you, Mr. Flint and Mr. Merriam ? They're going to do dreadful things to him, if you don't stop it."

42 A LITTLE MAID OF CONCORD TOWN.

'•The girl seems to have something on her mind," said Mr. Merriam, jumping from his chair, "connected with Tory Lee." He hastened to the window and looked out. " Ah, Brother Wood, see there!" he pointed to the crowd around the Lee mansion.

"In that case our conference must wait a bit," observed Mr. Flint, getting out of his chair — "until we subdue this tumult, whatever it is." He glanced out the window, then reached for his hat where he had hung it behind the door. " It is about time to put a stop to all Tory sentiments, in my opinion," he said, a heavy frown settling over his face.

Brother Wood was already out of the door. "We have need of great judgment to proceed aright. This day of all days it would be disastrous for a riot to begin." He strode off with long steps, his two colleagues coming after as best they might, and only overtaking him as he entered the Lee grounds.

The clamor seemed to proceed from the space surrounding the back door of the mansion, and to this spot Mr. Ephraim Wood and his two associates now betook themselves. No sooner had they turned the corner of the large house than the scene that presented itself awakened all their ire. The leader, who towered so above his fellows, thundered out, his usually calm face working fearfully, "Fellow citizens,

I command you in the name of God Almighty to disperse."

The riotous element, at this juncture attempting to force the heavy oaken door, was composed ot young men; and seeing the fathers of law and order in the town, headed by such a formidable specimen as Mr. Wood, advancing toward them in a way that meant business, each one began to fall back on the other, and to wish himself well out of the affair.

"God knows we have enough to bear," went on Mr. Wood sternly, "without disgracing the fair name of our town. Riot and disorderly conduct doth not belong to Concord."

"We've suffered through this man," spoke up one of the young farmers, more clever with his tongue since he'd once ventured to air an opinion in one of the town meetings which were being constantly held. "No one knows what evil he will do if not restrained."

"Leave that to those who can perform the work better than you," commanded Mr. Wood more sternly.

"Rioting and personal abuse are not allowable in this town," said Mr. Merriam. "We will take care of Dr. Lee at the proper time."

44 A LITTLE MAID OF CONCORD TOWN.

"Another instant's work and you would have made yourselves liable to be clapped into jail," cried Mr. Flint with anger. "Away with you!" he swung his knobby stick, which he had taken the precaution to bring, around his head,— "and never get into such work again. You'll have fighting soon enough,.God knows, when we Can all band together as good citizens of a town that has never been disgraced. "

"Softly there, my good friend Flint," said Mr. Wood, cooling down as he saw the other firing up, " let us take the names of these disturbers of our peace, so that we may know who they are who would threaten the good name of Concord." He swept the whole circle of young men with his eye, some of whom on the outskirts were endeavoring to duck and steal off unobserved. "No, you needn't hurry away, Jedediah Platt," he remarked grimly to such an one, "since I know you perfectly well, and your name must go down along with the rest." From the breast pocket of his coat he took out a big red leather wallet much worn, as it had belonged to his father before him. Its strap ran around to the opposite side, holding the papers close and safe within. It was lined with faded blue paper, and contained three pockets. Out of one of these Mr.

Wood secured the necessary bit of paper, using the end of a letter for that purpose; and taking out his pencil, he proceeded, in the leisurely judicial way peculiar to him, to note down all individuals before him, to their great disgust and shame.

When he came to Abner Butterfield he looked up in surprise. Mr. Flint gave an uneasy ejaculation, while Mr. Merriam showed his disdain by a contemptuous silence.

" Indeed, sir," protested Abner hurriedly, while the scarlet flew into his brown cheek, " I had nothing to do with this unhappy business. I came to try to stop them."

"Poor influence you've had, Abner," observed Mr. Wood with irony. " I should have supposed your words would have carried more weight."

Haskins sneered, and ground the heel of his boot into the grass. At least Abner would be disgraced in the eyes of these good and influential citizens. That was something to be rejoiced at anyway.

"Your name must go down," said Mr. Wood calmly, "with the others, as long as you are found here with them." And Abner set his teeth together hard at the first record of what to him meant everlasting disgrace.

"And now away with you all!" roared Mr. Wood

at them, the taking of names being finished. And what with this command, and the swinging again of Mr. Flint's knobby stick that somehow in the style of his performance seemed a terror, the crowd dispersed, and hurried off to town—all but two members of it.

Those were Abner Butterfield and Jim Haskins. The latter, not content with the sight of the gloomy, set face overtopping the stalwart figure of the first-named young man, chose to wait for him, as he walked slowly, evidently with a desire to avoid a meeting.

"Seems to me you're awful glum over it," remarked Haskins with an unpleasant grin, stepping to Abner's side. "I d'no's it's any worse for you than for the rest o' us. But what do I care? Confusion take 'em !" He snapped his fingers off toward the three dignitaries who had just read them the law.

No answer. Abner strode gloomily on, never looking at his companion. This nettled Haskins, who at least wanted the consideration of hail fellowship with Abner, which thus far in his life he had never been able to obtain; but now, dragged together in the common bond of misery, he looked to the fulfilment of his desires in that quarter. "And I'm monstrous glad you've caught it! " he went on, at sight of the

cold face turned away from him, while his companion's head was carried high.

"Will you have the goodness, Raskins, to go your side of the road," said Abner, "or in front, I don't care which. I want no words with you of any sort. All I desire is to be let alone." Still he didn't look at him.

"And that's just what you won't have," cried Has-kins, irritated beyond measure at the scorn of Abner's words and manner. Then, impelled by the working-power of the double draughts of hard cider with which he had fortified himself since early morning, and without a bit of warning, he yelled out, " You'll never get Debby Parlin if you try all your life; she'll play with you as she plays with all; a curse on her and on you."

Abner Butterfield turned like lightning, his face a stormy sea over which tossed the waves of white wrath. He seized the coat collar of the man before him, and shook it till he could shake no more; the figure within being lifted from the ground, its legs and arms flying out like those of a puppet. The end of the performance saw Haskins in the ditch in a heap, and Abner striding down the road after saying, "Another word about her from your dastard's throat, and you'll never speak more."

48 A LITTLE MAID OF CONCORD TOWN.

Haskins gathered himself from the ditch, looked carefully around to see if there were any witnesses, then shook his fist at the departing figure, his face swollen with passion. There were no words to come from his mouth.

Meanwhile Mr. Wood gave a vigorous clang of the knocker on the oaken front door of the mansion. "It is I," he said, at the same time, reassuringly, "Mr. Ephraim Wood. Do you,

Brother Flint, step to the window and speak within, and you to another window," nodding to Mr. Merriam; " verily; they are all so frightened that they will not admit us, thinking we are come to molest them."

"The curtains are all drawn tight," reported Mr. Flint, after a careful reconnoitring of the mansion, in which statement Mr. Merriam concurred.

"Then we must resort to sterner measures," said Mr. Wood, " to announce who we are ; for get into this house, where we can deliver our message, we must and will." He stepped off to the greensward in front of the door. "Approach the window, Dr. Lee," he called in stentorian tones, "for I have somewhat to say to you. You know me ; I am your neighbor, and these are your fellow-townsmen. Surely we have not come to harm you, but to a peaceable conference." All this he delivered as if to a large assembly.

It had the effect, before it was half through, to bring a long, nervous hand to the curtain-edge, which was pulled aside hesitatingly. And then, by the time the address was over, the window was open, and Dr. Lee's head appeared.

"We have come to speak to you, Dr. Lee," said Mr. Wood, his neighbor, dropping his voice to its accustomed note of calm consideration, "and we beg that you will open the door and give us admittance."

It was impossible to refuse this ; and the big oaken door was soon ajar, and the self-invited guests were passing down the wide wainscoted hall lined with family portraits.

Dr. Lee nervously threw open the door to the spacious room on the right. "Walk in, gentlemen," he said, motioning them within. He was very pale ; and his upper lip, well pulled down over the lower, concealed where that had been bitten in the ordeal of suspense and fear he had just endured. Me waited silently for them to speak, and followed them into the apartment, seating himself in its shadow as much as was consistent with his ideas of hospitality, that was in duty bound to present a show of pleasure at t? e visit.

"Our errand is on a most unhappy subject," began Mr. Wood, as the two gentlemen looked to him to

begin the conversation. " It is useless to ignore the fact that a disturbance has been made in your house-place this morning, even to threats to force your door." Mr. Wood was not one to mince matters, but usually he went to the heart of the truth at one bound.

" You say well — there has been a disturbance," began Dr. Lee harshly; and rolling back his upper lip, the little stream of blood released, trickled down by a slender thread to his waistcoat.

"You are ill, Brother Lee," exclaimed Mr. Flint, starting forward. "Pray do not try to talk," said Mr. Wood in commiseration.

"A paltry thing," exclaimed Dr. Lee hastily, to shut off the sympathy he saw coming to the mouth of Mr. Meriam, "only a lip-cut. Yes, the outrage committed on my house and grounds °s a dastardly thing. Let me tell you, gentlemen," he clinched his shapely hand, and brought it down heavily on the table laden with rare china, and what was rarer still in that day, fine books, and thrust his pale face over toward them, "such an outrage is subject to the extremest penalty of the law. Concord shall pay for this."

"Softly, softly, Brother Lee," said Mr. Wood in a large, calm way. The other two men hitched their chairs nervously forward, while their thin lips

trembled with their eagerness to speak. " Extremes! penalty of the law are hard words to use, and threats toward your town harder yet. Let us look at this matter." He crossed his long legs, and folded his large hands together judicially. " A number of young and hot-headed youths have committed a disturbance on your place, — a disturbance, Dr. Lee, urged on by certain fixed and growing opinions held to by many good, reliable residents of this town, that you are not loyal to her interests, nor to the interests of the Province and the Colonies."

" I am loyal to her, and to the Province and to the Colonies," broke in Dr. Lee excitedly. His pale face trembled with his eagerness, and again he clinched his hand fiercely. " I am, as we all should be, a good subject of our king. And no man can point to anything I have done, who dares to say otherwise."

" Common report has aired many dubious things on this point about you, Dr. Lee," said Mr. Wood soberly. "God grant they may not be true."

"They are not true," declared Dr. Lee in a shrill voice. "Enemies have followed me, and perverted many things from their rightful meaning. I can explain them all satisfactorily."

His visitors regarded him gravely. He ran on with the air of a man desiring complete re-establishment

52 A LITTLE MAID OF CONCORD TOWN.

in good favor, and cried passionately, " And if I have let slip at any time an unguarded opinion, surely every man can hold his own opinions, and I am supposed to be among friends."

"Too many opinions on the subject dear to our hearts, American liberty, cannot be allowed, Dr. Lee," said Mr. Wood quietly; " there can be but one opinion. Whoever does not hold to the right one, with the rest of his fellows, must be content to be ranked an outsider. He puts himself there by his own hand."

Dr. Lee cringed an instant, but immediately rallied. " And again I say," he boldly asserted, straightening himself up in the tall, carved chair, "that every man is entitled to his opinions. Liberty! what does the word mean but that? And, Brother Wood, pardon me if I express to you my belief that you may come to see the matter as I do. It is a poor time, let me tell you, for this outrage to have taken place this morning, when our king has sent us fresh warning of his power to quell our aspirations for American Independence, — an unpropitious moment truly for a good and loyal subject of his to be maltreated." He laughed triumphantly. Mr. Flint and Mr. Meriam sat with flashing eyes, erect on their chairs; but they held their peace, knowing that their turn to speak would soon arrive.

"And hark ye, Dr. Lee," Mr. Wood unclasped his large hands, and leaned his immense height forward while he sought the depths of the other's eyes, "it is mayhap in the sight of God the best time, if the disturbance must come, that you should be brought to see on this very day what a temper we are possessed of. Hardly any other morning could it have occurred. It is just because the news has aroused every soul in this town that the excitement has proved unbearable. It must vent itself on anything that points to even the slightest suspicion of disloyalty to our hope and our belief in ultimate freedom."

"We are waging a fearful struggle," cried Dr. Lee to gain time, and to feel his way, while he controlled his passion at the leaping forth of that of the other.

"We can but die — and, hark ye!" Mr. Wood thundered out the words, while he brought his large hand on the table with a noise, which, compared to that produced by a similar cause on the part of his host, was a Niagara roar beside a purling brook. Every article on the table danced and quivered. Dr. Lee involuntarily moved back his chair. " But we will die free men — hark ye that! " He brought his large face forward with a thrust at his neighbor — a face in which an innumerable host seemed to speak and protest their willingness to fight for what was

54 A LITTLE MAW OF CONCORD TOWN.

dearer to them than life. And for a minute, while the ponderous old corner clock ticked off the seconds, the two looked at each other, and no one spoke or stirred.

"And instead of the extremest penalty of the law,"

it was Mr. Meriam who broke the silence,— "let

me tell you, Dr. Lee, it is you who have cause to fear. There are laws that once broken cannot be forgiven. Arraigned before the bar of an insulted and outraged town, one who broke such a law would stand but a poor chance. I advise you to meditate well on this point."

"And it is in your power to protect yourself," observed Mr. Flint incisively, "but not much longer in our power to protect you. We have done our best this morning, as you very well know; but the times are getting more troublous, and we cannot answer for your safety if increasing suspicion points to you."

"Brother Lee," said Mr. Wood, getting out of his chair, and drawing himself up to his great height, " I pray you to ponder well our words. We have much business before us in the coming hours, and we will wish you good-day." He signed to his associates, who went through the same form of leave-taking, to be dismissed at the big green door with punctilious politeness by the pale-faced man, the little blood-stream still trickling over his waistcoat.

IV.

ONE LITTLE CARTRIDGE.

IT was a stormy night, wild and forbidding. The rain poured down pitilessly upon the scattered farmhouses, and beat about the windows, against whose panes the sodden branches were tossed by the wind that arose at nightfall. In about an hour it blew a gale.

Three men were wending their solitary way to the farmhouse where their deliberations were to take place. The countenances of all were animated by a stern resolve, as if, by slow accretions of strength, their owners had arrived at a determination, that, once fixed, became unalterable. The firmly set mouth, the eye glowing with the fire of resolution — each and all bore the same expression; yet in build and general make-up the pedestrians were widely different.

At last the paths of two of them converged in the road leading to Captain James Barrett's house, the place of meeting. And they fell into conversation, and spoke out of full hearts.

56 A LITTLE MAID OF CONCORD TOWN.

" The times are troublous to that degree that nothing worse can come to us than death," said one. "We are slaves in reality, though bearing all the semblance of free men," he added bitterly.

"That is so," assented the other gloomily, letting his head drop on his breast.

"Yet we must not despond," the first man made haste to reply, as he saw the effect of his words, "or all is lost. It is only by keeping our heads cool, and preserving our resolution, that we can strike the blow when the time arrives. And that time will soon be here."

"Thank God! " exclaimed the other, rousing out of his temporary depression; " to strike would be heaven indeed. It is this delay that is killing us all, when we see each day is but the season for fresh indignity and privation. My very soul burns within me for the fight to begin."

"You would not have us strike the first blow, Brother Whitney? " ventured the first man, more for the opportunity of a remark, than because he doubted the answer. " Surely that would be certain death and disaster, besides being wicked. We are a righteous people and law-abiding. Let the tyrant strike first, and begin the war; then we will show him we are ready for it."

In his excitement he bared his head to the pitiless storm, while silently invoking the aid of that God in whom he believed.

"I agree with you wholly, Brother Hosmer," said Mr. Whitney, "only I am for such plain and square statements now from the people of Concord that there can be no doubt as to our way of looking at the matter."

" I did not think there ever had been much occasion for doubt in our former words, when opportunity hath given us power to speak," remarked Mr. Hosmer dryly.

"True, true," cried Mr. Whitney. "And now," clinching his good right hand, "they shall hear it more than ever from our town. Concord shall speak as never before, although I grant you we have been plain and square of speech. We care not for the British foe on land or sea. We are free, despite King George himself ! "

The other repressed the sigh that was on his lips, and gazed in sympathy at his fellow-citizen, as the third man, whose approach in the rain and darkness had not been observed, now drew near.

"I could hear your words," he said, " and I am with you, Brother Whitney." He carried the same dauntless front, although his words were quiet

58 A LITTLE MAID OF CONCOKD TOWN.

" So are we all, I believe," declared Mr. Hosmer. "And we shall soon have a chance to prove our speech, Brother Heywood. Well, here we are," as a candle gleaming in the Barrett homestead beckoned them on to light and warmth.

"We have a task to do to-night that, please God, will help forward the work," he added, as they passed over the greensward before the door; "anything is better than this wretched suspense. Our words, as we write them to-night, must be strong, to arouse every soul who shall hear them to his duty."

The big door was thrown wide, and the good man of the house stood before them.

He was over sixty years of age, yet his countenance glowed with the enthusiasm of youth. He held the door wide, as if awaiting them impatiently. "Come in, friends," he cried, drawing them from the storm and the wind ; " lay off your wet garments in here." He led the way through to the big kitchen, where the large logs were crackling in the fireplace, and the kettle steamed suggestively.

Mrs. Barrett, a goodly matron of stately mien, rose to greet them; and by her side was Miliscent, the eldest granddaughter, a tall, slender girl with beautiful dark hair and eyes. With kind intent, they soon assisted the new-comers to dispose of the dripping

cloaks and hats, that presently sent out in the warmth, induced by the hot fire, a steam that proclaimed the drying process well advanced.

" It is a sorry night," observed Mrs. Barrett to open conversation.

" To say the truth, madam, I have not been troubled by it," said Mr. Hosmer; "nor, I venture to say has either of my companions. We carry about with us continually such a storm in our hearts, that the elements might war about us, and we should call it child's play in comparison."

Mrs. Barrett sighed; and Miliscent, who stood near, felt her young cheek glow, while she said, and her eyes blazed, " I hope you will do something to-night," including them all in her glance, "that will make the wicked king see he cannot grind us any more beneath his tyranny."

" Miliscent! Miliscent! " reproved her grandmother.

"I do! " asserted Miliscent stoutly, though usually she was most submissive to those in authority. " O grandmother! do let me say it ; I should die if I didn't."

Captain Barrett looked as if about to answer her, but said instead, " You must take your hot toddy, friends, and drive the cold out. Wife, bring the decanter and the boiling water."

The making of the toddy was religiously believed in through all the Colonies as a neighborly and family rite of universal distinction; and the old silver tankard and the decanter must necessarily take the post of honor in the setting out on the buffet. To-night the manner observed in partaking of the steaming tankard seemed like that of a sacrament. Each man sipped his portion silently with that abstracted and fixed gaze that showed him lost in thought. All the joy and neighborly gayety were lacking; more like to the pledging of vows it was, as the cup was passed around. And at last the silence became so painful that Miliscent stirred uneasily in her chair, and looked as if the tears were about to fall over cheeks blanched with efforts to keep them back.

"Well, friends," said the host, breaking the pause, " if you will not take any more toddy, we will adjourn to the muster-room. Wife, see that there is no noise, for we shall need all our thoughts in uninterrupted quiet."

The men rose and filed out silently. Miliscent gave a low cry as the last one disappeared. "O grandmother! how can you sit so still. I can't bear it;" and she sank down on the floor, and buried her head in Mrs. Barrett's lap.

"Dear child," said Mrs. Barrett with a low groan,

while her fingers smoothed the soft dark hair, "my heart is sore and affrighted, but it will not do to give way. Your father and Mr. Hosmer, Mr. Whitney and Mr. Heywood, need to be encouraged, and it is all we women can do to stay their minds and hearts. If they saw us fretting and repining, it would only burden them with useless sorrow. We must prove ourselves worthy of them and our town, and we must do our part to save it."

Her eyes glowed as much as the young girl's; and her heart beat fast, although her fingers, moving in and out the soft hair, were steady and cool.

" But think what we have suffered — see what we are enduring now! " cried Miliscent, raising her head in a flame of anger. " Can we — ought we to bear it longer before we openly rebel? Say, grandmother. Oh! why doesn't God help us?" She brought the last words out in a wail, and her head sank again to Mrs. Barrett's lap.

"Listen, Miliscent;" the woman's face was very pale, and her inward prayer for wisdom to speak, unloosened her lips. "The Lord is mighty and will prevail."

" Oh ! that is what Parson Emerson preaches," broke in Miliscent impatiently; "but why doesn't God help us now, grandmother? We've borne all we can."

" No!" Mrs. Barrett's voice rang out clear and true. She raised her eyes to heaven. " Thank God, we can bear everything for him. ' If he slay me, yet will I trust him.' Miliscent, stop at once " — and her tone was of authority that the girl knew allowed of no disobedience — " all this foolish repining. The Lord's hand is not so heavy that it cannot save. He will come, and that right early, in his own good time, to our relief. Do not be afraid."

The girl stole a glance at her grandmother's face, and was awe-struck to see how it shone, as if Heaven's own light were really on it.

" And now sit down to your spinning at once," said Mrs. Barrett, rousing herself to speak in her usual brisk manner ; " nothing drives out the desire for useless repining, quicker than work. Sit down and do a stent." And the whirring of the wheel proclaiming her command obeyed, she went to her bedroom, buttoned fast the door, to fall on her knees by the old four-poster, and pour out her soul in prayer for the deliberations going on in the muster-room.

The next morning dawned bright and clear, with no trace of the late storm, save that here and there branches strewed the ground where they had fallen twisted from the parent trees.

Miliscent had remained over night. In truth, she was as often at the
old homestead as at her father's house next door; for she was a favorite grandchild, and she fitted well into the ways of the older household. She threw wide the shutter of the little room, that was always hers when she stayed at grandfather's, and looked without. The svm was coming up bright and golden, a rosy flush pervading the sky to mark his advances. The fresh, sweet air poured into the chamber laden with that peculiar resinous quality that follows a heavy rain, and all the shining landscape lay fair and wholesome as a maiden's dream could depict it. Miliscent leaned her elbows upon the sill, and rested her head upon her hands, to drink it all in.

" War — and bloodshed! Oppression and distress ! " the smiling scene seemed to belie the very existence of such facts in God's universe. And Miliscent for the moment felt as gladsome as a child, simply in the delight of living. As far as her eyes could reach, were the broad acres belonging to her grandfather. No evidence was there of aught but peace and plenty; all was repose. The cattle off in the barnyard were lowing at the gate, preparatory to their departure for the luscious pasture across the road, and the fowls stepping about and picking up the early worms beneath her window had the same soothing air of content and security that broods over farm-life.

64 A LITTLE MAID OF CONCORD TOWN.

The girl looking on at the window caught this restful spirit, and it seemed as if an uneasy dream had been the occasion of all former disquietude. Here was reality.

But presently she started back as if struck by some unseen hand. " O God! " she cried, " how can I forget, even for an instant? Our homes — what do they mean to us? Only that we can keep them on sufferance, and in obedience to wicked mandates. Any instant they are likely to be taken from us, and we to become the slaves that we really are. Oh! if I could do something to help my poor, suffering country."

She suddenly left the window, and threw herself down by the bed, burying her young face in the dimity counterpane. "Dear God," she breathed brokenly, "give me something that my hands can do, to help forward our righteous struggle. Hear me, O God !" Then she hurried over to the old-fashioned wash-stand in the corner, and from the basin dashed up the clear water on her flushed and tear-stained face.

"Grandmother," Miliscent went up to Mrs. Barrett's side as she bent over the morning meal of ham and eggs frying in the spider; "I am going to get the rest of the breakfast. Sit down in the keeping-room, do, you look so hot and tired."

" Miliscent, it is good for me to have my hands occupied," said Mrs. Barrett. Yet she turned and looked long and lovingly into the face beside her. In truth, it was a comely sight.

Miliscent's dark hair was braided away neatly from either side of her shapely head; there was the glow of health upon her cheek, and a dewy light in the dark eyes, that had a deep and tender look in their depths as they rested gravely on her grandmother's face. It was as if she had, while losing none of her youth, grown suddenly alive to the responsibilities of the hour, and glad to feel the weight of them upon her strong young shoulders. There was altogether such a new expression on her face, that Mrs. Barrett hastened to add, "Don't worry, Miliscent, nor take all this trouble too much to heart. You are young; it is for us who are old and experienced, who should bear the burden and the distress."

"I do not worry," said Miliscent, throwing back her head as she spoke. "And I am glad to cast in my lot, and endure suffering with all the others, who perchance are old and experienced. Grandmother, I hope God is going to give something into my hand to help forward this struggle for freedom." Her delicate nostril quivered and her bosom heaved; but there was a light in her eye, and her grand-

mother gazed at her, the fork with which she had been turning the ham poised in the air.

"Child, child, what has come to you?" she exclaimed, not without admiration.

" I cannot tell, grandmother. I only know that God will hear my prayer to be allowed to help onward this mighty struggle against wrong and oppression."

"You do help — you are a tower of strength every day!" cried Mrs. Barrett. "In these two houses you are light and sunshine and hope. And your grandfather was saying but the other day, that to hear your step and to see your face were rest and comfort to him. It is no small thing, Miliscent, to be the stay of such a good man as he is."

Miliscent's cheeks glowed, and the tears ran down her young face. She put both arms around her grandmother and embraced her, a proceeding that astonished them both equally, for New England reticence forbade many endearing expressions of the affection that lay deeply hidden in the heart. Then she said, and this time she took the fork not ungently from her grandmother's hand, "Do you go and rest. At least this burden I can take from you;" and she pleaded with her dark eyes till Mrs. Barrett yielded, and left her with the task.

Miliscent had run over home to help her mother

with the morning work, and having finished the last duty required, that of inducting Patty into a clean checked apron, and seating her at a stent on a sampler, she was hurrying back to Grandfather Barrett's, skimming over the greensward that lay between the two houses, her thoughts busy with the ever-present topic, and her heart beating with her new and highborn hope, unconscious that she had reached the little path that led up to the old door, till she heard a light and musical laugh, and looking up, she espied a young and decidedly handsome British officer gazing at her with ill-concealed admiration.

He was just before her in the path, and advancing to the door. He stepped back; his hand went to his cap, while he made her a deep bow, and then stood with uncovered head for her to pass.

"You desire to see my grandfather, I presume. He is not at home, but will probably be in soon," said Miliscent, preserving her self-possession, and looking more like a wild-flower than ever, her head erect on its graceful neck. "Pray walk in;" for it was the custom for Captain Barrett and his son James to furnish oatmeal and other provisions through the Commissary Department of Boston, young staff-officers being sent out to Concord in connection with the transaction of the business.

"I do; but pardon me a moment, time is not so pressing, I am sure," said the young officer hastily. "I pray you to give me a few words."

"Time is pressing with me," said Miliscent, pausing with one foot on the flat door-stone. " We are poor people, sir, and need to work with our hands for our subsistence." She spoke with a sweet serenity, and a dignity that made him again bow involuntarily.

"Ah," he said with a smile, and the color leaped to his cheek as he spoke, " you would refuse me the right of conversation, and treat me as if I were an outcast, merely, forsooth, I presume, because I am a good subject of my king and yours."

"Not so," said Miliscent gravely; "you do wrong to say I refuse to talk with you. . Indeed, I am glad to speak my mind, and to say what is on my heart. You will but take offence at it, though, I am sure."

" Nay, nay, fair Rebel," said the young officer with a laugh, while his color heightened and his blue eye was clear and sunny; "you shall say what you will, and I promise you on my good sword here," he tapped the hilt as he spoke, and he looked at her long and earnestly, "that I will recognize no affront in your words."

"A rebel I may seem to you," Miliscent tossed her shapely head. " I am proud to rebel against the unjust mandates of such a king as you seem glad to serve. I would live on bread and water all my days rather than to submit tamely."

" I believe you," said the young Briton, all the laugh dropping out of his face, while his eyes grew grave. He rested his right foot on the step above him, upon which Miliscent stood, and laid his palm on his knee. "And yet, Miss Barrett, do you know," his voice dropped to a low tone as he said earnestly, " there is not the smallest chance that you can ever be victorious. Better be warned, and give up the struggle."

"We shall be victorious!" cried Miliscent defiantly, while her eyes flashed. "Do not say such dreadful things to me. We shall — we must conquer in the end !"

The young soldier shook his head sadly, like one who hates to say unwelcome truths. Yet he repeated, "You do not know whereof you speak — you are like a child if you entertain a thought of victory. And your fathers and brothers are mad to attempt it."

His pitying look changed to one of scorn at the thought of those men who, instead of being the

70 A LITTLE MAID OF CONCORD TOWN,

guard and protector of just such defenceless maidens as she, were exposing them to dangers untold by the defiant insurrections to which they were goading themselves.

" I do not for an instant believe, neither do any of us believe," said Miliscent, warming as she proceeded, " that we can ever be conquered. God will not allow it. He brought us over here to this country because we could not worship him in England, and do you think — can you believe, that he would desert us?"

Her face glowed, and her bosom heaved. She stood erect before him, and as she waited for a reply, some sort of an answer was necessary. He brought his foot to the ground, and turned away abruptly to examine the distant landscape. As he did not believe in the God of whom she spoke, he was at a loss for words, yet unwilling to dampen such a faith as shone in her eyes and glowed on her cheek. And for the first time, strange to say, he felt a shadow of impending evil, too intangible and vague to be put into words, settle over him, while the slender young daughter of the house of Barrett seemed a representative of a mighty power, indefinable, but terrible, whose opposition was deadly. The doughty old farmer-soldier, her grandfather, and others like him, who were putting

themselves to the front with their insubordination, loomed up now with a hitherto unknown quality that was to be respected if not feared.

Finding himself in such a predicament as to experience this uncomfortable sensation, he dashed out the first thing that came in his head, and glad to find a reaction in his mind as he proceeded, he said abruptly, " Well, then, if you persist in your rebellion, you bring its consequences on your own head. The king is not to be blamed in that event."

" The king ! " retorted Miliscent scornfully; " talk not to me of kings. We want no king but God. He is merciful, and does not grind his creatures to the dust. If we die, why we must. Better so than to be slaves." She turned away, her bosom panting with suppressed feeling, and her eyes flashing with scorn, yet her lip trembled as if her woman's heart had borne all it could.

" Stay, Mistress Barrett," cried the young officer, stepping to the flat door-stone beside her, " my words seem cold and hard, I know. I was only endeavoring to warn you. You have, I know, much influence in this home and this village, and you might even now turn the tide of bitter feeling into something more reasonable and befitting your condition."

"And I would not turn my little finger to influence

one of our brave townsmen to aught but deadly combat and resistance to our foe, King George, and all you whom he sends over here to oppress us," she flung at him over her shoulder. Then she turned swiftly, and a beautiful and grave expression settled over lip and cheek and brow, " Listen, sir; you do not seem to know the stuff the men of Concord are made of. It is because you wilfully determine not to know. I tell you this is no child's play at war, nor any sudden determination to fight you, and tyrants like you, to the death. We have grown for many long months and years into preparation for it; we have prayed to God, and we have held counsel together; we have studied it all better than you, who are only occupied in donning your gaudy coats and trappings." She glanced in derision along the brilliant surface of his uniform, although, truth to tell, poor Miliscent had sore trial with her feminine leanings toward the trickery and splendor of fine apparel, not to admire it strongly, and the bright face above it. Yet now she rose superior to all such weakness, and her tone gathered scorn, whereat the young Briton wilted perceptibly. "You have no thought beyond your gay clothes and gewgaws," she said bitterly; "to you it is doubtless a pretty pastime to come over the sea to subjugate poor farmers; but we — ah! you will find that

Concord Town, and all our other towns, are full of men, ay, and women too, who are fully prepared to meet you. Sir," she drew her tall and slen4er figure to its full height, " I give you to understand that we will fight till we die, but we will never give up to you !"

"I believe you," exclaimed the young man involuntarily, and with an admiration that he could not conceal. "Well now, my pretty maid," he took refuge in a bantering tone to hide his real feeling, "there is such a thing as a brave spirit, but no material to work with. What will you do when your ammunition gives out, as give out it surely will? Our ships think nothing of crossing the sea; our arms and accoutrements can never be exhausted. Why, your men do not know how to make even a cartridge. What will serve you then ? I give you a tough question to answer."

"We will make good use of our powder-horns and our bullets," said Miliscent calmly; "and we will shoot any invading enemy just as we shoot fierce and hungry bears that molest us."

"That would be cruel in the last degree," exclaimed the young man. "At least, if you are to slay us all, do it, I pray, in a civilized manner." He suddenly turned and swept the ground with his

gaze. "Ah, I have it," and he picked up a pine stick; quickly, with deft strokes with his pocket-knife, he fashioned it to a shape suiting his fancy, then thrust his hand into the breast-pocket of his coat, and drew out a letter. Across its back was the superscription in a woman's hand; on the front was the big red wafer that had sealed it closely. The young officer whirled it open, searching for a blank space. "My mother's letter," he said, and a shade swept over his mobile countenance. "I thought to find a clean bit to tear off."

"Stay," begged Miliscent, with a pang at thought of harm to the mother's letter, "I will get you a piece of paper." She ran into the house, and came back, bringing it, and a pair of scissors from her work-bag.

"You are a good girl," said the young soldier, shutting up the letter with emotion. "I have been reading it again. My mother says, ' My son, remember to keep your feet from evil ways, and be not led by your companions into aught that would bring discredit to your family name — or to your early training.' Ah! if she knew in what company I am thrown, and how all evil is around me, she would realize that I had need to keep this letter." He folded it close, and set it back carefully within

MII.ISCENT BARRKTT AND THE BRITISH OFFICER. " She leaned over to allow no movement of his to escape her."

ONE LITTLE CARTRIDGE. ?$

his pocket, this time taking the precaution to enclose it in his leathern wallet.

"But you can keep from being led into evil, though it may be around you," said Miliscent, her thoughts on the absent mother, doubtless this moment praying for her boy. " You surely can follow her entreaties."

" Ah, you little know," said the young man sadly, and his bright head drooped. " Well, let us get to this killing business," he exclaimed suddenly, by one of those quick transitions in which, from dejection, his buoyant spirit rose; "now, it is like this." He seized the paper and the scissors from her slender fingers, and rapidly twisted the former over the shapely pine-stick until it suited his fancy. "If you are determined to kill us, let it be by some humane process, and not like so many wild beasts of the forest."

Miliscent, with dark eyes dilating, drew near. He could not see her above his bent head that, absorbed as he was over his work, he did not lift. Her red lips parted, and she held her hand over her heart to still its beating, as she leaned over to allow no movement of his to escape her.

"There," he paused for its inspection, and held up the finished article, like a boy pleased with

his work, and smiled saucily into the face above him, now intrenched in its accustomed expression, though with every iota of color fled; "that is the way we make our cartridges," he cried, waving it before her, as Captain James Barrett drove up to the house-place.

THE OLD TOWN GETTING READY FAST,

V.

THE OLD TOWN IS GETTING READY FAST.

THE conflict of arms, that ultimate struggle that should once for all determine the governing power and vouchsafe, or deny, to the colonies the rights of freemen, was not much longer to be delayed. The sky was already tinged with that glow that was to proclaim the dawn of American liberty, and to usher into the world of nations a new republic.

Events had been rapidly marshalling their forces to an inevitable conclusion. Affairs were becoming so complicated by the continued oppression of the Province, without apparent reason other than a determined and deliberate desire to oppress and to enslave, that there was no evading the question of liberty or slavery. The situation had become intense and dramatic, and allowed of no greater delay in parleyings or entreaties. Either the colonies must stand by their continued utterances of belief in the God, to worship whom in .freedom and truth they had come across the sea, and defend their rights as free-

men, or they must take the alternative, and yield. There was no middle course now.

So Old Concord men thought, and so had they spoken, making themselves many times in the past, as they well knew, marked rebels for future retribution when King George became victor. Seven years before, in 1767, the citizens of Concord had come out boldly for liberty, failing not to express their sentiments at the offensive stand of the British parliament. Accordingly "the town had instructed its representative to oppose the operation of the Stamp Act, and to unite in all Constitutional measures that might be taken to obtain its repeal." And two months later, in December, "the selectmen were chosen a committee to consider and report on these measures, which threaten the country with poverty and ruin." After accepting their report, the town voted "to encourage industry, economy, frugality, and manufactures at home and abroad, and to prevent purchasing so much as we have done in foreign commodities." Thus did Old Concord early fire the torch of Liberty.

And she kept the flame burning steadily and high through all the five years thereafter; so that when in 1772 the address of the citizens of Boston on the 2oth of November, concerning the state of distress in which

the Province was plunged, came before the town, it awoke a spirited response. And the reply, prepared by the committee with instructions to the representative of the town, "after being very coolly and deliberately debated upon, was unanimously accepted in full town-meeting." So much for those early days, when to speak and to act, and to fire the hearts of others to patriotism, was to be a leader indeed. We shall see how she lived up to her teachings.

"Debby," cried Miliscent, springing into the little old kitchen of the Parlin cottage (her sunbonnet had fallen from a face pale with excitement, but luminous from her splendid dark eyes),—"I want you to come home with me at once."

It was the time of sudden summons, the air of every day was charged with excitement, and Debby did not look surprised nor question why.

"Can I, mother?" she appealed to Mrs. Parlin, hurrying "from pillar to post," as she always expressed it, now coming in from the woodshed.

"Yes," said Mrs. Parlin with a quick look at Milis-cent's intense face. She threw down her load of kindlings in the wood-box behind the stove, and shook her apron free of the chips. ".I know it's for something special," with another lingering gaze into the pale face.

For answer the tall girl went swiftly up to the mother's side. The lovely color spread over cheek and brow. "Forgive me for not telling you, dear Mrs. Parlin," she said; "it is a secret. If you will only trust me," she implored.

"I'll trust you, Miliscent, wherever you are," said Mrs. Parlin heartily. "Debby shall leave her work and go."

"This very minute," cried Debby, tearing off her apron to hang it behind the door; and taking out a clean blue-and-white checked one from the table drawer, she hastily tied it on, feeling now well dressed indeed. "Mother, don't you touch to spin my stent. I'll do it all to-morrow. Promise me."

"I won't touch your wheel," promised Mrs. Parlin. "I can't; for I'm up to my eyes already with work. Go along, child; it's all right."

"May she stay all night?" begged Miliscent, her arm around her friend. "Say she may, Mrs. Parlin, do."

" I suppose she might as well," assented Mrs. Parlin. "Yes, yes, go along, Debby. Only be home bright and early in the morning. Then you'll have to fly to your spinning in good earnest."

Debby tied on her sunbonnet, not without a good glance in the cracked looking-glass in the corner, and

throwing on her shawl, she ran off with her friend, with whose long steps she could scarcely keep up.

" What is it ? " demanded Debby breathlessly, as they clambered the Ridge, and were now on the even plateau back of the Felton homestead, ready to strike into the cat-a-cornered trail. "Whatever in all this world do you want me for in such a queer way ? Why don't you speak up, Miliscent Barrett?"

" Hush, hush ! " warned Miliscent, drawing her cloak tighter around her. " It is no time for speech till we get safely home."

" I should think you'd be safe enough in this wood," said Debby scornfully. "Only a bird or a squirrel to hear, and they won't tell."

"Debby, I don't dare to tell," said Miliscent under her breath. A red spot glowed on either cheek. She seized Debby's plump arm, and pulled her along faster. "This wood may be full of treachery. How do we know ? One Tory Bliss or Tory Lee would ruin it all. It is too much to risk. Don't ask it. Wait till we get home." She struck off now down the slope; and Debby, whose young feet were used to climbing, had all she could do to follow the tall, slender girl, whose swift foot-falls seemed not to press the ground.

At last Miliscent deserted the trail, and made a dtiour through a meadow, finally reaching a small yellow house well set back in its own farmyard. Here she paused. "You wait here, Debby," she said abruptly; and running nimbly up to the farmhouse and into the kitchen, she made the same request, only this time it was for the two girls of the household. A request that was speedily granted, as were all those made by a granddaughter of Captain James Barrett; and Lucinda and Jane came out presently, and down the box-bordered path, tying on their checked aprons, sure sign that they were going visiting.

This performance was repeated at one or two other houses. In some instances the girls were to follow as speedily as possible when certain household tasks were completed. But it was quite a goodly number of Miliscent's mates who hurried along with her to her home on the old Barrett Mill Road.

" James has gone over to tell Perces Wood to come," said Miliscent to Debby, as the other girls naturally fell back a little to let the two friends walk together.

" Of course I knew you'd send for her," said Debby. "Seems if Perces was older'n we are sometimes, she's so big and steady. Dear me, I'm thankful to goodness, Milly, that we're almost there;" and she gave a yawn that was not weariness, but she

ached in every bone of her body to know the reason for such mysterious actions. "I can't wait another minute, seems to me, to know what you can want of us." The two girls were together now, walking with their arms around each other as was their wont; so Debby whispered this against the slender neck of the taller girl.

"Poor dear," said Miliscent fondly, "your patience sha'n't be tried much more ;" and she turned her glowing eyes affectionately on her friend. " How good you are ! Now, I couldn't have done anything with those other girls," with a toss of the head toward their mates in the rear, " if you'd have teased me to tell. Just see how amiable and nice they come along."

" It wouldn't have done any good if I had have teased," remarked Debby calmly ; " that I well knew, when you looked like that, Milly. Well, I'm thankful to gracious that we're most there, and the secret can be told."

" I can't bear not to tell much longer," cried Miliscent suddenly. " Let's start and run. Come, girls ! " she called back to them in her high, clear voice.

A wild chase now ensued down the road, past Captain James Barrett's homestead to Miliscent's home beyond. Into the house that seemed pervaded by

84 A LITTLE MAID OF CONCORD TOWN.

an intense though quiet excitement, the girls flew led by Miliscent and Debby. Mrs. Barrett, calm and pale, met them.

"You're to go into the keeping-room," she said. " Then you better button the door to keep the children out. When my back's turned, I can't answer for them. Button the door after you, Milly."

"No fear but I will, mother," said Milly. "Come, girls."

No need to tell them. Every one scuttled in like rabbits, and turned to face her, with wide expectant eyes. She slipped the wooden button into place, then set her back against the door, and surveyed them all. "Girls," her voice throbbed with excitement, yet it was low and deep, " I've something to tell you that will make you very glad. But first you must each one promise solemnly you will never, never, never, in all this world, tell the secret until I give you permission to. Promise, now, each one in line, beginning with Lucinda."

"I never'll tell in all this world," proclaimed Lucinda, on a high key; "black and blue, hope to " —

"Hush! " warned Milly; "what we say in this room must be spoken low. Traitors may be

lurking beneath the windows," she glanced again at them— '• a loud
voice may warn them of our purpose. Begin again, Lucinda."

" I'll never tell in all this world," said Lucinda, in a gruff, heavy voice, as effective in its way as the high key; "black and blue, hope to die if I do, so there! "

"Now, Susan," said Miliscent nervously, to a thin little maiden standing next, clasping and unclasping her fingers in excitement, " do see if you can speak low, and not make such a noise as Lucinda. Will you promise?"

Susan whispered out her promise in terms as deadly as her neighbor's. And Milly passed down the line till she reached Debby, who stood last.

" I promise," said that damsel loftily, with her head well in the air. " I sha'n't say any of our play words; this is a different matter. But I won't break my promise."

"I know you won't, Debby," said Milly affectionately, "for you never did yet. Well, now, girls," and she drew a long breath, " you shall know the secret."

She picked up a pair of scissors that lay near at hand on a table, and whirled them before their eyes.

" See, see," she cried, under her breath, "these will

A LITTLE MAID OF CONCOKD TOWN.

help to cut our way to liberty! O girls! we have longed to be of use to our poor country struggling to get free from the tyrant King George. Now we can. I know how to make cartridges " she added in a whisper.

A silence like death fell upon the room. The girls stared at her brandishing the scissors, and then at one another. Suddenly the line was broken; and Debby rushed out and threw her arms around Miliscent. " O Milly, Milly, Milly!" she cried brokenly, having no further words at her command.

"And if we can't go and fight in their battles, we can equip our brothers and fathers," went on Miliscent, her pale face shining. " Oh ! the battles are surely coming. Girls, girls, we've so longed to help. And now we can! Quick, draw up your chairs. I'll sit in the centre, and let us get to work ; I'll tell you how — I'll tell you how."

She uttered all these commands in a short, quick voice, tense with feeling. And presently the ring of chairs was formed ; and her mates, their cheeks still rosy from their speedy run, and glowing with the emotion that found an answering gleam in their bright, clear eyes, were ready for the work that she soon put within their hands, as Miliscent seized the pine stick for the initiatory cartridge, and shaped

the paper over it, cutting it with her scissors into the requisite pattern.

They held their breath, and watched her silently.

" Oh, oh! " exclaimed Debby, wild with excitement, and beating her hands together, " we may not be allowed to fight, but we can make the cartridges."

Miliscent dropped her scissors to clap her hand over Debby's mouth. " Don't speak the word again. You may ruin all. I have told you once. Now, don't one of you breathe it." Her eyes blazed, and she stood tall and stern above the ring of chairs.

Then the latch of the door was rattled, and a voice called softly, " Milly."

" It's the children ! " exclaimed Lucinda, in alarm.

"Open the door, Milly," said her brother James, with his face close to the crack. " It's Perces and I." Whereat the wooden button was slipped back, and there was great rejoicing as Perces and James were drawn in.

It was now but the work of a few moments to get them all busily occupied; and while the fingers flew, Miliscent divulged the whole of the secret whereby she and her mates were to help the brave men who were to fight for liberty.

" See, see, I have the pattern," she cried exult-ingly, and holding it high. " He cut it with these

very scissors," and again she waved them. " Oh, thank the Lord for such an enemy as he!" and she fell to busily on the paper, while the circle of bright heads drew close about her fingers to see how it was done.

"Milly wheedled him into telling," said James, whittling more pine sticks into the required shape of the one formed by the young British officer. " I saw the whole thing from the barn-chamber window."

"Tell us, James, do; that's a good boy," begged the chorus of girls. James needed no urging.

"Foolish boy," said Milly, with heightened color. "Don't listen to him, but put your minds on the needs of your country."

"Foolish boy! " snorted James. "That's what she always says when I tell about the fellows and her. And here I have been ever since, whittling the pine sticks. Now I will tell, anyway, Milly." And he set the story forth to its last syllable; Debby, all her soul in her fingers, turning, out of loyalty to her friend, a cold shoulder toward him as she worked.

While this meeting was in progress, another was in session around the Common. It could not be said to be disorderly, yet there was that temper pervading it that boded ill for any'interference. Almost to a man,

ihere was an expression in face and attitude and gesture that bespoke intense determination of that cooler kind that results from a slow and cautious decision. It might be that among this company, scattered here and there, or massed in solid groups, or hurrying to the scene with long and determined strides, was to be seen occasionally the violent fellow whose quickly fired blood was not mixed with its requisite, essential-to-success power to control himself. He would bawl to every chance comer, as he ran quickly on, gesticulating wildly as he ran, "Down with King George's troops! Damnation to the Reg'lars !"

But he was quickly, and as effectually as the circumstances would permit, where the spirit of freedom was gro'wing rampant, quenched by the sober and sturdy fathers of the town; and while some of these hoi-headed fellows were walked off to cool their blood, others were well watched, lest their excited utterances should break forth to the disadvantage of the temper and mind with which the old town meant eventually to win.

There was the inevitable small, boy, of course, as omnipresent then as now, dodging here and there, and massing into groups wherever the crowd was the thickest; crowing and chuckling with delight at the noisier demonstrations of the turbulent element,

and saddening when the excitement was in any waj checked or diminished. But there was a way our fathers in 1774 had of making the small boy "mind his p's and q's" that is conspicuously absent to-day. Truth to tell, there was less of him in the earlier day, but that should be no detraction to the skill of knowing how to manage him. So, beyond their excessive exuberance over the situation, which after all was a secret stimulus to the fathers and older brothers, the small boy of Concord Town might be said, on that day, to present no bad feature of the citizens' meeting on the Common.

The women and girls, removed to a proper distance, as was the correct feminine attitude of that day, watched and waited, and hung about with bated breath for any chance news that might befall as to the progress of the meeting of the citizens thus congregated. But amidst all the babel and excitement, the women caught little but scraps of isolated talk, as the groups waited with only a show of patience for the messenger despatched in the early morning to Boston for the latest news, who should have returned by this time. And as the moments passed, and he came not, the delay seemed to verify all those fears raised by news of the recent " acts for the better regulation of the government of Massachusetts Bay"

that had so roused them to indignation but a short time before.

At last, when it appeared impossible to endure the suspense much longer, the small boy so largely in evidence espied, what was not discernible to the other eyes, a horseman wending his way down the old Bay Road. He announced this fact by a shout that was taken up by the rest of the boy throats with a heartiness that communicated itself to the waiting men ; and presently, after what seemed a small eternity to the impatient congregation, although the rider was spurring on his horse faithfully, the animal, dripping with perspiration, stood before them.

"What news? What news? " cried a dozen throats, while the men massed around him, pale with excitement and dread.

The rider, a young man of undaunted face and mien, drew a long breath and hesitated, as if unwilling or unable to speak.

"Give it to us to the last syllable," thundered Mr. Wood, forcing his way through the crowd, and laying his large hand on the bridle. The young horseman glanced into his face, and blurted out, " The Act dooms us all. The council is to be appointed by King George. All other civil offices, not filled by him or his tools, to be done away with."

92 A LITTLE MAID OF CONCORD TOWN.

Mr. Wood started back with a deep groan as his hand fell from the bridle. All his determination to bear ill news was unequal to the blow.

" For God's sake, fellow-citizens," cried another with white face, and sweeping the circle with his flashing eye, " are we to be ground, lower than slaves, to the dust? Can we submit tamely to this last act of despotism that would reduce us to a slavery than which there could be no meaner on earth ?"

" No! no!" came from a hundred passionate throats. "We will never give up our rights as free-born Americans."

" Our natural and charter rights have been invaded over and over," continued the speaker in a terrible tone; "the hand of despotism has been over the colonists with a constantly tightening grasp; the harbor of Boston has been blocked up; bodies of soldiery have desecrated the Province under one pretence or another, but with one end constantly in view, —our complete subjugation. And now these two last Acts just passed by Parliament are intended to, and will if submitted to, reduce us to that condition that no power on earth could rescue us from. Are we men to take all this and not resist? No. To arms! To arms/"

He flung his hands to heaven, and raised his face,

gaunt and terrible to look at. The men crowded around him wild with passion, but stilled for a moment at the sight of his face, depicting so strongly what each one felt was in his own breast. At last the silence was broken, and one cry broke forth, "Yes! yes! To arms! to arms! Away with the tyranny of King George I We are free men ! "

94 A LITTLE MAID OF CONCORD TOWN.

VI.

A CRISIS.

IT was a terrible moment. The whole earth seemed to open to Mr. Wood, and for an instant everything turned black around him. He strove to speak, but no words came; and he looked helplessly around for that assistance that might turn the tide in this evil crisis of reckless undoing of months and years of wise and patient patriotic work. Was Concord to ingulf herself and others in a wild and premature passion that would only hurl the thunderbolts of war upon unprepared and defenceless heads, and make herself an object of pity and contumely for all history to deplore ?

There were many citizens of like mind scattered here and there in the turbulent crowd; but they were swallowed up by the struggling, yelling mass, and their voices drowned in the general tumult. There was not an instant to lose.

"Gallop for your life!" gasped Mr. Wood into the ear of the young horseman, " and bring Parson Emer-

son." And seizing by the flying jacket one of the small boys, he bade him in a hoarse voice to run and ring the meeting-house bell. Which the youngster, wild for action of some sort, did as if by magic.

" One — boom — two — boom — boom!" out rang the bell, clear and true. The crowd, thinking it the signal for a massing together, perhaps for military instructions, and in their excitement eagerly welcoming any call, stopped shouting and yelling instantly, and hurried off in irregular groups to the meetinghouse, just as the young parson, breathless from the canter that landed him at the church-door, entered, and commanded them to sit down.

It was impossible to evade him. Parsons were obeyed in those days. Far ahead in authority of lawyer or captain or schoolmaster, was the divine, who seemed to stand so near to God that a wholesome fear possessed all souls of breaking any commands he might make. So the men silently settled into the corners of the big square pews — some of them as far off from the pulpit as they dared; while the young parson rapidly mounted the pulpit steps, and took a survey of the situation.

"Men of Concord," he began in a high, clear voice, and looking into their wild, excited faces with cool eyes, "listen to the word of God from this sacred

96 A LITTLE MAID OF CONCORD TOWN.

desk. What means this turbulent crowd ? Think ye that into hands that tremble with passion, and are lost to reason and judgment, would be committed the power to plunge this town, this good old town, and the Province, into the red gulf of war before the time is ripe! God knows the war is coming, and no man among you will welcome it more gladly than I." He flung back his head, and brought his hand down on the big Bible with a resonant clap. " For we are not slaves! We are free as the air above and around us, and so will we die. Ay, every soul of us will die with our faces to the enemy before we will give up our rights as men."

They were cooling off now; and, hearing such warlike words fitting into their boiling indignation, they began to listen eagerly. And for a good half-hour the reverend gentleman gave them wholesome advice, squarely, without mincing or dilution, as to the propriety as well as wisdom of following the leadership of the citizens of the town who were empowered by their fitness and the suffrages of the townspeople to take the lead in all matters, and certainly in such a momentous one as this before them. "Be ready for war, and to quit you like men when you are ordered to war," he thundered, with another resonant clap on the big Bible; "and think not for an instant that to em-

broil yourselves and us in a wild and unprepared onslaught on our enemies is war. Verily there is great and pressing need that wisdom for each man shall be added to his courage, that so our glorious old town may gain her well deserved honors of war, whenever she shall be called to action." There was a movement to depart, the passion in the faces of the men giving place to quiet and steady resolve, more deadly to the future peace of the enemy, and biding its time to strike. But the parson had not done with them yet; for, opening the big Bible, he read in a clear and sonorous voice that woke the echoes in the old meeting-house, a chapter from the Old Testament, supplementing it with another from the New — well chosen for the time and the occasion. And then, shutting the leaves, he led them in a lengthier prayer, with eloquent and impassioned fervor. After that came the by no means short extemporaneous sermon. When at last, about two hours later, they filed out of the square meeting-house, they might be said to be thoroughly subdued. What could not be accomplished otherwise to stay their brute force, the parson, by his liberal quotations from Holy Writ, not to speak of his seventhlies and eighthlies that ever commanded immense respect, had done, and done well. And they filed out, and dispersed quietly.

98 A LITTLE MAID OF CONCORD TOWM.

"The fight's begun! The fight's begun!" a voice yelled out beneath the window, — the window behind which Miliscent and her mates were working, — as a man ran down the old Mill Road. " Where's Cap'en Barrett?"

Miliscent threw down her scissors to the floor, and sprang to her feet, her face white as death. James jumped up with a whoop, and dashed out the door, his pine stick in his hand.

"Oh, don't stop working! " cried Debby in an awful voice, so full of tears that there was no time to shed. " If the war has begun, we must get these done," pointing to the little pile on the table. "Oh! why didn't God tell us how in time to make enough " —

" Listen ! one of us must go and carry these over to grandfather's, and if he has gone, must take them to him wherever they are fighting," said Miliscent. " Now that James has gone — poor boy ! — he will feel badly enough he forgot them. "

"I'll go," said Debby eagerly, jumping up with panting bosom. " I can run the fastest ; give them to me." She spread her blue-checked apron, and the girls brushed the cartridges within it with hasty hands ; and with Miliscent's last injunction, "Give them to nobody but grandfather," ringing in her ears, she sped off, first to Captain James's house, and failing to find him, and no news save that he was down to the Mill-dam, she fled along the Barrett Mill Road to the town's centre, her heart on fire with rapture that she was really going to the battle and with aid to the men.

She was speeding along with head bent down over her apron bunched out with the precious result of the girls' work, when suddenly she came full upon a person running in the opposite direction. He put out his hand to save her from the collision. " Why, Debby ! " he cried in surprise, as he saw her.

" O Abner! " cried Debby breathlessly, her hair blown about her face, " where — where is the fight ? "

"There isn't any fight," said Abner, setting his teeth hard. "There was danger of the men's losing their heads, and getting their muskets to rush off to Cambridge or Boston; but Parson Emerson has quieted 'em down now. Still, there'll always be the fear of it, as long as we hear this wicked news." And he told Debby what word the messenger had brought of fresh evil piled upon the Province.

Every vestige of color fled from her cheek, and she clinched her little brown hand.

" O Abner! I want to tell you; but I've promised, and I must keep my word."

"Is it anything I can help you about?" asked Abner eagerly, forgetting for one instant war and his

country's sufferings. "Do let me," he begged in his big, awkward way.

" Oh, no, no, no!" said Debby, unable to stop herself. She leaned for an instant on the railing. They were pausing by the Spencer brook, on whose edge stood the Barrett saw and grist mill. " No, no; do not ask me, only tell me where I can find Captain James. Oh, do tell me, Abner, I must see him at once!"

" He is down in the Centre at the Common. I've a message from him to take to his home, Debby;" and not allowing himself to look again at her, he strode off to set into a run.

Debby took two or three steps, then stopped impulsively to look after his retreating figure. As she did so some one jumped noiselessly up the little incline by the bank beneath the bridge, and coming up behind her, seized her arm.

"O Jim, how you scared me!" exclaimed Debby, with a jump, and holding to her apronful of cartridges.

" What were you saying to Abner Butterfield ?" demanded Jim, looking down the road where Abner's tall figure was fast disappearing. " Hush, don't you call him here, or I'll kill him! I've sworn to be even with him yet. What were you saying to him?"

" I sha'n't call Abner Butterfield or any one else

DEBBY AND JIM RASKINS. "'O Jim, how you scared me!' exclaimed Debby."

to help me," said Debby in white scorn. "I guess I can take care of myself, Jim Haskins. Now go your way, and I'll go mine." But he gripped her arm.

"Not so fast, Miss Debby Parlin; I've got done with all your playing with me."

" I've never been playing with you," denied Debby, in greater scorn than ever. Yet she saw in dismay that Jim had been drinking, and she cast about in her quick little mind how best to get rid of him quietly.

"Jim," she said, "aren't you ashamed, when our country is in such need, to be acting so? Don't stop to talk to me, but go your way and be about your business, whatever it is."

Jim laughed, a joyless, harsh note, in her face. "Didn't I see you talking with Ab Butterfield a minute ago ? Time wasn't so precious but that you both had a plenty. I don't care for the country." He swore a great oath that turned the girl's cheeks whiter yet, and made her eyes dilate. But she answered spiritedly, "Then you've a small, contemptible soul, and not worth my talking to you here or any other place." And she tried once more to pass him.

For answer he seized her other arm, and shook it smartly. The apron-end loosened where it was doubled up, and down rattled several cartridges upon the ground.

"Cartridges!" swore Jim, looking at them with drunken eyes. Then he picked them up and examined them, meanwhile twitching roughly at the blue checked apron to secure the rest. But Debby held it with tight little fingers. "I'll scream, Jim, and have the town around your ears. Give me back my property this instant."

But he laughed again, and plunged into the thicket, carrying the few cartridges with him, and snapping his fingers at the girl as he disappeared in the bushes.

Debby rushed along in dismay. How unfortunate that Jim, of all people, should see the cartridges ! Folks said that he had lately been acting queerly — certain it was that he had taken harder to drink, and that he had been heard to utter Tory sentiments on more than one occasion, despite his outwardly violent denunciations of Tory Lee and Tory Bliss. She redoubled her speed, and met Captain James just as the men were released from the old meeting-house, and were straggling off to their homes.

"Well, my little maid," he said sadly, taking the small heap of cartridges from her apron, while something glistened in his eyes, "we shall need them and as many more as can be made, God knows, before long. But not to-day. Run home, child, and get to work again with Miliscent."

There was no time to tell him of Jim's discovery and possession of the cartridges, for Captain- James was now immediately besieged on all sides. And threading her way out of the crowd, she ran backwards toward the Barrett Mill Road. But she did not reach her destination.

Jim, after leaving Debby, grasped the cartridges tightly in his big sledge-hammer fist, and swore several great round oaths to himself, in the bushes that skirted the river, that he would be even with the girl, Debby Parlin, who had so bewitched his heart, and pay off at one and the same time the deadly grudge, that still haunted him, against his rival.

"My country — well, that t's a good one!" laughed Jim, snapping his fingers again, "my country! What's she ever done for me, except to get us in this fix. I vum! I'm for King George every time now, since the turn affairs have lately taken. What's th' use o' kickin' against the pricks? King George has got the best of it. An' now that officers are to be set over us, an' we not to be allowed to say boo to anythin', why, it's easy to see th' end. I'm goin' to get what I can out o' it, an' be on the right side o' the fence. Who knows but His Majesty'll give me a commission. Anyway, my pretty Debby, here's a precious lot o'

information against you; an' that slab-sided old scoundrel, Ab Butterfield, a-makin' ammernition, an' preparin' secretly for war. The sooner I git news to Cambridge, an' spoil all your game, the better fer me, an' the worse for you and your busted cause, — the rotten old rebellion agin the king."

He scratched his head in a drunken sort of way, undecidedly, then turned and struck out in a bee-line down the river-edge, completely concealed from all eyes, so he thought.

Debby ran on with light feet, retracing her steps, but with a sad heart. All the excitement and glow attendant upon the expectant fight had vanished, leaving a dull little ache and fear of, she knew not what. The dread of what Jim might do with the secret so cruelly wrested from her was uppermost in her mind, although the horror of suspense in the face of this last tyrannical act of oppression weighed down her young soul in bitterness to the earth.

"All that is left to us," said Debby in the gloomy depths of her own soliloquies, " is to work as hard as we can, and make all the cartridges possible. It may be that we women and girls will finally fight, and use them up. Who can tell? At least we'll make them, and enough to last."

Suddenly, with an unconscious influence, that was

not altogether dread of meeting Jim upon the road, she turned and ran off down the river, to follow its bank, and come out beyond at a point somewhat near the turn to the Barrett Mill Road. She ran as she had before, with head down, wholly engrossed in her own melancholy thoughts, now stopping to pick her way more carefully along the river-bank, and again occasionally to refresh herself with a sight of the pure, gently flowing stream that seemed to breathe peace to her soul.

It was at one of these pauses that she heard voices; and with that involuntary caution that times of trouble and danger had taught our impulsive little maiden, she stopped instantly, and brought her lithe body up to a listening attitude. It was Jim's voice that was speaking.

" I tell you, Squire, it's a good chance to show our allegiance to our king."

The reply was slow and cautious, and too low for Debby to catch a syllable, although she strained every nerve to do so. From the position where she stood, she could not see the face of either speaker. Only she could have sworn to Jim's voice, and she could see his big leather boots as he carelessly leaned on one foot. And there was his right hand on a tree-trunk, as if supporting himself in a half-

106 A LITTLE MAID OF CONCORD TOWA:

intoxicated condition, — his right hand with the big ring — the girls had always teased him about it when Jim had been a better companion, and not so given to drink, saying that it was brass, partly to awaken his ire, as he had as bright a temper as the color of his locks. The figure of the other man now and then came partially into view as he moved restlessly about. It was that of an older man, and he was not Tory Lee. At last she ventured to move a few steps nearer, still keeping well within the shadow of the thicket.

" I tell you, Squire, I'm fer goin' to once down to Cambridge," said Jim, in a dogged, guttural tone, "an' givin' them warnin' that our town is a-prepar-ing to spring war on 'em. It'll be a rich thing for them who want to stand well in the king's good books to be up an' a-coming now."

" Stay, my good fellow," said the older man, in a tone of remonstrance; "you say well that the time is opportune, but it is best to observe caution. A little lack of it would be disastrous indeed."

"What do you want to have done?" asked Jim still more doggedly. When he met this man unexpectedly, he considered himself a lucky fellow indeed, as who better could help him to understand the safest and best way to dispose of his secret.

But now he did not attempt to disguise his lack of appreciation in the other's slowness of action. "Air you goin' to let th' fellows arm themselves, an' git all ready, as you saw on th' Common for yourself they mean to do, before you give warnin'? How much would that story bring then? " He laughed sarcastically, and shuffled his big boots. "Hey, Squire Bliss?"

It was Tory Bliss! Debby clasped her hands until the nails pressed into the flesh. Oh ! was God to let her brave countrymen be hounded to death by enemies within the border? She prayed to know what to do, her lips not moving, while the quick little ears watched like sentinels on duty, to hear. "Softly, softly there, my good fellow." Mr. Bliss was saying propitiatingly. "Your heart and disposition are all right, but you must let me plan for you. Do you go to Mr. Lee; he knows the lay of the land perfectly, and how to inform the Council at Cambridge. Do you go to him; he will probably start at nightfall, and carry the news."

"Tory Lee!" exclaimed Jim with a smothered execration.

"Speak of Mr. Lee in that manner again," cried Mr. Bliss warmly, "and I will give warning of you as a turbulent fellow, and one given to drink, and

have you locked safely in the jail, where you will trouble no one."

"I didn't mean no harm," said Jim, cooling down as the other warmed up.

"Then see that you obey instructions," said Mr. Bliss curtly. "Do as I say; carry the news to Mr. Lee, and give him the cartridges as proof. Then you shall be rewarded, never fear, when, as I firmly believe, the king will be intrenched in his power over the Province, and these deluded fellow-townsmen of ours will suffer the penalty of their foolhardi-ness." He stopped suddenly, and without another word stole softly off, and was lost in the covert.

"You're a sweet one, ain't you 1 " cried Jim in an exasperated way after him, when there was no longer any danger of being heard. "You'll save your mean skin, will you, until you're quite sure it's safe to holler for King George, an' send me troopin' an' trainin' to that other old skin-flint, Tory Lee, whom I'm not to call Tory yet, till it's safe to be known as a Tory. Confusion to you both! "

He slouched off a few feet, — and Debby drew a long breath of relief, — turned, wavered on unsteady, drunken feet, lurched a bit, and suddenly whirled with an astonished cry around into the very face of Deborah Parlin.

VII.

"1 SHALL GO OVER TO THE SIDE OF THE KING."

MRS. PARLIN hung the kettle on the crane for the hot cup of checkerberry tea for supper against the time that her good man should come home. All through this long, troubled day she had gathered what news she could from various persons passing up the Old Bay Road, the thoroughfare constantly travelled since the first settlers built one side of it against the protecting hill. And she had resolutely "baked and brewed, boiled and stewed," spun and sewed, keeping the little cottage neat as a pin, as was her wont, and filling the place in the world God evidently intended for the women of 1775, with no thought for the town's centre and the news there to be obtained.

" Glad am I that Debby is with Miliscent this troublous day," she said to herself; " for the child with her love of country and eager mind would have been miserable enough tied to her spinning-wheel. It is cold comfort to a woman to sit with none but her own

thoughts for company, though Heaven knows the children are a blessing. But to a young creature like Debby bursting with eagerness to be free, it is intolerable distress. Where the child got her nature, I cannot see. Surely not from John or me."

Mother Parlin never said a truer word. John Par-lin was, his neighbors and townsfolk said, "the salt of the earth," meaning he was wholesome, and had sterling qualities that would keep well. But he was slow to exasperation, and as heavy-mannered as one of his oxen, whose great brown eyes looked exactly like his. And he had gone down in the village records as " Sot as a mule," the New England parlance for having a will of one's own. And Mrs. Parlin, she that was Lyddy Thompson, was of the same build, —square and upright, and honest in body and mind.

Where little Debby of the peach-bloom and dimples, and light dancing feet and sunny smile, with the eager soul looking out of her laughing eyes that could be fired with sudden purpose, ever came by it all, was a mystery of mysteries. None of the other children were like her. There was Johnny, more lumpish than either father or mother had been at his age, a boy of ten, who if he had enough corn-meal griddle-cakes and doughnuts to eat, and a good store of nuts laid by for winter nibbling, seldom cared to stir from his beaten tracks. And Doris, the girl who came next, seven years old, went soberly around the kitchen and woodshed, in reduced pattern, like her mother in feature and figure. And to wind up the list, the baby was the roly-poliest little object, just fat and stolid; calmly blinking at the world, evidently intending to pattern after his immediate predecessors when he got big enough to strike out for himself on his own two feet.

But Mrs. Parlin did not waste much time over mysteries. It wasn't her way to bother over them, having enough to do to keep the daily work " down from around my ears " she often said ; so now, as she filled her kettle with fresh water from the well beside the cottage door, she followed the course she had observed all through the troubled day; rejoiced her soul with thankfulness that Debby was with her friend, and in the stimulating atmosphere of the Barrett household ; was glad that things were no worse, and that the lawlessness of the morning on the Common was subdued, and that she and her family still had a house-roof over them that they could call their own. "Though how long that will be, Heaven only knows," she sighed.

Clearly, where everybody was necessarily reduced

to such a state of constant worry as were the homesteaders in the Massachusetts, or Old Bay, Province, in the stormy days preceding the war of the American Revolution, there was a place and a mission for such good souls as Mrs. John Parlin, whose very existence seemed to promise strength and solidity and repose to the community.

Mr. Parlin strode heavily up the little path that led by the enormous elm, within his enclosure, to the cottage door. His wife met him with a mild and placid brow. " Come in, John," she said, with a kind hand on his arm. "You're dreadfully tired. Doris, get father's slippers."

" Yes, I am, Lyddy, and that's a fact." John Parlin sank down heavily in his chintz-covered chair, that creaked in every joint, as it had done for years from the same cause. "And I shall be tired'n this before long, I 'xpect. Wife, give me my dish o' checkerberry tea right here."

"O father!" expostulated Mrs. Parlin, "ain't you going to wash up? " all her spirit of neatness quite in alarm. "Doris, fill mother the tin basin with water, and bring it and the towel."

"No, I ain't," said Mr. Parlin decidedly; "not till I've had a good drink of checkerberry tea, anyway." He held out his hand for the bowl, and drained it dry.

Then he wiped his lips deliberately, and got out of his chair, motioning Doris away, who was coming across the kitchen with slow, heavy steps, bearing the washbasin and towel. " Bring it back," he said briefly, going into the woodshed for the wash-up, which was always performed with conscientious and painstaking deliberation. Then he came back, and drew up to the humble repast now set forth on the table.

"There's going to be a war, sure enough," he said calmly, and looking over his slice of brown bread to his wife, with calm, bovine eyes; "so you and me, Lyddy, 's got to get ready for it."

"Yes, I s'pose so," said Mrs. Parlin, with an air of quiet assent that accepted the inevitable. "Well, John, it is to be, and God will see us through it."

Mr. Parlin nodded reflectively and returned to his brown bread. "Give me the Bible, wife," he said at the conclusion of the meal, when she and Doris put away the remains of the frugal repast, and swept up the crumbs; "and we'll have prayers."

" I was thinking you'd tell me what's been going on to-day," said Mrs. Parlin, pausing, broom in hand, a moment; "seem's if every one going by here had dropped in with something worse'n the last one, and I said to myself, ' I'll wait till father gets home, and know the truth.'"

For answer, Mr. Parlin asked abruptly, "Where's Debby?"

"She's over to Miliscent Barrett's," said his wife: "I told her she might stay all night. Miliscent came for her this morning."

Her husband looked around the kitchen as if missing something, with as much longing as his face ever expressed; but there was an expression of relief, after all, as he said briefly, " Well, reach me the Bible, wife, and come to prayers."

So the big old Bible, its leathern lids encased in a dark red spotted calico cover, was lifted reverently down from the shelf, and put on the father's knees; the tallow candle was trimmed, and John and Doris folded their pudgy hands. Mrs. Parlin sat decorously by her husband while he sonorously read a long chapter, then knelt to offer a longer prayer.

After this was concluded, Mrs. Parlin reached down her knitting-work, the long blue-yarn stocking, and began to clack her needles. She did not suggest again any communication from her husband. Once expressed, such a thing was never repeated. But she looked at him anxiously. He was different to-night, that she clearly saw, from any other home-coming. He looked up at last, and saw her regarding him.

"Send the children to bed, wife," he said. "I want to talk with you."

"Go to bed, Doris," said her mother, "and you too, Johnny. Good-night."

Both children went out, Doris across the hall, over the landing of the stairs, to the little room that jutted into the greensward, and Johnny to the gabled loft above. The baby was already asleep in the trundle-bed in the bedroom.

"Shut the door," said Mrs. Parlin. " Now, John," as they were left alone by the fireside, "tell me all that is on your mind; for that something is, and weighing heavier than the coming war, there is no manner o' doubt."

"You say truly, Lyddy, " agreed John Parlin; "and yet 'tis occasioned by the war that has set me to thinking so I scarcely know myself to-night."

" I should give you a dose of boneset if 1 didn't know the troublous times had made so many folks queer-actin' and thinkin'," remarked Mrs. Parlin, not relaxing her even and monotonous clack, but making her blue rounds just the same, so that one, looking on, might be said to see the stocking grow. " Now, the sooner you get it off your mind, whatever it is, John, the better you'll feel."

" I must lead up to it, Lyddy," said her husband.

"easy like. You know I never could be driv. So let me take my own way." He put one foot slowly over the other, and gazed at the fire a moment without further speech.

Mrs. Parlin made at least three rounds on her stocking. Then because, even to her slow nature, some movement was necessary, she got out of her chair, and went and looked at the clock in the corner, taking a longer glance at her husband's ruminating figure on the way back.

"Yes, the war is surely coming, Lyddy," at last he said.

" I know it."

" And we've got to get ready for it, you and me."

"You said that before."

" Folks who have children," observed John Parlin, not noticing her remark, "have a sight to think of, Lyddy, in these times that try men's souls."

Mrs. Parlin made no reply to this. Her husband proceeded.

" If the war comes, and it is a-coming, what will we do, Lyddy ? Where's the provision for our children ?"

"We've got the same provision, I s'pose," said his wife, "as everybody else in this town has; just nothing at all, when it comes to that. The war, when it is once upon us, will use us all up alike; and if King

George beats, why provision, if we had any, wouldn't be of any earthly good to us nor the children after us."

"That's it/' said John Parlin gloomily, staring at the fire; " we might as well be all dead then, and that's a fact."

He continued to ruminate over this last idea; and his wife, uncertain how far to interrupt him, clacked away vigorously at her knitting, wondering at this most unusual mood. The big cross-log cracked with bright little snaps that proclaimed the penetrating flame pushing its path into the heart of the hickory, and lighting up the pewter on the dresser opposite. Everything in the kitchen was outwardly bright and cheery, except the figure of the farmer, who, as he thought on, settled down in his chair with a depressing droop, that, despite her habitual placidity, made his spouse conscious of nervous little creeps down her spinal column. At last she dropped the knitting into her lap from sheer inability to k-ep still, and said, "Now, John, tell me all without delay. What are you thinking of?"

Her husband set down both feet to the floor, raised himself in his chair, and looked at her long and deliberately.

"Lyddy," he said, with that slow utterance that

gives token of the choice of each word, "I've always been fer liberty and our rights, and I've been a good citizen of this town, hain't I?"

She kept her eyes on his face, unable to reply. A vague notion of all the war-talk having gone to his head, and unsettled his wits, crossed her mind; but one glance at his. clear blue eyes, and she dismissed the idea, and held her breath while he went on,—

"Well, Lyddy, I've stood it day in and day out, working and toiling, and praying and hoping. I'll live on bread and water all my life, and you know it, Lyddy, to live and die a free man. But to-day, Lyddy, when that accursed news " — his big face was very white now — " came, and I see how useless and wicked 'tis for those of us who've got children to provide for, to hold out longer, when King George has got us body and soul, why, Lyddy," he drew in his breath hard, and spoke through his set teeth, "I've made up my mind to go over to the side of the king."

The woman sprang from her chair. " O John ! stop where you be. Stop, not another word! See, I'll go down on my knees to you, but you shall take that back." She slid down to the floor, and clasped her hands over his hard and knotty ones. "You're not well," she cried, crouching low and fondling him, while she writhed on the floor. "You're all worn

out; this is the reason you say such dreadful words. Come to bed." She essayed to draw him out of the chair as she tried to regain her feet.

"Yes, I be, Lyddy; well as ever I was in my life," declared her husband solemnly. "You let me be. I've ben thinking this all out to-day, and it's best said to-night. Get up and set in your chair. You must hear me."

" No, I'll kneel to you; it's the best place for me," she cried, "so I may be able to turn you from such speech, when it shows you how your wife can beg on her knees. O John ! take back those words. Better to struggle, to face death, ay, to die, us and the children, than to hear such words. Oh, my husband ! "

She did not cry — far worse was it to hear the tearless sobs; and John Parlin turned his face away, and his big hands shook.

" Lyddy," his voice was determined and low, like that of a man whose mind is made up, "

I tell you solemnly that the struggle is useless. We have no right to condemn our children to what will surely come if we persist against the king. Our farm will be confiscated, and our children will be beggars."

"Let such a fate come." She raised her head proudly. " Beggars we may be, but we will never eat the bread of traitors."

He winced at the word, but went on doggedly, "And to hold out at such a time, believing that God himself has left us no alternative, I know is downright wickedness. I shall go over to the side of the king; there is no more to be said."

She sprang to her feet once more, and drew away from him. She was a large, square woman, and now in the bright firelight she seemed to tower over him from a terrible height.

"John Parlin," she said, "when I married you I gave my faith and my love to a man who feared God and loved his country. I've served you faithfully, John, as God will testify in the last great day. This night you have said words that have made a bar between us that nothing can lower until you take them back." She stepped forward, lighted another candle from the one on the table, and left the kitchen, leaving him immovable and stiff as he sat staring into the fire.

VIII.

WHERE IS DEBBY?

HE was there in the gray morning light when she came out of the little room, where alone with Doris, fast asleep in fat, pudgy innocence of trouble or sorrow, she had fought out her battle. To a woman like Lyddy Thompson, brought up in the most rigid belief that by love of God and of country, one held to all that made life endurable or honorable, the shock that she had received had dealt a most awful blow. Her hair did not turn white, it is true, in this single night; but her vital force had suffered in a way that she knew meant for her to be thereafter a different woman. And she arose from her knees where at intervals she had thrown herself during the long hours of her agony to bury her face in the patched bedquilt in that voiceless entreaty that is swifter than any words, and passed out to take up her round of daily work with full realization of being this changed creature. All the blood of her ancestors, who had fought to plant the Colonies, who had struggled to maintain them, and who by prayer and precept had died exhorting their children to so fight and struggle, now seemed to assert itself in her throbbing veins. She shut her lips tightly, and with a marble front, that had hitherto been stolid and comfortable placidity, she proceeded to the duty nearest at hand.

Her husband turned heavily in his chair, and scanned her from beneath his thick light eyebrows, and for the first time in his life almost started in surprise. To any one who had seen Mrs. John Par-lin the day before, it would be impossible to believe the matron now performing the household tasks to be the same woman. John Parlin stared at her as he had previously stared at the fire, but she appeared to take no notice of him. When the breakfast was ready, she simply announced the fact, and drew up her chair, and tied on the baby's eating-apron with an unmoved face.

" Father, come to breakfast," said Doris. Johnny was already in his place, with his eyes on the plate of hot smoking buckwheat griddle-cakes.

"I don't want any breakfast," said Mr. Parlin in a gruff voice.

Mrs. Parlin folded her hands, and offered the grace herself. An observance that astonished the children

so much that Johnny transferred his attention from the griddle-cakes to his mother's face, on which he hung open-eyed and open-mouthed.

"Eat your breakfast," she said. So both children betook themselves to their plates and mugs. The baby slapped his spoon into the molasses cup, and succeeded in overturning it, which made a diversion, and a relief to the overstrained woman, as it necessitated quick movement on her part for repairs, and took her out of the reach of curious eyes. When she came back with the cloth to wipe up the sticky mess, her husband was gone from the chair. She showed no sign of feeling at the discovery.

"Father hain't eaten any breakfast/' said Doris, laying down her knife and fork in slow but decided amazement. " He's gone out."

" He hain't eaten any breakfast," repeated Johnny, between his mouthfuls of dripping cakes.

"You eat your own," commanded Mrs. Parlin in a stern, cold voice. " Did you hear me tell you ? I speak but once, you remember."

They ducked their heads, and again addressed themselves to their plates, with an occasional side glance at the tall, stern woman whom they had never seen as their mother, and finished the meal in silence.

Everything was attended to as usual, with the most

scrupulous care. And Mrs. Parlin at last sat down to the mending-basket and an overstocked supply of sewing. And then for the first time she began to wonder why Debby was late, and what could have kept her from obeying the injunction to be home bright and early; for the girl never disobeyed the slightest wish of father or mother. All through the terrible night had been the one only cause for thankfulness that the girl, the loved one of the household, had been saved the shock of hearing from the father's own lips that he was a traitor to his country. " It would have killed her," the mother moaned within her parched and silent lips. But now the mother, her heart wrenched at one awful strain away from its natural abiding-place, turned with unspeakable longing to the bright presence who was the light and comfort of the house, and she cried aloud once to herself as she sat there, "Deborah — O Deborah!"

But the clock ticked on, and she came not. At last footsteps were heard, light and quick. Mrs. Parlin's heart gave a great leap of dread now that the eventful moment had really arrived; and she sewed nervously as a light figure, too swiftly to distinguish it, came around the cottage.

"Mrs. Parlin," called Miliscent Barrett, coining quickly into the kitchen, "why did you not let Debby

stay all night? I want her to come up again this morning."

Mrs. Parlin's work dropped to her lap, and she stared in speechless amazement out of a white face into the blooming one of the girl.

" If it troubles you to let her go — oh ! are you ill ? " as the woman sent out her long arms and beat the air with her hands. " Debby — come, come quickly — your mother! "

"Where is Debby?" gasped the mother; "where is my girl, my all? Where is Debby?"

"Where is Debby?" repeated Miliscent, her own cheek blanching, "why here, of course. She left my house yesterday afternoon to go down to the Common to find my grandfather, on an errand ; and she came home, didn't she ? She didn't come back to us."

" She is not here — she never came back ! "

Miliscent was only conscious that a tall figure stood over her calling in wild accents on God to restore her daughter, that she, Miliscent, rushed out of the kitchen and summoned the children to stay with their mother, while she prepared to run on anguished feet up to Captain James for help in this distressful moment.

" What's the matter ? " A voice that came from the other side of the stone wall dividing Mr. Parlin's farm from that of his next neighbor caused her to look

126 A LITTLE MAID OF CONCORD TOWN.

up into the yellow face, under its big inevitable handkerchief, of Aunt Keziah.

Miliscent was not afraid of her, as were most of the village young people, nor had she any particular reason for dislike, not being a neighbor. She recognized gladly the fact that here was a woman who probably could look after the half-crazed mother better than two small frightened children. So she said quickly, " O Miss Felton ! Mrs. Parlin is sick — she has had-bad news. Will you go in and stay with her while I go for help?"

" Yes, yes," grunted Aunt Keziah, not ill-pleased at an opportunity to display her medical lore ; " as soon as I have got my herb-pot, which, thank fortune, is ever steeping by the fire, I will be right over."

She disappeared within her own house before Miliscent could remark that the case was not one for medicine save that required for an anguished heart; and the girl, with her own misery of the dread of ill befalling her best-loved friend haunting her every step, hurried on, the hot August sun beating down on her unprotected head, for she had dropped her sunbonnet in the Parlin cottage.

Where was Debby ?

" Ha!" Jim Haskins had exclaimed, and seized both of Debby's supple wrists before she had time

to move, " been listening, have you ?" He brought his drunken face so near to the girl that she recoiled in disgust. "Well, you shall have no chance to tell what you've heard."

"Jim," cried Debby in a passion, "unhand me this instant." She shook his hard hands in her efforts to get free. But he was too far gone in drink and the fury of passion at having all his plans thrown out by this girl, Abner Butterfield's sweetheart. It was gall and wormwood to him, and a thousand times worse than having it found out by any one else. He took both of her hands in one of his big ones, and held them as in a vice, with the other whipping out of his pocket a leathern string. "Here you'll stay, ha, ha! You needn't think your news, that you've so cleverly got, will do any good." With a few swift passes (Jim was quick and handy at a knot) he had her safely bound, her hands behind her, to a tree, the cruel string cutting into her young and tender flesh.

Debby gathered up all her soul into one mighty scream; but she regretted it the minute afterward, for he turned suddenly from regarding his work, pulled out his red cotton handkerchief, and thrust it in her mouth. " Now you can scream all you want to, or try to, Miss Debby Parlin." He gave a

parting laugh, and then loped off, plunging deeper into the thicket, and was lost to view.

How long she stood there before she was conscious of making any effort to free herself Debby never knew. She was in such a dense forest, with the underbrush thickly filling up the interstices, that there was no opportunity to tell by the sun's rays, for all was dark and cool. She was first brought to herself by the stinging pain in her hands, and an intolerable sense of anguish from the gag in her mouth. It was useless to pull against the leathern string and struggle to be free, for every movement only strained it deeper into the flesh. She at last, after several worse than useless attempts, resigned herself to waiting until some one who missed her should come to her release.

It was madness to think of word being carried to Tory Lee, who would deliver it to the council at Cambridge, warning them of preparations for warfare, and possibly an uprising by the people. Debby felt her brain swim at the thought of what the effect of those words might be, if only to anger the leaders of the Regulars, and swell the already aggressive spirit of the enemy to more oppression.

" I will die, but I will make one more attempt," she determined; but the swoon that it produced made her

see, when her brain cleared and she came to herself, that it must not be repeated.

It must be near nightfall now. Yes, the birds were twittering about her poor head in that sleepy fashion that bespeaks the nest and the folded wing, as they fluttered to their resting-places. Debby closed her eyes and tried to pray. The good Father would take care of her, and let some one find her. But that was not so much matter now, since it would soon be too late to keep Tory Lee from his mission. Oh 1 she would pray once more for the evil she feared to be averted. " Send some one, O God ! for Christ's sake." She looked up, and saw a man regarding har with a fixed and curious expression as he stood behind a tree. The next instant he had torn the red cotton handkerchief from her mouth, and was cutting the leathern thongs.

"Poor little one! " he said; and he made an involuntary movement as though he would smooth the rings of sunny hair lying across her hot and aching brow, then his hand fell away, and he stepped back, and told her she was free.

It was exquisite torture at first for Debby to move her arms, so long bent back in their unnatural position, and she nearly fainted from the trial, as she sank upon the ground; seeing which the stranger

ran lightly to the river-bank, and brought water in his hat, with which he laved her face and poor arms until she opened her eyes. Then he withdrew as before, and regarded her closely. He was dressed in peddler's attire, having his pack resting against the tree behind which he had first seen the girl. He was tall and slender, now standing quite erect; his head, on which was a wig of long, straw-colored hair, thrown easily back. "What wickedness is this," he cried in deep, rich tones of indignation, "that has been perpetrated here? Do not try to speak, poor girl;" for Debby was making ineffectual efforts to move her poor swollen mouth. " Enough that I have been able to rescue you."

"Oh, I thank you, kind sir!" mumbled Debby, trying to regain her feet. The peddler sprang forward, and put forth his hand to help her, with as much deference as if she had been a duchess. The hand struck her particularly; it was long, with tapering fingers and nails that certainly looked like those of no peddler who had hitherto crossed her path. She gave a little start, but quickly recovered herself. It was — it must be — a British spy in disguise. She must be on her guard about giving information.

" Can I — can I — help you ? " asked the peddler

awkwardly, and speaking in a high, squeaky voice. " I am going through the country, miss, at my trade of selling goods to the farmers' wives. If I might see you safely from this wood to your home, for it has been perilous enough for you here." He glanced about, as if for sight of lurking foe, and waited for her to speak.

"I can get along," said Debby, with a hot flush rising on her white face ; and she staggered a few paces off, then stopped a moment by a friendly tree.

He did not offer to assist her again, but waited till she should recover freedom of motion. Nor did he attempt to question her; but turned his back on her, and seemed to be absorbed in contemplating his pack, resting where he had left it. Soon Debby essayed again to move on.

" I will follow you," said the peddler, leaving his natural tones into which he had been betrayed when lost in pity over her condition, and addressing her in the squeaky voice as before, "at a distance, miss; then if you need assistance I can give it." He slung his pack over his shoulders, which now looked bent and worn, and dragged on hastily a pair of old black cotton gloves, although the day might be said to be unnecessarily warm for such an addition to a peddler's costume, then motioned to her to lead the way.

132 A LITTLE MAID OF CONCORD TOWN.

Debby went off very well for some paces. Suddenly she turned swiftly, went back to the peddler's side, and put out her bruised little hand. " I thank you, sir," she said, in a sweet, serious way, and raising her blue eyes to his face, " for saving my life, and for all your kindness."

" May God bless you, miss!" (again the stranger forgot to care for his voice, but he soon recovered himself with a cough. He took the outstretched little hand in one of his, and covered it for a moment with its black-covered mate), "and keep you from all harm forever. Now lead on, please," he squeaked forth suddenly; and the two went forth, the peddler slouching along well to the rear, his head bent as if wholly occupied with thoughts of his travelling gains; while Debby, as her wonted strength returned to her with the exercise, stepped off faster and faster, her mind laying rapid plans meanwhile.

" It won't ever do to go to Captain James's house now, nor to Milly's," she said to herself. " If he is a spy, and oh, he must be — but how beautiful he is 1" Then she pulled herself up with a remorseful twinge. How could any British young man be beautiful, even if he had wondrous dark eyes and long taper fingers ? He was good, certainly. Debby was glad her conscience would allow her to admit that, for he had

saved her from a terrible fate; indeed, she thought, she must have died before morning but for him; perhaps there yet was time to keep Tory Lee from taking his message. At this thought she struck into a run. But where? She must not let the peddler, whoever he might be, find the way to Captain James's; yet it was imperative that some trusty person should hear her news about Tory Lee as soon as possible. Where? Oh, to Abner Butterfield's, of course! His tidy farm, where he lived with his widowed mother, was but a mile or so farther on; and if she could only get this peddler to put aside his care of her, she should do quite well enough, and reach there safely. But no; there he was — she could see in the turn in the road, as she glanced backward — coming on. He did not seem to run, but to get over the ground all the same easily enough with long, masterful strides that kept about the same distance between' them as at starting; and the distance was traversed in this fashion, till at last the candle twinkled out from a window of the old brown farmhouse set back from the road that was known as the "Butterfield Place."

Debby stumbled up the box-bordered path to the kitchen door. She could hear the peddler stop out in the road opposite the house and wait, as she rapped with a tremulous hand. Then the candle was with-

drawn from the window, and heavy steps sounded in the entry, and the green door was thrown wide.

" Why, Deborah Parlin!" the peddler could hear Abner Butterfield's mother say in her high-keyed voice; "for the land's sakes, what brings you clear over here ? "

IX.

AT THE BUTTERFIELD FARM.

« A BNER!" Debby did not heed Mrs. Butterfield's 1\. exclamations nor her look of surprise, but rushed past her into the kitchen's depths.

" Why, he isn't to home," said his mother, coming back to set the candle on the table and look at her curiously. She knew well enough her son's love for this little blooming damsel, for he had freely confided it, but not by any means so sure was she that it was returned. Indeed, it had been hinted to her many times that Deborah Parlin looked down on Abner, and made fun of him, even to his face, for his big hands and feet and awkward ways; and Mrs. Butter-field had tossed her head, and said she guessed her boy needn't to go seeking very hard for company. When he got ready to settle down and get married, she'd lay a shilling he could have his pick from the best girls in Concord Town. So now she eyed Debby sharply, and with no particular favor, waiting for her to speak.

But Debby did not seem to notice aught amiss in face or manner. " O Mrs. Butterfield!" she seized the good woman's arm, thus bringing into view the poor cut hands and wrists, along whose surface little drops of blood had trailed; "where is he? I must see him."

" Oh, my good gracious me ! " ejaculated Mrs. Butterfield with a sharp look at them ; " what's the matter with your hands ?"

"Nothing," said Debby, twitching back to tuck them under her apron. "Never mind. Where is Abner? Oh, dear 1 I tell you, Mrs. Butterfield, I must see him."

"He isn't to home I told you," repeated Mrs. Butterfield testily; "but, you poor child, lemme take your hands — they're all cut up dreadful. I must wash 'em, and bandage 'em up for you in opodeldoc."

" I don't in the least mind my hands," cried Debby crossly, with another twitch; " and you will oblige me, Mrs. Butterfield, by not mentioning 'em again." And in stalked Abner, to find his mother flushed and combative, and Debby in a pretty pet, standing before her.

She flew to him at once. " Abner," she said in an authoritative way, vastly becoming to her, thought the young man, but it made his mother grind her gums in the absence of many important teeth, to see it. " I

must speak to you at once on a very important matter."

Abner looked at his mother, who stood her ground valiantly. Debby went swiftly up to her. " I want you to forgive me, Mrs. Butterfield," she said, "for speaking so; but I've been through a good deal, though that's no excuse, and I've something to tell that no one ought to know but Abner."

"You can take her into the keepin'-room, said Mrs. Butterfield, bobbing her large head at Abner. "All right, child; now you speak some way decent." And Debby, in a tremor to get her news delivered, fairly ran after him as he led the way, and shut the door behind them.

"We'll, if I ever!" exclaimed Mrs. Butterfield, left alone in the kitchen ; " well, there, there, there ! " she cried gustily, quite unable to stop herself. " No, I never did in all this world; I declare to gracious, I never did." Then she sat down in the big calico-covered rocking-chair, and swung back and forth breezily.

" Abner," Debby kept her hands well behind her back, as she told all the story hastily; as it was done, imploring him to hurry, and prevent in some way Tory Lee from carrying the inflammatory news to Cambridge. He stood still a moment, thinking in his slow way.

138 A LITTLE MAID OF CONCORD TOW*.

" O Abner! why don't you start ?" cried Debby impatiently.

" It is too late to keep him back," said Abner. meditating a minute or so; " for he has already started, probably. But I ought to follow him, and track him to Cambridge, and see if he really does meet any of the council. But where did you come from ? You must get home, Debby." He bent an anxious look on the young girl's face.

" Oh, never mind me !" exclaimed Debby more impatiently than ever. " Besides, I wasn't going home to-night. Mother said I could stay with Miliscent Barrett."

"Then I ought first to take you there," said Abner, a sudden light in his face.

" No, no ! I can go with Pompey, can't I ? You ought to hurry off this minute, Abner."

" I s'pose so," said Abner, the light dying out. "Well, I ought, as you say, to hurry;" yet he made no movement for the door.

" Yes, yes," cried Debby nervously. There was no time to tell him about the peddler, nor was she certain that it was a subject to be mentioned. Surely the first thing to be done was to finish the business in hand, and that with as much despatch as possible, without wasting time on any other story. She had given

the lightest of touches concerning the way in which she had become possessed of the plan, and only mentioned Jim's name incidentally as talking with Tory Bliss when she had overheard the conversation. She now almost pushed Abner to the door. " Do hurry,'* she begged.

" Mother," said Abner, going into the kitchen, " Pompey must take Debby down to Cap'n James's. She was to stay there over night."

"All right," said Mrs. Butterfield, rocking noisily. "You goin' away?" seeing him pick up his cap which he had thrown down on the table.

"Yes; and I sha'n't be home before morning. Take good care of yourself, mother." He went over and planted a kiss on her wholesome cheek.

"And you be careful of yourself," she said; "for these are troublous times." But she didn't dare ask him his errand.

"Good-night Debby;" he put out his hand, which she pretended not to see, and a hurt expression came into his face as he turned away.

"Abner, don't be angry," she began — "nonsense ! " and she gave a little laugh, too nervous now to care for anything, as the reaction was coming.

"Well, I must wake up Pompey," said Mrs. Butterfield as Abner's footsteps sounded down the road, and she got heavily out of her chair.

" Oh, dear me! has he gone to bed ?" cried Debby in dismay.

"Why, yes; what do you expect at this time o' night," said Mrs. Butterfield ungraciously; "long after nine o'clock." And she went out the door. Debby could hear her calling up to the barn chamber to rouse the negro man who had been the faithful servant of Abner's father. He had been, some folks said, a slave when a boy, but no one knew for certain. Mrs. Butterfield now called and called, but in vain; and then she mounted the stairs and searched for herself.

"Pompey ain't in bed nor nowheres," she announced, coming back with a puzzled face to set her candle on the table. "Whewl how hot I bel Now, what's to be done ? You was to stay at Cap'n James's, was you, over night ? "

"Yes," said Debby in a miserable little voice. All her brave spirit had suddenly oozed out of her, and she presented a very abject appearance indeed. " Miliscent was going to sleep at her grandfather's, and mother promised her I might stay with her." At mention of her mother, she looked ready to Cry, and one or two tears did fall on the red tablecloth.

"Well, you can't now," said Abner's mother, who didn't see the tears; "you've got to stay all night here, as there ain't no way to get you down there; it's black as Egypt out, 'cause there's a thunder-storm, I guess, coming up." She spoke harsher than she otherwise would, thinking of Abner out in it, driven somewhere by this girl, on some fool's errand maybe. "You can take a ni'gown of mine; it's the only way," she added shortly.

"I ain't afraid to go by myself," said Debby, twisting her poor hands hard. Yet she thought of the peddler; he wouldn't hurt her, even if she should chance upon him, for he was good, but — and she hesitated.

"Well, I guess," began Mrs. Butterfield in a loud, high key, "that I know better'n to let you go streaking off alone this dark night, Deborah Parlin. I shouldn't want to meet your mother afterward, that's all I say."

"Where shall I sleep?" asked Debby in a broken little voice, longing for some bedclothes to pull over her head, or she would disgrace herself and break down altogether.

"You can sleep along of me, or you can go up in the back chamber,"' said Abner's mother.

"Oh! I'll go up in the back chamber," said Debby quickly; " if you please, and you don't mind, Mrs. Butterfield," she added humbly.

"It don't make no difference to me; the clean sheets is on the bed. You can take that candle," pointing to one in a tin stand on the shelf.

"Good-night," said Debby. "I hope you'll say you forgive me for being cross," she said, pausing a minute on the way out.

"Well, I will," said Mrs. Butterfield, not looking at her. Her thoughts were all on her boy, off somewhere this black night, she'd give a good deal to know where.

Debby went up the crooked stairs unsteadily, and set the candlestick on the bureau before the cracked looking-glass, got off her clothes as well as she could for her hands, that now began to bleed afresh, and curled in between the sheets, which she pulled well up over her head. Then she burst into a torrent of tears.

"Mercy me, I forgot all about that child's hands!" exclaimed Mrs. Butterfield. After shooing out the cat, and tying on her nightcap, she was just about to step into her own bed, and with a stab of remorse that was genuine and deep, she toiled over the stairs and into the back chamber. Without any preamble this time, she advanced and .gave a hasty twitch to the bedclothes, — " I'm a-going to see your hands now, for I won't have it on my conscience not to do for

'em," — to see a face convulsed with sobs, the pillow drenched, and Debby in an agony of grief.

"You poor, blessed little creeter, you!" Abner's mother bent her nightcap over the bed, and just lifted the little figure up until it rested in her arms. "There, there, there !" She cuddled her against her large neck; and Debby nestled there, a hurt little thing, without a show of resistance. " Don't try to talk, nor say anything. I'm a-going to take care of you. You're a pretty creeter as ever lived." She was passing her large hands over the sunny hair now with even, soothing strokes. How like to Abner's hands they were! Debby thought her own mother's could not be softer nor more gentle. "I wouldn't cry if I was you." But Debby was beyond all power to help it; and Abner's mother soon began to be dismayed at the stream of tears that flowed down her neck, and the sobs that shook the slender little frame.

"And so you come up here after supper," she said, to make diverting conversation. "Well, there, you must be tired."

"I haven't had any supper," said Debby involuntarily.

"Land o' Liberty!" exclaimed Mrs. Butterfield. "I b'lieve the child's hungry. Hain't had no supper!

144 A LITTLE MAID OF CONCORD TOWN.

Now you just lie there," she slipped the bright head on the pillow, "and don't you cry no more, like a pretty creeter, and I'll bring you up something to eat, the first thing I do, says I."

Debby, with a big flowered calico wrapper over Mrs. Butterfield's "ni'gown," soon sat up in bed, with a generous blue-edged plate on her knees, while Ab. ner's mother sat at the foot admiringly watching her eat, and alternately suppressing a groan of dismay as she saw the full extent of the bruises on wrist and hand where the large sleeves fell away.

Debby looked up as the last scrap disappeared, and a wan little smile stole over her face. "I think you're awfully good to me," she said simply.

" There, there! " cried Mrs. Butterfield, quite overcome ; and setting the empty plate on the bureau she began to cuddle her again. "Don't say nothing about it. How can I help it? You're as pretty as you can be, and I hain't never had a daughter."

"And I was ▓▓ross to you," said Debby sorrowfully, and feeling it time to steer clear from dangerous ground.

"Don't you speak of that," said Mrs. Butterfield peremptorily; "for I've forgot about it long ago."

"But I can't forget," said Debby, with a droop of her bright head.

"And I warn't none too pleasant ▓▓▓▓ou," said Ab-ner's mother, " to be honest about it. So I want you to forgive me. You see, I was a-thinking of my boy. I'm bound up in him, Debby."

"Yes, yes," said Debby, realizing that the ice was becoming thin again, and it was best to skate away. "Well, I wanted to tell you, dear Mrs. Butterfield, what I'd come to Abner for; but it wasn't my secret alone, you see."

"And I don't want to know," declared Mrs. Butter-field most decidedly. "Now I'm going down for the old rags and the opodeldoc; and I'll have these poor hands of yours done up so nice, you won't know you got any hands when I get through."

It took so long before the process was ended of getting them where Debby was not to know that there were any hands, that the thunder-storm, that otherwise they must have perceived coming up, now broke in fury over the old brown homestead, that shook in its every casement.

"I don't want to leave you up here alone," said Abner's mother, after oh-ing and ah-ing for the last time over the poor hands, and viewing her work with great satisfaction as the big bandages lay up against the pillow. " Hadn't you better come down and sleep along of me ?"

"Yes," said Debby; "I should like it very much, Mrs. Butterfield."

"Well, then, says I, you just hop out of bed," said Abner's mother, very much gratified, "and I'll help you down ; might as well carry this pillar, I s'pose," bunching it under one arm as they went along.

" Oh! I can get down by myself," began Debby brightly. Then she thought better of it, and allowed Mrs. Butterfield to hoist her along in the way popularly supposed to be a great assistance, by tucking one hand under the arm, and bestowing a series of persistent shoves, indescribable to all but the one assisted. At last, to the great satisfaction of both, the journey was accomplished, and Debby lay back on the four-poster in the big bedroom down-stairs.

" I forgot to tell you that I always sleep on feathers," said Mrs. Butterfield ; "but then, la! it's best I do tonight, being there's such a thunder-storm. You ain't struck on top o' them."

"I don't mind the feathers," said Debby happily, and stretching out her toes comfortably as far as they would reach.

"Now you take plenty o' room, and stick out your hands on the pillar. Don't you be a mite afraid; they won't be in my way," continued Mrs. Butterfield, with a last critical survey of the" two white bundles that

finished Debby's arms, before extinguishing the candle.

She leaned over after she climbed into her nest of feathers that billowed up into a big ridge between her stout figure and the slender one. "You won't mind, I hope, if I snore some; it's kind o' comp'ny, I think, to hear the human voice in the night, and sociable like."

But Debby was beyond all the pleasures of such entertainment, being fast asleep on her pillow.

X.

AN UNUSUAL CONFERENCE.

" T 'CLAR to gracious, massa," Pompey shook in

JL every limb like an aspen leaf, " I'm skeered 'clar through. Oh, ▆▆▆! " as a terrific boom of thunder rolled over their heads; " s'pose the Almighty is after ole Pomp 'cause he done run away ?"

The peddler leaned back against the hayrick and said, " I suppose the Almighty has more important business on hand than looking after you, Pomp."

" S'pose so," said the negro, a little relieved; "▆▆▆Passon Emerson, he do say, he do, that there can't no one git away from God's big eye."

" Oh, well! you're in the way of duty now, Pompey," observed the peddler carelessly, " so take the comfort of it. I'd advise you to."

Pompey scratched his wool with anything but a happy hand. Still, in these dismal surroundings, with the rain descending in torrents around them, and the elements at war overhead, it was something to hear a word of encouragement.

" And as we are shut up to each other's society, we might as well enliven the time by conversation," the peddler went on in an easy voice. It was astonishing how soon he lost his squeaking tones. " So go on, Pomp, with what you began yesterday, or was it last week when first we met ? "

" Massa question a body up so I can't tell all de times," said Pompey in a discomfited way.

" Well, never mind, we won't be exact about dates," said the peddler.

" An' I'm a-goin' home, massa," said the negro with a sudden lifting of his head, "an' tell missis why I didn't come when I heerd her a-callin' me fit to split, an' I in the woodshed corner just a-goin' to streak it to meet you." He made a quick movement which the peddler's long leg intercepted, so that with a howl Pompey's round body rolled over and over on the sodden grass beyond. "████ massa!" he cried, "you needn't to kick so hard; you needn't to, shorely," as he rubbed his shin.

" I was afraid you wouldn't stop for a small kick," observed the peddler.

"Oh, ████ I ain't a-goin' to run, I ain't, massa," declared Pompey, coming back to huddle deprecat-ingly under the rick.

"No; 1 don't think you will," said the other; "and

150 A LITTLE MAID OF CONCORD TOWN.

if you did, I could easily come up with you, if there were miles between us."

" Massa he got such a very long leg," said ████y in still greater discomfiture, "he just like the ████ after a body."

The peddler took this compliment coolly, and indulged in a smothered laugh under cover of the dark ness, presenting an unmoved countenance in the sharp gleam of lightning that followed.

The negro burrowed deep in speechless fright within the rick, and shook again worse than before. ████

"You must remember, Pomp," began the peddler in a reassuring tone, "that you are now in his Majesty's service, a fact that should make you proud as Lucifer."

"I donno who Loosifer is," grumbled Pompey, "and I don't care fer the Majesty; I'd druther be back at Mis' Butterfield's. Oh, wheel I wisht I never lef her an' Massa Abner."

"Pomp," cried the peddler sternly, springing up to a sitting posture so suddenly that he nearly overthrew the darkey who was bunched up in a heap rubbing his big hands together, "do you know you could be delivered over to the strongest hand of the law, that would land you in a prison where you'd never see daylight again? Not to care for your king, his Maj-esty, is treason — treason! Lucky for you that I don't deliver you up at once to have your head cut off."

Pompey's eyes stuck out till they could protrude no farther ; and as the peddler made an involuntary movement, he cried, "Don't kick, massa," — protecting his shin with both black hands, — "████ don't massa, an' I'll do just everything you say."

" See that you do ; and there is no more talk about deserting your king, and going to serve these rebels," commanded the peddler, settling back into his easy attitude. "You've started with me now in his Majesty's service, and there is no drawing back. Well, now, to begin with, you know where I found you, Pomp."

"Yis, yis, massa," said the negro with a groan of remembrance which he speedily changed to a hee-hee; "down in the wood-lot a-cuttin' out the ole bresh. "

" Quite correct. That was — let me see " — said the peddler reflectively, " last week ; and I gave you some money, you remember."

"Yes, sir, yes, sir," said the negro. "Thankee sir, thankee," bobbing his head.

"Well, that bound the bargain, as we say; that is, you have had pay for accepting service for his Maj-

esty. So you see you can't back out without awfu. punishment."

"'Twas such a little money," said Pompey, squirming all over; "only a shillin', massa."

"It doesn't make any difference what the sum was," said the peddler with a return of sternness. "Take care, Pomp."

"Oh, yes, sir — oh, wheel Yes, sir, thankee, sir."

"Well, and then I came again, you remember, that was yesterday — or have you forgotten, eh? "

"No, sir, no, sir, I done 'member; an' I was in the wood-lot agin."

"What a good Pompey it is," remarked the peddler pleasantly; "and I gave you some more money."

"Only another shillin' — oh, thankee, sir, thankee."

"And that bound you again; so you see you are bound twice, fast and long, strong and hard. Really, Pomp, if you should attempt to run away now, I don't know what would become of you."

"I ain't a-goin' to run, massa; oh, ▬▬ I ain't!" cried the negro, creeping up in abject terror to his companion. "Keep the dreadful things from coming after me an' cotchin me, massa."

"I can't," said the peddler coldly. "If you take it into that thick head of yours to give me the slip at any time, I could catch you as easy as I can touch

you now." He sent out his long and supple fingers to close them around the darkey's wrist.

"Oh, ▬▬ massa, how they pinch! Oh, wheel Massa think my arm thick as my head — ee!"

"Just as I can touch you now," repeated the peddler, releasing the negro's arm, "so I could catch you 'f you tried to run. But I want to save you from the punishment that would be yours for trying any such game."

"Massa needn't be 'fraid," said Pompey, his teeth chattering in his head; " fer I'll stick to him just like a burr. 'Deed, an' I will, massa."

"Very well. Now, seeing that you understand the matter thoroughly, why, we can progress with our conversation. Only first I want to refresh your memory a grain more. You know when I saw you yesterday I made an arrangement for you to meet me to-night down in the wood-lot again as soon as it was dark. The storm favored us, and you came a little earlier than I had dared to hope."

"Yes, massa; but I didn't think I wasn't a-goin' back."

"What's that?"

"Oh, nothin', massa, nothin' 'tall!" said Pompey, ducking animatedly.

"Well, now that your memory is jogged up, we will

leave our starting-point, and proceed to our conversation. To begin with, Pomp, you know Captain James Barrett very well, you said."

"'Deed an' I do, massa; alwus know'd him since I live in this yere town; an' that's a many years."

"He's a very important person hereabout, I believe, eh? "

" What's that ar?"

"He's one of the best men here, and makes people do as he says? " explained the peddler.

"'Deed an' he do, sah. Capen James he have a way with him, they just got to, sah."

"And he keeps a loc of things that the soldiers use, I suppose," said the peddler, — "bullets now, and guns most likely, and maybe gun-carriages, eh? "

"There you're right, massa. He make those things, Capen James do. Oh, he awful smart! "

"Well, let us see. He keeps things to eat, most likely," observed the peddler, — "oatmeal and pork and rice, eh? — and maybe more? "

██████ massa, 'twould make your eyes stick out to see 'em all ; the corn chamber's full, and the south barn, an' " —

" And there is another person who greatly interests me in this town," said the peddler. "Among many interesting characters, I must say you possess a few

of remarkable claim to my regard. I refer to Mr. Ephraim Wood."

"Massa Wood awful smart, he are," rejoined the negro, bobbing his head. "He live up t'other end of the town."

" I happen to know his residence," said his companion dryly. " I was up there practising my vocation a few days ago, and had the honor to have his dwelling pointed out to me. Well now, Pompey, does Mr. Wood come down to talk with your Captain James very often, do you know ? "

"He ain't my Capen James," contradicted Pomp; "Mis' Butterfield's my capen."

"Was, you meant to say. Well, we won't split hairs. Captain James is one of the fathers of the town. Does he meet Mr. Wood very often to have long talks? "

Any reference to hair always made the negro mad ; so now he sat gloomily silent, not daring to exhibit any further displeasure.

"I asked you a question, Pompey," said the peddler, with a significant movement of his long right leg.

" Don't kick, massa. Oh, ██████████ don't kick! I'll tell, I'll tell. Yes, sah; he do, sah; a great many times, sah."

I$6 A LITTLE MAID OF CONCORD TOWN.

"Goon"

"Once when I was down to the capen's, Mis' Butter-field sent me fer " —

"Never mind what you went for."

" An' Mis' Barrett warn't in; an' I went along th' entry, an' I heard the capen an' some one a-talkin' — but 'twarn't Mr. Wood that ar time, 'twas Mr. Whitney, sah."

"And you heard what they said? " cried the peddler.

" Couldn't help it, sah. Mis' Barrett warn't there, an' I couldn't go home without what Mis' Butterfield had sent me fer. She told me to get some " —

" Yes, yes, that will do," interrupted the peddler impatiently.

" You told me to talk, massa," said Pompey.

" But I want you to tell things that I want to hear."

" Massa do ask sech a lot o' questions," said the negro discontentedly, and scratching his wool.

"What's that?"

" Oh ! nothin' — nothin' 't all, massa. Hee-hee! "

" You were going to tell me what you heard those two gentlemen talking about." The peddler bent his dark eyes full upon the round, black face clearly disclosed in the fitful lightning gleams that every now and then illuminated the heavens. The fury of the storm was somewhat abated; but it still thundered a sullen, persistent roar, and the rain showed little sign of holding up. " Now begin at once."

" They said they warn't a-goin' to buy no more tea."

" Anything else ? "

" An' that they'd fight; they wouldn't be slaves. I member that ar', 'cause white men ain't slaves."

" What did they say about fighting ?" asked the peddler eagerly. " Rememb▓▓▓▓▓▓ Be careful; you know what I told you."

" Yes, sah, yes, sah. Well, they said fer one thing that they never should submit,—that's the word, I know fer shore, 'cause I kep a-sayin' it over an' over arterwards, — they never'd submit to the disrageous commands of the king."

"Outrageous, you mean."

"Yis, sah, yis, sah, I said so; an' they'd fight fer their liberties, and they'd git ready."

"Ah, they would?"

"Yis, sah."

"Cuffee, do you believe the men in this town would really fight? " The peddler asked the question explosively, as if quite beyond his volition.

"My name ain't Cuffee," said the negro, in a dudgeon, "it's Pompey, sah."

"Well, then, Pompey, or Snowball, or whatever you choose, do you really believe they would fight? "

158 A LITTLE MAID OF CONCORD TOWN.

"I really think massa might give a man his right name," said the negro sullenly; "I ain't no snowball, an' I don' wanter be called one."

"That's a fact," exclaimed the peddler, bursting into a laugh. At this cheerful sound, the first that had enlivened the meeting, Pompey showe▓▓▓▓▓▓▓▓ies, of which he had a goodly supply, and grinned till his mouth might be said to almost meet behind his ears. When he had finished, his sullen fit had quite disappeared.

"Well, now, Pompey, I don't blame you for wanting your own name," said the peddler; "andafter this, I'll observe great care to see that you get it, when we are talking together, at least, and it is quite convenient. And we feel better now, I think, and more acquainted, after that little laugh. Well, now to business again. I will ask my question once more; please pay attention, and not oblige me to repeat it. Do you think the men of this town would ever fight, or would they run away?"

" Do you mean fight the wicked Bloody Backs, sah? "

" What?"

Pompey never could tell whether it was the thunder that roared so, nor what hit his shin with such a horrible force, for he didn't see the long right leg move from its place. But he was rubbing the place affected

by the explosion, he knew, with quick hands, the tears streaming down his face, and hearing the peddler say, " Never let such words pass your black mouth again; " so he could form a private opinion, though not publicly expressing it.

"Would they fight his Majesty's troops, think you? " asked the peddler searchingly.

" Yis, sah, they would. ▓▓▓▓▓▓ 'taint my fault, massa," cringed the negro, now thoroughly frightened, and beginning to blubber outright.

" Stop that, ▓▓▓▓▓▓ you'll not be hurt, if you keep a civil tongue in your black head for your king and his soldiers. So they would fight, eh, and not run away — sure ? "

•'Run?" exclaimed Pompey, and brushing off the tears from his cheek with the back of one black hand. " You don't know 'em, sah. Run ? "

It was enough to hear the tone, and the peddler forbore to question further. When he spoke, it was in a careless way, and on quite a different subject.

"Well, now, Pomp, I don't suppose you know anybody around here of the name of Parlin."

"Deed an' I do, sah," cried Pompey, with a chuckle. The turn of the conversation was quite to his liking, and he became communicative again.

"Why, that's the name of Miss Debby, that ar is, hee-hee."

"Miss Debby?" repeated the peddler carelessly; "I presume you mean Deborah."

"Yis, yis; Mis' Butterfield she call her Deb'rah, but she not like her much. But Massa Abner, he call her Debby."

" Does this Massa Abner, as you call him, like her, then? " queried the peddler, still without the slightest appearance of interest, but rather as if the whole thing bored him.

"No, sah, but he lubs her to 'straction; she's his sweetheart, Miss Debby is."

"Ah?"

"But I donno's she keers so very much fer him," said the darkey; " I donno, sah, I heerd tell that she laugh at him. But Miss Debby cain't help a-laughin', she cain't, no more'n a bird can help a-flyin' an' a-singin'. Miss Debby's alwus a-laughin' an' a-sing-in', an' the little hole in her cheek keeps comin' in an' out. My! but don't Massa Abner set by her, though."

"I suppose Miss Debby favors the king, and is a good Loyalist," said the peddler, after a pause.

"What that ar?"

" She feels that the king is right, and ought to be obeyed."

"Miss Debby feel that ar?"

"Yes."

"O **NO!** , Miss Debby ud fight like pisen if a redcoat come into this town. I've heerd her say a many times, how she wished she could fight 'em herself, an' she meant to when the war came. Everybody here would fight, but Miss Debby would be the worst of the hull lot."

"The storm is over, I think," exclaimed the peddler suddenly. " Get up, Pomp, we must make good travelling between now and morning." He sprang to his feet, and stepped out into the night, with an imperative gesture motioning the negro to go before.

XI.

"WE ARE WELL MATCHED."

THEY travelled two or three miles in silence, Pompey not daring to grumble aloud, but ejaculating "O massy," under his breath every minute or so as he stumbled on by the side of the long legs getting over the ground so evenly. The rain had now entirely ceased, the clouds giving way quickly to a bright starlit sky. The air was sweet and fresh with that resinous quality pervading a wood-section after a smart shower, and all nature gave out balmy odors that to an untroubled mind would have produced peace to a remarkable degree. It was impossible, from his imperturbable manner and expression, to tell what the peddler thought as he tramped on; certain it is that his companion was a good remove from placidity.

At last they came to an abrupt halt. "Your legs aren't in' as good marching order as mine,

I take it, Snowball, I mean, Pompey," observed the peddler, "so we will stop here a bit and rest."

" 'Deed an' they're not, massa," grunted the darkey, too sore in every bone to notice the slip in his name; and, without waiting for further invitation, he sank to the ground and began to nurse his feet.

The peddler cast his pack aside, and threw himself lightly beside him, plucking up some tender checkerberry leaves, which he meditatively chewed, and then became lost in thought.

Suddenly he lifted his head, and his jaws were set. " Get up, Pomp," he commanded; and the negro felt himself dragged, without ceremony, back from the roadside to a thicket, where the hand on his old coat was removed, and he slid to the ground. " Hist, don't move or speak, or I'll blow your brains out." The peddler by a swift movement threw open his long coat enough to let Pompey see a pistol end, as a traveller, long and lank, was proceeding with immense strides round a curve in the road, directly toward them.

It was well that Pompey's tongue stuck to the roof of his mouth in fright at this threat, else he surely must have bellowed out in fright, "Massa Abner — Massa Abner!" But all was still; not the faintest echo of a sound disturbed the traveller's thoughts, as his long steps carried him safely by the two men in the thicket.

When all danger of being overheard was over, the peddler bent over the negro.

"Do you know that farmer fellow?" he demanded.

"It's Massa Abner," gasped Pompey, putting up both hands to ward off a blow.

"Getup! " Pompey didn't wait to be assisted, but found his feet. The peddler was stripping oil his long coat. "Tear off your rags, and put on this." And the change was quickly made. Then the black man's old straw hat was on the peddler's tow-colored wig, but not before it was sharply scanned to be sure of no distinguishing marks to set it apart from other hats of its kind, and the peddler's was on Pompey's white wool; and as a finishing stroke, an immense bandanna was brought forth from the pack at his feet, by the peddler, who proceeded to tie up the negro's face so effectually with fold upon fold, that no one could see a feature of his face, except two black spots that might be supposed to be eyes as they were in the right places. The white wool even was effectually concealed, as the old black felt hat, which was of a generous pattern, was well drawn down over it.

" It requires some ingenuity to dispose of these pistols," observed the peddler, drawing out a brace, "so that they will not be intrusive, until wanted;

however, I can manage it, where needs must. Now then, we are ready. Hark ye, Pomp, if you open that black mouth of yours to utter a sound, I will send cold lead in you that instant. And one thing more, if you think we went on a canter before, you'll make up your mind to go on a worse canter now. You've got to keep up with me! Come on, Snowball!"

Away went peddler, and away went darkey as well as he could, being assisted by the peddler's long and sinewy arm, down the road after the traveller, who had by this time, being blessed by such excellent walking facilities, gotten a good piece ahead. But at last his tall figure could be seen silhouetted in the bright starlight; and although the pace of the two followers was slackened, they still kept up a goodly gait, calculated to bring them success. When this was in view, the peddler began to go slower. Moreover, it was imperative, as the puffs emitted from the black man's throat were by this time demanding attention ; so a pause was indulged in for him to secure the necessary second wind. At last, however, they joined the solitary pedestrian with a " Good-evening, sir," squeaked out so that Abner turned to the salutation.

" Good-evening," he said with no show of interest in the meeting, plodding on as before.

"Terrible rain that," volunteered the peddler, falling into step, Pompey on his other side.

"It was so," observed Abner, as something appeared to be expected.

"I hain't met another such in all my tramping," remarked the peddler, shifting his pack ostentatiously. No answer.

"It's hard work goin' from pillar to post," squeaked the peddler, "year in an' year out, to scratch up a living. You fellows who own your farms don't know nothing about it." Still no answer.

"What's the next town now?" at last he demanded.

"Cambridge," answered Abner shortly.

"Oh! likely place is it? Would I sell much, think?"

"That you could tell when you reach there," said Abner. "I'm sure I cannot say. Women's gewgaws and trinkets ought not to find a ready sale when our country is in such distress," he added bitterly.

"Oh, but I have more things than a few trinkets in my pack," cried the peddler eagerly; "those we must carry to please the ladies, and pins and needles and household things. But I have also many

other useful articles, as you shall see." He stopped suddenly, dropped the pack to the ground, and twitched it open.

"See, see!" as he knelt beside it, and rapidly held up one thing after another.

Leathern wallets, cheap snuff-boxes, bandanna handkerchiefs, comforters, suspenders, tobacco-pouches, and a general odds-and-ends collection of what might be termed the necessities, not to say luxuries, of that day. " Here are many things that you ought to see — cheap. I'll sell 'em cheap." He stuck out a big green leather wallet. "No?" as Abner shook his head; "well, then, this. It's dirt cheap—only a ninepence; you can't get it in Boston shops lesser'n a shillin';" and he tried a tobacco-pouch.

" I want nothing," said Abner decidedly, and going his way.

The peddler clapped to his pack in an angry fashion, and slung it on his back. " Hard times it is," he said, "when honest folks can't get a livin'."

"You speak truly," said Abner gloomily; "but blame not us farmer-folk."

" Who is to blame then ? " squeaked the peddler.

" Who, indeed ? Ah, and can you ask me that ? Your travels through the country have brought you

little knowledge that sharp wits might have picked up, I should think."

The peddler scratched his long straw-colored hair in perplexity. "I go about to sell things, not to get knowledge," he said with a stupid laugh.

" So I should say."

"And I see farms" — he stretched his longhands, on which were now his old black gloves. — " in every direction, and cattle and nice houses. Surely there must be money and plenty of it. Whew! but I wish I had one of these homes! "

" And how long are we sure of these homes ?" cried Abner, in a burst of bitterness. " In a moment, in the twinkling of an eye maybe, all that a man, and his father and grandfather before him, have toiled to earn and to save, may be swept away at the behest of a tyrant king."

" Eh ? " the peddler gazed at him vacantly.

" And all for what ? " cried Abner, careless whether or no he had a good listener, now that the pent-up emotion had found utterance. " Because, forsooth, we have been obedient to our God and our king — because we have obeyed his Majesty's slightest wish, and given him the allegiance our consciences told us was right. Ay, more, we went beyond the letter of the law — we obeyed in the spirit; and we

trusted him and the Parliament of Great Britain to do the right thing by the Colonies. How have we been rewarded ? By oppression and obloquy and scorn; all our charter and natural rights trampled down. Our ports have been stopped up —• look at Boston Harbor; we have been taxed without the privileges of all tax-payers in a civilized land; and now, after untold tyranny, we are met with this last proof of the perfidy of the king and his ministers."

" What is that ?" asked the peddler with open mouth.

" The Act, the Act, man, — where have you been not to know it? — by which our officers, appointed by the vote of the people, are put out, and their places filled with officers of the king's choosing, or that of his minions. This makes us nothing but slaves, and reduces us, and our children after us, to bondage. Nothing now remains for us but death or freedom."

" Would yo\.\ fight ? " asked the peddler drawing near, and bringing out the word in a long-drawn syllable of astonishment.

"Fight? Ay, that we would 1" replied Abner. u Fight?" he threw out his long arms and clinched his hands. " Pray God it may come soon, and the world will see how we will fight. We will fight as a man does who has nothing to live for unless he can

I/O A LITTLE MAID OF CONCORD TOWN.

win. We will fight so that those we love better than life may live in freedom and safety."

" I s'pose now you're thinkin' of your wife an' children," said the peddler meditatively.

"I have no wife," said Abner shortly. The hot color rose to his brown cheek, and he stalked on impetuously.

"That so. Well now, I got ten — I mean children," said the peddler; "an' my wife she finds it hard work to get along, I can tell you, an' me trampin' round the country to scratch up a livin' for all of us. It's mighty hard I tell you, mister."

Abner walked straight ahead, lapsed in gloomy thought, and for some moments neither spoke. At last the peddler began.

" I sold a lot o' things in Concord Town, but then the folks are rich there ! My gracious ! but it's a nice town. If I hadn't got my trade, I'd bring my wife and children an' settle down there myself. Be you goin' far ?"

" A short piece," said Abner curtly, with a manner that invited no further questioning.

" Yes, they're awful rich," continued the peddler, shifting his pack again. " Here you, Simons, s'pose you just carry this thing a spell now; it's your turn. Rim's my partner," he volunteered, as he slung the

pack over on Pompey's back; " we've tramped it together for years now. An' sometimes we each takes a pack an' goes about country, but this time we left t'other pack in Boston Town. ████████████ ! " he stretched his long arms, " ain't I glad to get red on that ██ thing! Have a chaw, mister ? " He twitched out a chunk of tobacco, and held it out invitingly.

Abner shook his head, and plodded on.

" Be you 'quainted up to Concord Town ?" asked the peddler, breaking the pause.

" Somewhat," answered Abner.

" I s'pose you don't happen to know a fellow named Butterfield now, do you ? "

Abner did not reply for a minute, till the peddler repeated the question.

"Yes, I know such a person," said Abner. •

" Well, what sort of a fellow is he, anyway ?" asked the peddler.

"Oh, I always thought he meant well enough," answered Abner.

" Rich, maybe ? " asked the peddler insinuatingly.

" No ; he's poorer'n a good many there. Rich ? how can a farmer be rich who's ground down to the earth; who has to put a mortgage on his farm, and nothing to pay the interest with ? Rich ? I tell you, the peo-

pie are rich only in one thing, and that is, love of freedom."

"Well, now, p'raps this man Butterfield,—•! heerd talk of his bein' a likely sort of a fellow, — might git his mortgage off, an' be a risin' citizen, ef he only knew which side his bread was buttered on."

"What do you mean?" thundered Abner.

"I mean jest what I say. I've tramped around country so I've picked up a few things that are o' use to some folks, maybe, if they ain't to me ; an' if I hain't got book learnin' and the idees you have in your head, I know a thing or two, maybe."

" Explain yourself, if you can," cried Abner in contempt.

"Well, I heerd yist'day, or maybe 'twas longer ago," said the peddler composedly, "that there was a mighty good chance for a young farmer like they said he was, to come back to his allegiance to th' king if he'd been lively the other way ; an' if he did, why he'd git his house an' lands saved free to him, beside bein' on the winnin' side, an' " —

" Hold your ▬▬▬ tongue ! " cried Abner in an awful voice, and squaring up before the long figure of the peddler, "or I'll knock you into kingdom come !"

" Why, I hain't said anythin' about you," exclaimed the peddler coolly, " I'm a-talkin' 'bout that Butterfield they told me of" —

" How dare you speak of the king's tyranny being the winning side," cried Abner, all his usually slow blood racing in a fury in his veins. " And it's an insult to mention one of the men of Concord Town as sunk so low as to think of turning his back on honor and truth."

"P'raps this Butterfield chap don't think as you do," insinuated the peddler, facing him unmoved.

"He does — he does. They all think alike," cried Abner, in a passion; "that is, all but two or three, who are confessedly traitors," and his face darkened.

"Well, stranger," said the peddler, with a triumphant smile, "there's where you are wrong. You've got one man in your town, for I see you are a Concord cit'zen, who's been a rebel, dark and bitter, but who has just come out strong for the king."

" Name him," commanded Abner, with glittering eyes, and coming dangerously near.

"John Parlin."

"You liel " Abner made a rush, but the long arms kept him back.

" Softly, softly there," said the peddler. " No man tells me that to my face without he gives me satisfaction. You must fight."

"Willingly," cried Abner, in a white heat, and stripping off his coat and waistcoat. Pompey, standing like a statue whenever they paused, now groaned within the folds of his bandanna, and wrung his hands.

The peddler cast his eyes quickly on all sides. "We shall be more to ourselves, though as yet we ain't troubled with folks passin', in this pleasant business," he squeaked, "if we get beyond that grove. Come on, Simons, you ain't in this, but you can look on. Now, I'm agoin' to do the square thing, stranger, an' jest have a knock-down with our fists, bein' as you an' I ain't neither o' us armed. Be you ? "

" No," said Abner; "but I have some fists that you will see are able to avenge insults."

" Here we be," said the peddler in great satisfaction, as they reached the spot, Abner with his coat and waistcoat over his arm; and with a sudden movement he quickly divested himself, behind a tree, of his outer garments, which he laid carefully at the roots. Pompey got behind some bushes, where he continued to wring his hands and groan without intermission.

The two men gazed at each other a moment as they rolled up their shirt-sleeves. They were just of a height; but where not an ounce of flesh that could be spared to grace and beauty of outline was to be ob-

served on the peddler, on the young farmer the frame carried more weight beside that of brawn. Yet he had the muscular arm and the fist of a deadly foe. The black eyes gazed into the flashing blue ones, and the pedler forgot to squeak, as he said, " Lay on, stranger! "

For the first few minutes the negro didn't dare to look out of his covert. All he was conscious of was the regular breathing, the thud, thud, of the blows and the stamp and straining of the feet against the ground, like that of angry animals when in combat. But at last, as he became accustomed to the sounds, he ventured a frightened glance, to acquaint himself with the progress of the fight. If Massa Abner would only kill the [redacted], or his emissary, whom he was sure that his companion must be, he would be well content to witness an even worse battle. But all Pompey's terror was, with the intimate acquaintance he possessed of Abner's antagonist, that the combat must end the other way. And what with his stabs of remorse at letting his own Massa Abner be slain, and his perils that he ran from any interference, the negro was in such a pitiable plight that he soon was reduced to a mere quaking body of terror, unable to render any assistance, had he decided to give it.

But after a few moments of this sort of work, the combatants stopped suddenly, drew off, and looked at

176 A LITTLE MAID OF CONCORD TOWN.

each other. Pompey gave a great gulp of joy, and the tears ran down his black cheeks, soaking the bandanna drawn over his mouth.

If the [redacted] wasn't to be killed, at least Massa Abner was safe, as Pompey said, over and over to himself, in excess of thankfulness, "They've done got done now for shore."

But there was a tightening of band and girth, that proclaimed other plans on the part of the combatants. And the drawing in of the breath, and the setting of the jaw, as well as the flashing eye, showed that the truth was the contest had but just begun.

"We are well matched," said the peddler.

"Yes," said Abner, through his set teeth; "you may know how to parry better, but I'll hold on longer, for I've something to fight for."

" Are you ready? " asked his antagonist briefly.

" Yes," said Abner; and the fight was renewed.

Pompey must have lost consciousness about this time, as he huddled on the ground, in abject, witless fright. When he came to himself, and was conscious of the stage in the affair, the two men were wrestling. The muscles of their arms stood out like whipcords, as they swayed back and forth in a deadly embrace. The ground was torn up and stamped, and worn for a large area, as one or the other dragged his contestant

from his position. Pompey even imagined he could see blood dripping from nose and mouth, as occasionally he obtained a glimpse of the strained visage, every nerve alive to victory, the flashing eye, and locked jaw, of each adversary. At last the labored breathing of the panting, struggling combatants became so distressing to hear, that the negro thrust his black fingers in his ears, and the sight being so dreadful, he covered up his eyes, so that he lost the ending which now could not be much longer delayed. The peddler by a dexterous twist, and with a lightning rapidity of action, was achieving what mere strength could not do, and Abner— • "O Lord!" cried Pompey — Abner was falling with a heavy thud to the ground.

The peddler drew off, and folded his arms, and looked at him ; for Abner's eyes were open, and he was by no means in that condition that required help. He was simply a fallen hero.

"We are well matched," said the peddler, his heaving bosom attesting his struggle. " I could never have beaten you, I will frankly say, had I not been acquainted a little better with the rules of wrestling," and came forward and stood over his foe, whose great frame he gazed at in admiration, and offered his hand. " Let us call it even," he said.

But Abner's eyes were fastened on his antagonist's

head. Quick as a flash, the peddler's hand sought the spot toward which the gaze was directed, to meet his own waving locks, the long straw-colored wig lying at some distance on the ground, where it had been thrown in the thick of the battle.

XII.

ABNER ACCOMPLISHES HIS MIS.SION.

" r INHERE is small use in attempting to deny that -i- for purposes of my own I chose to assume a disguise," said the peddler, with a slight smile. "Well, you are a brave man," and his face dropped back again into its grave expression. "Will you shake hands ?"

But Abner got up to his feet. "You beat me," he said slowly, " in a fair fight. I'm not ashamed to own that I like you, and you took no mean advantage. But you've said words that are an insult; and you are, I believe from my soul, an enemy to all my poor struggling countrymen, and an adherent to that tyrant, King George. I cannot take your hand."

" As you will," replied the other curtly; " the time will come when you will be glad to have me offer you my hand, — sooner than you think," he added, with rising anger.

"And now permit me to go upon my way without company," said Abner, resuming his outer garments.

"I have the pleasure to wish you good-night." He strode off into the night, not with the ill-temper of a defeated man, but as carrying a deeper hurt in his soul, harder to bear than any personal misfortune, and was soon lost to the view of his late travelling companions.

"Well, Pompey," — the peddler had resumed his straw-colored wig, trusting to chance and to the negro's terror, that the mishap of its displacement had not been observed in that quarter, — " our friend and your late employer seems to have gotten the worst of that encounter. ████████, I wish I had dealt him some harder whacks," his ill-temper gaining on him.

Pompey had evidently noticed nothing, being far beyond wigs and such trifles, and his teeth chattered as he tried to speak.

"We will give him a chance to stretch his legs well toward Cambridge Town before we start on our journey thither. Of a truth, this young fellow is spared to see greater sorrow than this night's defeat has brought him. He will wade in blood, I fear, before long, and most ineffectually spilt, if ever it comes to the fight, as he thinks it will. But pshaw! what fool's nonsense is this! These country bumpkins will never raise a rifle nor draw a sword. It is all well enough, forsooth, for them to con their tales by the fireside, and believe they are ready for war. But war—what do they know of it? Poor innocents !"

So he ruminated, lost in thought, and oblivious of Pompey's presence. When at length a sufficient time had elapsed to give, in his judgment, the right start to his late opponent, the peddler, for so we must continue to call him, since he has given us no right to describe him by any other name, rose from the ground where he had thrown himself, and commanding his companion to do likewise, took up the pack, and struck off down the road toward the town of Cambridge.

Abner, with head bent down, and the air of a man lost in sorrowful thoughts, went swiftly on his way. That he had missed Tory Lee at his own home on account of the lateness of the hour, was not to be laid to his inefficiency; and that his horse, which, after Debby's tale, he had hurried out and saddled, leaping to its back, and riding hastily off to the Tory's residence, and then away on the wings of the wind to the Cambridge road, should rear in a mad fright at a blinding lightning flash, plunging into a gully, was certainly, again, his misfortune, and not his blunder. Poor Dobbin had gone lame at the mischance; and Abner had left him at the nearest farmhouse, and set forth on foot for the remainder of the distance, vowing to himself that he would track Tory Lee, at

182 A LITTLE MAID OF CONCORD TOWN.

any rate, although he was denied by fate the power to stop him. Then he met the peddler.

Who this person was, and why thus disguised, Abner did not at present bother his head about. It was a time when many new and strange people were shifting into view; and in the presence of the low-hanging cloud of war, the mind was callous to their effects. What was knotting Abner's honest brow and clinching his brown hands as he strode on, was this fellow's mention of John Parlin's name. Of course it could mean nothing. John Parlin was as stanch a patriot as any in Concord Town. Imagine Debby's father — and the hot flush again rose to the young man's face —- being any but a thorough-going patriot, who would die for his country, if need be, but never give up to a traitorous thought! Why, Abner had heard him many a time raising his voice in town-meeting in that slow, deliberative way of his, that was all the more effective when used to impress zealous sentiments, urging the citizens to stand by their rights, and not consent to be further ground down under the tyrant's heel. And how well he remembered that Debby had quoted in her pretty way, often and often, with loving pride, what father had said as being the end of the matter, that if only followed, would lead on to victory and freedom. Oh ! now how bitterly he

regretted that he had not been able to punish this insulting fellow as he deserved — one of King George's dastardly minions, who, because he had the knowledge of the tricks of the game, had beaten him in the wrestling. Abner knew in his heart that his combatant's statement was perfectly true, and that courage and strength had been well matched. It was gall and wormwood to his sore heart now to reflect that the fellow who had uttered the lying statement concerning Debby's father had been spared the lesson of the farmer's good right fist, that should have felled him to the ground.

It was the early morning twilight when Abner entered the town, and betook himself where he knew he could get some glimpse of the man who had gone to warn the members of the Council against the preparations to resist that were being made in his own town, and the temper that was rapidly possessing his own townsfolk. And at last, after some hours, he found himself standing in the shelter of near-by buildings, to be soon rewarded by a sight of Tory Lee emerging from the dwelling of one of the most prominent of the Council, who stood upon the steps of the mansion, profuse in his appearance of gratitude and satisfaction at the interview. The horse of

Tory Lee was then brought around to the door; and with more

satisfaction expressed on both sides, the Concord man vaulted into the saddle, put spurs to his horse, and struck into the turnpike leading to his home. Abner, having thus got all that it was possible to acquire, also started homeward, bu-t on foot.

" Why ?" Debby woke up with a start, and stared at the bed tester of brown-and-white linen, on which remarkable pictures of stage-coach trips, village merrymakings, and men on prancing steeds, greeted her eyes. Then she gazed at her hands, or rather the bundles that adorned each wrist, and it all came back to her.

"Mrs. Butterfield!" she called.

That good woman, with a throb at her heart at the sound of the young voice, dropped her dish-pan with a clatter in the sink, and hurried to look into the rosy face and the eyes dewy with slumber.

"Well, I never!" she ejaculated in great satisfaction. " If you hain't slep'!"

"What time is it?" asked Debby, raising herself to lean on the elbow of the big "nigown." "Oh ! I hope it's not late, because mother told me to come early."

"It's ten o'clock," said Mrs. Butterfield, "if 'tis a minute. But never mind," as Debby sprang from

the bed with a dismayed little cry, "your ma wouldn't expect you if she knew; an' you must git a good breakfast first. I've kep' it hot for you down by the fire."

"But she doesn't know," said the girl, dressing rapidly. "Oh! I mustn't stop, Mrs. Butterfield; thank you so much for keeping my breakfast hot. I must get home as quick as I can."

"Drat that black Pompey, he ain't at home this morning. Where can he have gone ?" exclaimed Mrs. Butterfield. "I've screeched and screeched till I've most split my throat, and no more good than to call the dead. He's took too much cider, I'll be bound, somewhars, and has stayed to sleep it off. Now I depended on his turning up this morning, and I'd 'a' sent word to your mother. If there was only a team going by now." She ran to the window, as she had run forty times before that morning for the same purpose; for the mother's secret worry, if she should find out before her arrival home that her daughter had not passed the night at Miliscent Barrett's, weighed heavily on the good woman's heart. "Well, if you won't stay to eat a bite, you must take some breakfast and eat it on the way;" and she pressed some doughnuts, a piece of pie, and some fried ham and potatoes, done up in a clean old towel, into Debby's hands, which were now undone from their bandages, and after a

hurried inspection were pronounced wonderfully better. "Which is all owing to that opodeldoc — sup-posin' I hadn't 'a' made you have it on, child!"

"Good-by," said Debby, bending down over her bundle of breakfast, and putting out her pretty lips; "you've been so good to me, Mrs. Butterfield, I can't thank you."

" You pretty creetur, you!" exclaimed the good woman, highly gratified; and she opened her motherly arms, and gathered the girl in. " I wish you was here always, Deborah, I do. Now if you only could "-

"Oh! I must hurry," cried Debby, in a fluster; "mother is in a worry, you know."

" Oh, dear me ! if there was only a team," cried Mrs. Butterfield again; and stepping out after her on the flat door-stone to scan up and down the road, "that's just the way! never is one when you want it, and when you don't, always a-clatterin' round. Something like men, teams is; can't put your fingers on 'em when they could be of use, and la! when nobody wants 'em round, there they be. Well, good-by," she shouted, for Debby was already nearly out of sight at the turn in the road. " It's a mercy that the Barretts would s'pose, of course, that Deb'rah had gone home last night, or there'd be a dreadful piece o' work up there. Well, I do wonder where in creation the child got her

hands so cut up; must 'a' fell, and is ashamed to tell, young folks is so queer. Well, I do wish that she and Abner'd take to settin' up in real earnest; she's old enough now, and I alwus liked her," for Mother Butterfield was not the first one to discover lifelong affiliations that were born of an hour, out of the past absolute chill. All this she kept saying to herself throughout the morning hours that now seemed so dull, as if the old brown house had suddenly all its sunshine withdrawn.

Debby, running across lots to Miliscent's to tell her why she had not come back from the errand to the centre, saw young James, and hailed him.

"Tell Miliscent," she began; but he ran up to her, crying out, —

"Oh! where have you been? Everybody's looking for you," which meant his immediate family, as Miliscent had confided the fright only to her own home people.

"Tell Miliscent," she said, "I'm all safe," and ran on, to hear him screaming after her,—

"Your mother's took sick; she's got a fit, I guess; " which sent the girl, with terror at her heart, off like the wind.

When she arrived at the little cottage on the Old Bay Road, she found every thing in the direst con-

fusion. The baby, usually the most stolid specimen of placid content, was screaming lustily; Debby could hear him long before she reached the top of the Ridge. And when she entered the kitchen, her mother, always the one to greet her eye, busy and cheerful, lay stretched out on the bed, just beyond, Debby could see through the bedroom door. Aunt Keziah was bending over some mess stewing before the fire, and the children were sullenly weeping in the corner.

"O mother!" cried the girl, rushing to the side of the bed, and burying her face against the poor drawn one, " surely you are not worrying over me ?"

Mrs. Parlin raised her tearless eyes, and a sob shook her.

She put her hand up, and smoothed Debby's hair. But she did not smile, and she looked so strange that Debby shivered. "Dear mother," and she comforted her again, " I'm home now, and father will be in soon to dinner, and" —

" Don't speak your father's name to me," cried Mrs. Parlin, her eyes flashing, and she sat up in bed. " Remember, I command you;" then she fell back to her pillow.

Debby staggered out to the kitchen, and leaned against the table.

" O Debby! " mumbled Johnny, coming out from his corner, " I don't like that old woman; send her away — old Miss Feiton."

" She scares me," said Doris, hurrying, as fast as it was in her nature, to Debby's arms. " Make her go home, sister."

Debby mechanically comforted them, and turned her face to Miss Keziah, "What is the matter with my mother ? " she asked.

" I can't tell the nature of her disease, but she'll be better when I get some of my herb tea down her," answered Aunt Keziah. "Of all times in the year not to have any! and I thought I had a pot-ful at home. Put it's most steeped now," — stirring the mess with a long spoon, —" then this will reach the trouble, whatever it is."

"I do not wish her to take it," said Debby firmly; "and thank you, Miss Keziah, you are very good to come, but now I can do everything for my mother," as the children huddled closer to her, begging in loud whispers that the old woman might go home.

Debby hurried, with John and Doris at her heels, to quiet the screaming baby, who kept his eyes as if bewitched on the yellow face under the big handkerchief, and roared, without stopping to draw breath, steadily on.

Aunt Keziah in much passion twitched off her brewing mess from the bed of coals, "And if you had the smallest amount of faith in this, the only thing that can cure" her," she said, "your mother would be well. Silly child! well — well-a-day. The Lord have mercy on you, and all who doubt the herbs he has made! " And she went off, mumbling to .herself vigorously.

The children drew long breaths of relief. Debby had now succeeded in quieting the baby, but he wouldn't let her put him out of her arms. So she beckoned to Johnny and Doris to follow her to the woodshed, where out of reach of the mother's ears she might arrive at the bottom of the truth of this mysterious illness.

But Johnny and Doris knew no more than she did, and by a few well-directed questions Debby soon found this out. Then she went back to the mother's bed, the fat baby in her arms. Mrs. Parlin lay there dry-eyed, and staring at the opposite wall.

XIII.

LEADING EVENTS.

AND now Debby went no more to Miliscent's to ±\- make cartridges, where the busy circle worked day after day. And affairs progressed swiftly to the great fulfilment so sure to come. And the county convention was held, of delegates from every town, and the fire of liberty burned brightly, each man charging his spirit with fervor, till the whole town was as one family—all but the two or three now openly avowed as Tories, and shunned accordingly. " It is evident to an attentive mind," rang out the report to this convention, " that this Province is in a very dangerous and alarming situation. We are obliged to say, however painful it may be to us, that the question now is, whether by a submission to some late Acts of the Parliament of Great Britain we are contented to be the most abject slaves, and entail that slavery on posterity after us, or by a manly, joint, and virtuous opposition, assert and support our freedom. . . . Life and Death, or what is more,

Freedom and Slavery, are in a peculiar sense now before us, and the choice and success, under God, depend greatly on ourselves. We are therefore bound, as struggling not only for ourselves, but for future generations, to express our sentiments in the following resolves; sentiments which we think are founded in truth and justice, and therefore sentiments we are determined to abide by. ...

"These are sentiments [the nineteen resolves which were passed] which we are obliged to express, as these Acts are intended immediately to take place. We must now either oppose them, or tamely give up all we have been struggling for. It is this that has forced us so soon on these very important resolves. However, we do it with humble deference to the Provincial and Continental Congress, by whose resolutions we are determined to abide, and to whom, and the world, we cheerfully appeal for the uprightness of our conduct. On the whole, these are 'great and profound questions.' We are grieved to find ourselves reduced to the necessity of entering into the discussion of them. But we deprecate a state of slavery. Our fathers left a fair inheritance to us, purchased by a waste of blood and treasure. This we are resolved to transmit equally fair to our children after us. No danger shall affright, no difficulties intimi-

date us. And if in support of our rights we are called to encounter even death, we are yet undaunted, sensible that he can never die too soon who lays down his life in support of the laws and liberties of his country."

Such was the spirit fired by town-meeting, county convention, and private assembly of citizens one with another, that now took possession of the old town by the river of her name. It was impossible, being given over to it, for the march of events to be other than they were; and September of 1774 saw the entire community aroused to the necessity of action, and only awaiting the word of command, to fall in. But while they held themselves in readiness, they were law-abiding to the last degree, and determined to give no excuse to the hot-headed and the reckless, for any premature explosion of indignation.

The vote recommending a " provincial meeting," to assemble in Concord on the first Tuesday of October, had also been passed at the above mentioned county convention; and all eyes were looking forward to this with great hopes that their deliberations there to take place might afford some means of relief. At all events, the citizens would be instructed what next steps to take.

Meantime John Parlin had not been seen by the

townsfolk, but had so effectually disappeared from their life that no one could say what the cause might be, with the exception of his wife; and she lay on a bed hovering between life and death, unable to tell, had she so desired. And Debby, withdrawn from the life of the village, and fastened in the little cottage with the children and the sick mother, felt the days go by with stunned senses, that seemed only mechanically to do her bidding. She heard, when Miliscent or cousin Simon or Jabez dropped in, as one or the other did daily, the common news of the Centre, or the last reports from Boston Town, as they had gathered them, and then ran on swift and sympathetic feet to give them to her. And Abner came of an evening, always awkwardly, more often silently asking with his eyes to be allowed to help her, than by any words; and Perces Wood in her steady and mature way would come and move around the little cottage like any old woman, sending the half-fainting girl to bed, while she kept house and minded the children. It was astonishing how they looked up to her; for, let her speak never so lightly, and Perces had a smooth voice that never adopted surprises, they immediately made it their first business to hear it, and to do as she said, obeying her a thousand times better than Debby, who.was only "sister."

And Mrs. Butterfield came at once, as soon as she heard of the illness, wild to help her " pretty creeter " (already destined in her own mind to be her Abner's wife); but she knocked down with her big body, accustomed to the freedom and breadth of her large farmhouse kitchen, so many things in the little cottage rooms, that at last she got frantic, and came to the conclusion herself that she was much better away.

" And how you ever do any work in this little tucked-up place, my dear, I don't see," she would say in her loud whisper next to the sick woman's door. And Debby would run and shut it, and try to smile patiently, as she thanked her, till the good woman fell into despair; and one day she clambered into the wagon when Abner came to fetch her, saying, " I can't come here never no more, Abner; tain't a bit o' use."

"What's the matter, mother? " asked Abner, paling at the lips.

"I'm too big," blurted out Mrs. Butterfield, slapping the ends of her shawl together in her lap; " I warn't cut out for a lettle mite o' room; an' 'tain't any use, not a mortal bit, at my time o' life, to try to git along in a three-inch corner when the Lord's made such a lot o' creation. My!

how that girl does it, Abner, I don't see ; but she just slips round as easy, an' lo and behold, the work's done. But I

tell you what I'm goin' to do; I'm just goin' to take those children, Johnny and Doris, home to-morrow. You may come down an' git 'em."

" That's a good idea, mother 1" exclaimed the young man; "why haven't we thought of it before? "

"I don't know. I s'pose because the Lord only gives just so much common sense at a time to one in-dividooal," said his mother; "an' you an' I hain't got enough gumption to claim our share. Well, Debby says they may come to-morrow, so you be sure to be on hand with the team in the morning. She can weather it through with the baby, I guess. It's a mercy he's got so many teeth; he can eat quite like folks."

And Debby never made any inquiries, not even of Abner, for news of her father. With that terrible sentence of her mother's ringing in her ears night and day, she must hold her peace, and wait for recovery to come to the one who alone could unfold the mystery. Better was it for the townspeople to guess at a cause that had carried her father away, than for her, the daughter, to fan the curiosity of the village by any useless questions. Probably they would think his absence was all understood in the family, and the curiosity would soon die down. So although her heart was bursting with sorrow and dread, Debby

would meet Abner at the door of an evening, quiet and patient as ever, with a face on which there appeared to be no unanswered questions. And he never dared ask her aught of her father, but feasted his great brown eyes on her, feeling her never so sweet and winsome as in the gravity of her trouble and distress. And so the days slipped by.

The sessions of the two courts were to be holden on the i3th of September; but a stormy meeting of citizens of the town and neighboring communities, on the Common, the great rendezvous of the day, decided that " if it proceeded on in the old way " the sitting of the court should be allowed ; " but if under the new organization, they were determined to prevent it, agreeably to there commendation of the late convention;" and through their committee chosen from these towns they voted, "as their opinion, that the Court of General Sessions of the Peace ought not to be opened or sit at this time," the justices of the court being waited on to this effect. And the court giving out a written declaration, which was read to the assembled crowd, it was declared satisfactory. This declared it " inexpedient to open the court lest it should be construed that we act in consequence of the late unconstitutional Act of Parliament." Moreover, a promise was attached that they would " not open nor in any way proceed to

the business of said court." This all the justices signed.

Affairs were now rapidly crystallizing. All persons who favored the mandates or authority of the new or unpopular judges were marked men. The people now were in that temper that confessions were drawn up, and persons who had offended in this way were obliged to sign them. And these confessions were, after being read to the public, published in the newspapers, and scattered broadcast. Truly the spirit of independence was working.

From this time on, the residents of the old town came together without waiting for any special call. " Eternal vigilance," they early concluded, " was the price of liberty;" and thoroughly awakened to the duty of watchfulness, they did not propose to be caught napping, nor to let their praiseworthy caution outweigh their zeal and promptitude in action. So each man, a " son of liberty," obeyed the covenant of the town, had a sharp eye for Tories, controlling them without resource to mob-law, and got himself, and kept himself, ready for all such action as his country should need at his hands, whenever the time was ripe and the command given to thus act.

A Tory to be watched was now Jim Haskins: openly bragging on the Milldam, when in his cups too much

to observe proper caution, of his allegiance to the king; so much that the other young fellows of the town, polishing up their old muskets and taking account of stock of powder and balls, had hard work to keep their hands off him, but were more than once inclined to treat him to a coat of tar and feathers. But older and wiser heads forbade, and the hot-headed element was forced to submit. As for Abner Butterfield, he not knowing how much more reason he had to hate the man, took special pains never to meet Jim, knowing well that if he did, one or the other must fare badly. And Jim, feeling sure that certain plans would result to the complete routing of his rival in goods and estate, if not bring him to an English prison when the king should count up his victims and his victories, as there was now not a shadow in the young Tory's mind but what that must be the case, leered in his sleeve, and thought he could afford to wait. So the two kept apart by a tacit consent.

One night in early September the sick woman turned uneasily on her pillow. All day her eyes had followed her daughter in a way that Debby could not shake off. And now. as she took the cooling drink for her parched throat, she said, as she gave the mug back, "I must say something; it is on my mind, and I best have it over with."

2OO A LITTLE MAID OF CONCORD TOWN.

"Mother," Debby put up her hand as if to ward off a blow, " not to-night," she began.

"To-night," said Mrs. Parlin, with a.return of her old firmness. " Debby, I've lain here day after day, praying for strength to tell it. I shall never get off this bed until I do. Pray God to help you to bear it; for bear it, my girl, you must. Debby, my husband, and your father, is a traitor to his country. He declared to me, the night you were away, his allegiance to the king. And he is a Tory."

With a wild cry of despair Debby fell to the floor. Suddenly she arose and faced her mother. " You are dreaming, or your mind is clouded, mother," she began gently; "think no more of these things, for you are too ill to lie here and meditate on them."

But Mrs. Parlin put out her hand, now, alas, wasted and white. "Give me your hand, daughter. I solemnly swear," as she felt the young palm, " that your father declared over and over this fixed determination. Now will you believe ? "

"Yes," said Debby. But she could not feel that it was she, Debby Parlin, who was uttering this word. She seemed dead and cold, and to have no feeling or emotion of any kind. Truly she ought to be stung by the disgrace into a newer life, even if one of keenest agony. Her father, John Parlin, a traitor to

his country, a thing for all future generations to scorn as too bad to be mentioned save in terms of blackest obloquy, to be ever after held up as an example of the deepest infamy? Her father, who had held her as a little child on his knee, teaching her to prattle out childish admiration for the heroic deeds of his ancestors who had helped to plant and to save the new country. Her father, who had toiled every day since she could remember, with one aim in view, and one hope ever before him, — the aim to help that country when she needed him, and the hope that the day of resistance to the oppression of the king might come in his time and generation. Oh, no! she had been dreaming; and she would give her mother some quieting medicine, and put all this dreadful thought aside, and get out into the fresh air. She was over-tired, and the room was close. She must get out right away.

" I wouldn't talk now, mother," she heard herself say, as she measured the medicine out in the spoon, and brought it with a steady hand to the bedside; " to-morrow you can tell me all about it." And then she went out, climbed the Ridge, and sat down under the silent stars to think it all out.

2O2 A LITTLE MAID OF CONCORD TOWN.

XIV. IN THE BRITISH COFFEE-HOUSE.

A TORY — oh, hateful thought! — worse than if he were a criminal, who in a moment of passion had committed some crime for which he must suffer the penalty — he and his family with him. Then she could envelop him with her tenderness, and so would her mother have done, Debby well knew. Oh, how that mother must have suffered, bearing the first shock, and the weary days and weeks when it had eaten into her sore heart, as she lay on her sick-bed! Debby shivered, and her slender throat contracted convulsively.

And of course she must give up Miliscent's friendship; for the granddaughter of that stanch old patriot, Captain James Barrett, would never speak to a Tory's daughter, much less associate with her. Debby was quite sure she never would. And Perces Wood for the same reason must be given up. And Abner, oh, how he would look at her out of those great brown eyes of his! Debby hid her own for

very shame, and grovelled on the soft pine-needles in speechless misery. And all the townspeople would point at her mother and herself and the children with fingers of scorn, while every one else was doing brave things for their country — and Concord Town

— oh, if she were only a man who could fling himself into seas of blood, and peril life and home and family — everything, to help put down the power of King George, and to show the old town what love of country was, how her crushed heart would rejoice

— but now!

A little noise in the underbrush startled her at last. She looked up and saw her father.

"I don't s'pose you want to speak to me, Deb'rah," he said, in his slow way; "but I'm goin' to say somethin' to you, an' then I'm goin' for good."

"You better go first," flung out Debby in a hard voice, her young face pitilessly stern as she raised it.

"I've thought it all out many an' many a time when you an' the rest o' the folks s'posed I was satisfied in my mind. At night I couldn't sleep for the worry of it, and by day it bore into my soul. And when a man thinks out a thing in such a way, and comes to his conclusion slowly, he has as good a right to his opinion as anybody else has to theirs."

204 A LITTLE MAID OF CONCORD TOWN.

" Father," asked Debby slowly, when he had finished, and set his mouth hard together in that way that the villagers meant when they said "sot as a mule," "were you ever offered money to change your opinion, and did you take it ? "

The man started as if stung, and swore a great oath, the first his daughter had ever heard from his lips.

"What do you take me for? Money 1 Oh, my God!"

" A Tory can be taken for anything," said Debby bitterly.

"This hand of mine," John Parlin shook it in her face, "has never been soiled by touch of anything I couldn't proclaim to the whole world. I am not to be bought. You know that, girl."

"I thought I knew my father before," said Debby, in bitter scorn.

"I did think of you children," he began; but she interrupted him fiercely.

" Better that your children had not been born, than to have a Tory for a father."

" Our king is our sovereign appointed by God," he burst out doggedly. " Besides, any further resistance by the Colonies is useless, and worse than useless. Why, girl, the whole Parliament of Great Britain is

determined to crush us; this last act shows it; there was hope before, but now there is none, — they can do it as easily as I could crush an egg-shell."

" Father," said Debby quite calmly, all the storm hidden in her heart, "some one has been talking to you lately, — some one outside of this town, — that I can see. Who is it?"

He shuffled uneasily on his big feet. With all his obstinacy, John Parlin had the heart of a child, and could be as easily led. " That has nothing to do with it," he said shortly.

" Father," Debby went up to him and laid her hand on his arm, "you wouldn't refuse your daughter, would you, when she asks you such a simple question? Father, just think how you've always told me everything since you dandled me on your knee."

The man took a hungry look at her face. " Debby," he began; then he broke off suddenly. " It's nonsense for you to want to know. What difference does it make? I'm my own master, and no one can influence me. I've my own mind to make up."

" Father," said Debby, and her voice broke, " I never shall ask you anything more. And you won't tell your little girl this one simple thing, father;" she hid her face on his arm, and sobbed.

"I met a man two or three times," said John Parlin slowly; "and he has put the case to me plainly as I have never had it in my whole life. God threw him in my way. And he was not a tar-nal aristocrat neither; he was as poor as I, with only his hands to maintain him; not even a house over his head."

"Who was he?" asked Debby.

"A peddler," said John Parlin, "a poor" —

Debby thrilled from head to foot. All the scene of her rescue flashed upon her, — the long, tapering fingers with the exquisite nails; the high bearing and fine speech; the tones when dropped from the occasional squeak; and the beautiful manners, as if she were a duchess to be deferentially treated. Oh ! was this the way to subjugate the high spirit of the Colonies, to send out disguised serpents to lure their patriots to destruction ? The open field and the chance of war, — this was easy to face. Oh! if she could only have known the truth, and charged him with it, that he might have struck her down in the wood. Better than to live to such calumny!

"A peddler !"

"It is no disgrace, child," said John Parlin, mistaking her tone, " to consort with peddlers. Poor men are to my liking; and they know whereof they

speak. This peddler, child, from his very vocation, tramping about the country, gets at the heart of the truth."

•• Truth ?" cried Debby bitterly, " O father !"

•' I could hear from him what I could not have tolerated from an aristocrat. He hates them as much as I."

" Father," cried Debby, all in a glow with righteous indignation, that swept her as with a torrent, "I have seen this peddler; I know—oh! I am sure he is some hateful Englishman in disguise; he " —

"There is where you are wrong," declared John Parlin obstinately, and using a favorite phrase of his; "the man whom I saw is not disguised; he never could be, and cheat me. He was just what he was. You have ever been apt to jump at conclusions, daughter, and to imagine things."

" But in this case I am right, father," she argued, with the same spirit to meet his own, which sent him back into his old obstinacy. " He had such long, slim " —

"No more — no more," commanded John Parlin sharply; " I'll not have my own daughter contradict me. The peddler that I saw I could swear was an honest man. There are many of them, no doubt, God

help them in these limes, tramping over the country. Say no more. You were ever an impetuous little thing, Deb'rah, to jump at things quickly."

She flung aside the reproof as a trifle not to be noticed. "Go up and talk with Mr. Wood," she said at last, "or Mr. Whitney, or some of those whom you have always said knew the whole situation. Do, father," she begged.

But he shook his head obstinately. " They are intrenched in their own views; they never talk with outsiders to hear the truth about the whole country. They will plunge this town in blood, Deb'rah ; blood — and all spilt for nothing."

Debby wrung her hands. "Mother is very sick," she said hoarsely. " O father ! we thought she would die."

The man's face changed swiftly. " God help me," he groaned. "I've haunted this place, Debby," he said, under his breath; "many's the night I've watched under these trees to see your candle in the window, and you stepping about. Once when she was the worst, I almost went in. But I knew that would kill her, and I kept myself back. Oh, God knows I wish I could see it all as you do!"

She knew it was useless to urge further. "Where are you working, father? " she asked suddenly, glan-

cing at his hands, which showed a respite from farm-work.

He evaded this, and said presently, "And now she is better, and I've seen you, so I am best out of the way. Give me one kiss, daughter."

For a moment Debby drew back. Then she threw her arms around his neck and kissed him passionately. He strained her to his breast with a hungrier grasp than ever he had clasped her from a little child, —his first-born; then suddenly thrust her forth, and ran — this slow, heavy man — out through the trees and down the Ridge.

"Father, father," cried Debby, with empty arms. "Come back —O father" —

The entrance to the British coffee-house on King Street, the resort of the high Tories of the town, gave signs on the evening of the 2d of August of the departure of a guest of no inconsiderable importance. The landlord himself was on the upper step, obsequiously rubbing his fat palms, and casting about in his fertile mind how further to advance the comfort or the welfare of a guest whose appearance and bearing bespoke wealth and consequence. The horses attached to the governor's own carriage pawed the ground in their eagerness to be off, and shook their manes rest-

210 A LITTLE MAID OF CONCORD TOWN.

lessly. The equipage had been sent around as a last mark of respect, to bear the personage now taking his leave of Boston Town to the wharf where he was to embark. Rumor had it that this Englishman stood, in influence, near to the throne and Parliament; he was therefore naturally very close to the regard of Governor Gage, with whom both as governor and as commander-in-chief of the British forces in America, he had been often closeted in conference during his stay in the Province.

As this person of importance passed down the steps, and was about to place himself within the carriage, a tall, slender figure, in the uniform of an officer in the service of King George, came striding down King Street. He quickened his pace, and presently stood by the side of the older man, whose figure showed the portliness of luxurious middle life; and the cordial hand-shake indulged in, the smiles and chat of familiar understanding, told the onlooker that two good friends were about to part.

'• I will render good account of you, Bernard, to the different members of our family," said the elder man, as he stepped into the carriage, and he pausec to lay his hand approvingly on the young shoulder. "But best of all, our king, God save him, shall hear it all to the last word. I' faith, you may trust me."

"Spare yourself that trouble," cried the young officer hastily, and his face darkened.

"Tut, tut, man, you are too modest by half," cried the other. " The king shall know it all. You shall be so intrenched in his Majesty's favor, when this paltry matter of the Colonies is settled, that you can ask what you will, only to obtain it."

Bernard put his hand up hastily in protestation; but the elder man laughed, gave the signal to depart, and the governor's equipage rolled down King Street, the admiration of all eyes.

The young officer, whose face now grew darker than ever with suppressed dissatisfaction, paused a moment to recover himself, then, with his usual sang froid, he turned within the hostelry, to find a gay company of young British officers, having a roystering time at a near-by table, in the middle of which stood a steaming bowl of hot punch.

"Ha, Thornton," called one, as he entered the doorway, filling his glass again, "here's to you! Verily, you are a poor companion these days. Pray, where have you kept yourself? Come, and drink confusion to these poltroon Yankees;" and he tossed off his bumper with a gay hand.

The young officer thus addressed put himself into

the chair now pushed toward him, and partook very sparingly of the beverage as the toast was given. Then he set back his glass, and despite his efforts to lend himself to the conviviality of the hour, he was soon becoming lost in revery as the jest went on.

"Ho, here! wake up!" at last called out the young man who had first spoken; an officer whose commission ranked him as lieutenant, but with the eye of his superior officers upon him for his brilliant promise. "Egad, by my sword, I believe you're asleep, Thornton. It's this beastly climate that is pulling us all down; and the Yankees — pah! I wish we could mow them down and end the business, and get home to Old England."

Thornton glanced at the gay flushed face and unsteady hand that poured another full glass.

"Best not, Harry," he said, with a meaning look. "If we want to begin the mowing process, it needs be that we keep our heads cool."

"I' faith, that's not necessary!" spoke up a big hulking officer of more years than the most of them, interlarding his words with a couple of strong oaths; "these farmer fellows are easy game. If I had command now, it would be touch and go with every mother's sen of them."

"What a pity that you haven't the command," observed Thornton dryly, and with a sip at his glass.

"They'd have small chance to say their prayers and sing psalms through their noses," finished the other, heedless of the laugh that went around the table at his expense. "Confusion to 'em, say I, and rot their bones! The whole of their carcasses aren't worth one good Englishman; and the sooner they're punished for their mad rebellion the better."

"How King George can play along with them in this way passes any belief," spoke up another. " Egad! Buckthorne is right. Extermination is the only thing, if we can't subjugate them speedily."

Thornton leaned back in his chair and laughed. "To speak of exterminating full-grown colonies with such power as have these in this Province, is, forsooth, food for amusement that must be enjoyed" —

"But if the leaders were taken and hanged as they should be," struck in Buckthorne angrily, and bringing down his fist on the board till all the glasses rang, " I swear by my soul these rotten old farmers, that smell of their bogs, would all fall on their mouldy old knees and beg for any mercy that Parliament would give them."

" I swear it too, Buckthorne," said the other speaker.

"And I, and I," was taken up by a half-score of throats.

"These rotten old farmers, as you are pleased to call them, Buckthorne," said Harry, as the babel died down and he filled anew his glass, oblivious of Thornton's appealing eye, " have considerable and wholesome vigor, as I could tell you, who have chanced at some of them, on my trips to fill the commissary orders."

" Yes, to Concord. Isn't there a place of that name where you were despatched a short time ago, Her-ford ? " asked one of the half-score who had yelled so vociferously a moment ago.

"Ay," said Harry, nodding his bright head; then he drained his glass; " if you'd seen that old town and her men as I have, you'd know whereof to speak better than the drivelling stuff you've given us. I tell you, there's fight there ; and fight to the death."

" Hoh! Pah!" l breathed out the men derisively; "and if they wanted to fight — they must fight without ammunition. It's madness for them to think of it," cried several.

" Ay, ay," responded Harry, with an eye that was unsteady and glistened unnaturally, " that's it ; it is madness. Better to have the ringleaders here in Boston Town mowed down for their wild and senseless

rebellion, than that these poor villagers should be slaughtered like sheep." He pushed his glass away abruptly, and stared gloomily at the circle, who met the look with one of surprise.

" Herford's struck by one of the village beauties," cried Buckthorne coarsely, at a venture. " Some daughter of a horny-handed farmer has made love to him," coupling the words with ribald oaths. " Here's to the damsel of Concord Town ; give us her name, Herford," he said with a leer. He poured out a stiff bumper from a bottle standing near, and called to his brother officers to do the same.

Lieutenant Herford sprang to his feet, his hand on the hilt of his sword, his blue eyes flashing dangerously. " Speak not of any woman here, you who have mothers or sisters," he said hoarsely, his voice thick and unsteady with the wine; "your lips, Buckthorne, are too foul for such a use."

The heavy figure of Buckthorne sprang to an upright posture, as he dashed his glass to the floor ; and he swore a great round oath, as he put his hand to his sword, glaring at the handsome and heated face, that before he spilled the blood of the Yankees, he would have satisfaction for the words just spoken.

Instantly all the brother officers were on their feet, and the coffee-house was in an uproar, every-

body pausing in drink and speech to take in the brawl.

"Are you mad?" cried Thornton, seizing the young lieutenant's arm. " Harry, disgrace not yourself by another word. Think of your mother."

XV.

PREPARING AN ARENA.

:< TTNHAND me!" cried Harry, his flushed face LJ turning white with rage, and shaking off the grasp of his friend, while one of the high Tories, as the king's friends were called, in the corner, with his pipe and his grog, discussing the political situation with another of his ilk, roared out for a messenger to be despatched to the guard-house or barracks, but a short distance away, for a squad of soldiery to stop the dispute.

" By my sword," he said, his big, florid face suffused with an irritated flush, " these young blades assert themselves too noisily to suit my taste. Better that they stay where they belong, in the barracks, and leave this place to those who can conduct themselves like English gentlemen."

The landlord, hearing this from a quarter where similar speeches had been aired, and with no desire that such lucrative customers as " the young blades " should find other quarters, now deserted the bar, and joined himself to the circle to which all eyes were turned, where the two disputants, the table between them, were glaring at each other like wild beasts.

" Softly, softly there, young gentlemen," he began in his most conciliatory tones ; but the roar of angry voices told him the quarrel had gone too far for him to prevent, and his rotund figure was thrust unceremoniously aside as the young officers closed in around the two.

" Stand back! " commanded Thornton in low but passionate tones to them. " Buckthorne, cannot you see that Herford has taken a glass too much ? Listen not to words that come at such a time."

" He meant to insult me ! " declared Buckthorne sullenly, himself too far gone for reason, and glancing at his comrades in a blustering way ; " and who throws in the teeth of Jack Buckthorne aught but what he can swallow, will have to chew the consequences." He tapped the hilt of his sword significantly.

Thornton controlled his choler, and was about to reply in a way that would have made all well, when Harry drew his sword, and rushing toward Buckthorne, would have thrust him through on the spot had he not been seized by the two who were nearest, his weapon spinning over their heads to the flooi beyond.

" You braggart," he was yelling, " and black-hearted scoundrel, take that! "

In an instant some one rushed out across the street, bawling to the sentinel pacing back and forth on duty before the custom-house ; and another, running to the corner, met a squad of soldiers on their way to the barracks. These latter stepped into the British coffee-house ; and as Harry seemed to be clearly the aggressor, they hauled him off summarily to the guardhouse.

The florid-faced Englishman and his high Tory friend returned to their grog and pipes with great satisfaction after this diversion ; the former remarking that now matters were more to his mind, since one of the party was by this time well on his way to the guard-house, where, in order for his complete pleasure, the remainder should have been carried. And the other frequenters of the tavern, having seen the thing to the end, or at least to the quelling of the disturbance, now took their minds back to their own affairs.

" You will not deny me the satisfaction, I presume," said Thornton, going around the table to speak clearly into the face of Buckthorne, now red with triumph as well as liquor, as he leered his great delight at the ending, " of measuring your sword with mine in some fitting place, after I tell you that besides being a black-

hearted scoundrel, you are a coward, and not a decent companion for an English officer to associate with."

The words were low, and not a person beyond the circle of young officers could hear them. Yet nothing that could possibly be uttered could strike such dismay into one of the group. Buckthorne's face turned purple and then a livid white. "You know I didn't mean, — " he stammered thickly, — "didn't intend any offence, only to scare the boy."

Thornton stood silent and immovable, the picture of scorn, his determined front adding new terror to that already possessing the big, burly man he addressed. As the latter seemed unable to speak, one of the officers, who perhaps had as much regard for Buck-thorne as any, which was not saying too much, ventured to suggest, "You know, Lieutenant Thornton, that what you said for your friend Herford might apply here ; Buckthorne is in his cups."

"Yes, yes," muttered Buckthorne, catching at the straw; "I didn't know what I was saying; I had taken a drop too much."

"The case is different, Gardner, as you are well aware," said Thornton coldly; " the disparity in years is quite enough to make Buckthorne's behavior dastardly. When I add, what we all know, that Herford cannot take what other men can bear with impunity,

~ o

and that out of liquor he is a gentleman worthy of Old England, whose soul of honor has never been questioned, I think you will, to a man, bear me out in punishing the scoundrel who has brought this disgrace upon him."

A silence like the grave fell upon the circle. Buck-thorne did not move a finger, only stared helplessly into the face of the man whom, he well knew, as did they all, it would be death to meet in a sword contest. At last, after waiting what he considered a sufficient time for Major Buckthorne to accept his proposition, Thornton turned to the others,—

" Gentlemen, you will all be witnesses that I have offered Major Buckthorne complete satisfaction for my avowed estimate of him, and that he has rejected it. If any of you, as his friend, desires to take it up, I will be pleased to hear it."

No one replying, Lieutenant Thornton said with a smile playing around his thin lips, " I will be glad to meet you socially at any time and on any occasion when Major Buckthorne is not present. Now I go to the guard-house to report the truth of the case, and to do what I can for young Herford." Then he turned on his heel, and strode out of the coffee-house.

And now the number of white tents of the encampment on Boston Common increased as if by

magic. The quarters in Faneuil Hall were becoming too largely occupied for comfort, as the British soldiery were transported in greater numbers over the sea to re-enforce the Governor-Commander-in-Chief Gage. The rattle of musketry, with the fife, drum, and bugle, pierced the air of Boston streets, and awoke angry echoes in the souls of her citizens that the sight of the swarming redcoats was not likely to assuage. The Town House was now well supplied with soldiers, where hitherto had been the Merchants' Exchange, and the meeting-place of the judges and the governor's council. A British bayonet seemed to meet one at every turn, — peaceably, it is true, if not opposed, — and a British sentinel challenged whom he would. It was a despotic Crown and Parliament that spoke in this military display, the determination to enforce the new and obnoxious laws that were to break the proud spirit of the Colonists. And twenty miles away, among the farms, by a quiet river, there was this moment preparing an arena that should proclaim aloud to a waiting world, God's determination also, against which no Crown or Parliament could contend.

And now the days of petitions and memorials to the Governor, the Council, the Parliament, and the Crown, might be said to be over. All appeals that could be

made and yet retain self-respect, had been presented; every argument, clear, forcible, and patient, had been drawn up by the patriotic statesmen of the oppressed Colonies. The spirit and temper of the leaders had forced many expressions of admiration even from those who would have been glad to be avowed enemies. No opportunity was there for a deserved punishment to fall upon the faithful American subjects of their king; for they had served him with a loyalty that rose above privation, suffering, and oppression. Nothing now remained but slavery. Instead of petition to an earthly king, was now a last prayer to God, and a preparation for armed resistance. Action was now the word.

It became now a necessity to Concord Town to have the people often assemble for counsel and deliberation, and that interchange of patriotic fervor, that the spirit of liberty leaping to break its chains, must communicate by its divine right.

They now constantly called themselves and their neighbors together on their Common, made decisions as to those matters they deemed appropriately arranged in such meetings, and forwarded all important proceedings to the Continental Congress at Philadelphia, keeping in touch with that body with wonderful clearness of judgment and despatch.

And the struggle over the sitting of the court that was to hold its sessions in the old town on the i3th of September, was urged with such determination not to allow it unless it was carried on in,the old way, that the strenuous efforts of the committee chosen to wait upon the judges with this decision, won the day. The written declaration from the court was read to the people and then published, " declaring it inexpedient to open the court, ' lest it should be construed that we act in consequence of the late unconstitutional Act of Parliament.' " And then long-delayed attention was directed to discharging the debt of obligation to the Tory element in their midst, and to all who had, or were helping forward in any way, the " unconstitutional plan of government" proposed by King George and his Parliament.

It took Simon and Jabez both to run up over the hill and down the Ridge to tell Debby of the rousing big meeting, — "when we are going for the Tories, yes, sir ! " — and they wondered at the lack of animation this news elicited, although her eyes shone clear and bright in her pale face.

"Hush," she said, drawing them out from the kitchen where the mother sat now, wan and spiritless, her hands employed in sewing, while her thoughts were ever on the one subject near her heart; "don't

let mother hear you say the w6rd ' Tories.'" She closed the door, and faced them in the woodshed.

"Why not?" asked Jabez, breathless from his long run. "I sh'd think 'twas the best med'cine a sick person could have — to know there's going to be judgment come to those fellows; shouldn't you, Si ?"

Simon grunted some inaudible reply, taking his cue from Debby's face.

"Mother's very weak," said Debby, "and the least thing upsets her, so you just mustn't do it, boys." Her lips were set together hard, and she held the door firmly closed.

"All right," said Simon carelessly. "Now she's sick, Aunt Lyddy's like mother; we have to pick and choose, as you know, Debby, just what things we can talk about before her. Jabe and I hold our meetings out by the wood-pile or in the barn. Well, good-by, cousin; sorry you can't go to the Common. This is one of the times you'd rather be a boy, I expect," he added saucily, hoping to rouse her old spirit. But she didn't smile, nor seem to notice the remark; and the boys ran off, their delight over the approaching meeting considerably subdued.

"Beats all how trouble and work have broke her down," said Jabez, as they hurried along the Old

Bay Road to the "Centre. "I wouldn't b'lieve it could be Debby."

Simon snapped his jaws together hard. "What's the use o' talking about it? Of course till Uncle John comes back, she can't laugh and carry on." He was sorely put to it to explain to himself a certain attitude of mind in his cousin that did not seem to be the outcome of grief or worry. It was enough, he kept arguing to himself, to break down any girl, even one so self-contained as Debby, to have the double blow of the father's sudden disappearance, appealing as it did to the curiosity of the village, and the mother's dreadful illness; yet still, when the arguments were all in, Simon felt unsatisfied and restless.

"Come on," he added roughly, "or the best of the time will be over ; " which had the effect to make Jabez drop all other considerations save getting over the ground as speedily as possible, especially as he had long ago accepted the common theory now becoming settled in the town, that the troublous times had unsettled John Parlin's wits, making him wander from home beyond the long and careful search they had given for him.

It was a busy crowd that greeted their eyes long before they ran into its midst,— thoroughly determined,

yet not turbulent, knowing that full justice would be done, and the honor of the old town most thoroughly vindicated. All testimony was in against the offenders, and nothing now remained to be done, except, as one old farmer said, to " let them know there is a God in Israel."

They were choosing a committee to try the Tories, when the boys arrived, and the excitement was at its height. Suddenly a wild yell smote the air. Everybody started, and some men grasped their muskets for action if need be ; for by this time it was becoming quite the custom to take along the firearm if one so desired. It kept one in practice by the mere handling of it, and suited well the spirit of the day.

"Forbear to use violence," cautioned some of the fathers of the town, always in evidence at these meetings; and mingling with the crowd, they essayed to allay the fears the sudden disturbance had made. But men's blood was easily fired in those exciting days; and they looked in each other's faces and waited, prepared for action when the time arrived. It came, bringing not the thing they feared, but something quite different.

A man was seen running down the town centre to the Milldam pursued hotly by some half-dozen others, whose near approach to their victim had brought forth

228 A LITTLE MAID OF CONCORD TOWN.

the yell of anger and despair. He fairly ran into the heart of the crowd, panting and furious, and only drew breath when he felt it close upon him. It was Jim Haskins, now universally spoken of as Jim Has-kins the Tory.

" I've come to be protected ! " he cried in a loud tone, and pointing a shaking finger at his pursuers. " Is there any law that will hound a man for having opinions of his own ? "

" You've come to a poor place, Jim," said one of the older citizens of the town gravely. " In the temper of the time there is not much safety for one who gives allegiance to a tyrant, at the expense of his own townsmen. Keep quiet until the excitement of your pursuit has abated, then slip out as quietly as you can, and get to your home. It is the only way to save your miserable skin, I fear."

" They are the ones," cried Jim in a loud, vindictive voice, again pointing to the small band that had pursued him, now quietly waiting on the outskirts of the crowd, having run him to earth, as it were, well contented to bide their time, " who would break the law and molest me. Here are the officers of the town," — he looked around into their serious faces as he spoke,— "I am safe here;" and he smiled defiantly at his persecutors.

"You are safe not an instant," said the citizen sternly. "Can you not feel the righteous indignation, man, that is at last to break upon the heads of all who, like you, have turned traitor to their country." He spoke with suppressed feeling, but in a low voice, to avoid adding to the inflammable material around him aught that would hasten this man's doom.

But Jim was not to be silenced. And he continued to attract attention to himself by adjuring all persons before him to give liberty of speech and action to the individual who, like himself, chose to be a most loyal adherent to King George in all his plans for his subjects at home and abroad. So that at last the business of the meeting was for the time given up, to make way for his loud, sonorous speech.

This quite delighted him, to find that he had at last something to say which the people would hear; and he proceeded with a great degree of confidence to a louder burst, mistaking the growing silence which was now pervading all the circle.

'•Fellow cit'zens," he cried, thrusting out his right hand in the way he admired in oratorical attempts, yet had never had the opportunity to display, "I stand before you to-day to say I am proud to support the king, and" —

" Cut the miserable wretch short," cried a dozen

230 A LITTLE MAID OF CONCORD TOWN.

voices, that sent the cry out from as many different quarters; "and toss his carcass over here," yelled the waiting men who had followed him to the Common; " we'll teach him what it means to turn traitor." There was at the same time a sudden rush made; and the compact mass of men trembled as if a wedge had struck them in a vulnerable point, forcing admittance to the centre.

It was all done in a moment, but not before Jim saw the swiftness of his peril; and had there been room, he would have sunk to his knees entreating mercy. As it was, he seized and clutched and strained at all those who had the misfortune to stand near him, making the air again resound with wild, incoherent cries that upbore the discordant yells of the infuriated crowd. They had him at last, pulling and hauling several along with him in his frantic clutches of despair; but his captors speedily loosened his hold upon all such and bore him shrieking off.

THE SECRET MUST BE DISCLOSED:' 2$1

XVI.

"THE SECRET MUST BE DISCLOSED NOW."

IT was a fearful moment. The crowd parted enough to allow the strong hands seizing the unhappy man, to bear him with a rush through the howling mass of men that closed up and surrounded him and his captors. It was impossible to distinguish his cries for help, as he was thus borne along mid the yells of " Horsewhip him ! " "A tar-and-feather coat! " and "The river — To the river with him!'"

This last cry prevailed ; and off over the Milldam the throng swept, with small thought for any in their way, least of all for the comfort of the luckless wight in their midst who was at last to taste the penalty of being a Tory, and to know what it meant to turn against his country and his countrymen.

In the mad rush of the first moment, when shoulder was knocked against shoulder, and the triumphant crowd surged down over the Milldam bearing their captive, it was easy enough to drown the notes, stentorian though they were, of those in authority, left on the

232 A LITTLE MAID OF CONCORD TOWN.

Common, commanding the tumult to cease and that the victim be released. But after this first moment, the voice of the fathers of the town began to be heard with its old insistence ; and one after the other of those who, though not taking active part in the violent proceedings, had yet put forth no hand to stay them, commenced to bestir themselves on the side of law and order. The foremost one was a young man, tall and broad shouldered, up to whose honest blue eyes crept the flush of remorse at not sooner stepping into action.

" For shame!" he cried in ringing tones, that pierced like a clarion note far over the crowd, and made them for an instant haste over the road with redoubled speed, so fearful were they that he led an opposing force. " Would you thus deal with traitors ? Hold, and let the law take its course!"

When they, looking back, saw that it was Abner But-terfield alone who stood forth and thus defied them, they shook their brown fists in derision, and laughed triumphantly, and rushed on.

" Come on, fellow-townsmen who do not believe in riot!" cried Abner, all the blood gone to his head, and waving his right arm in the air; " or, by Heaven, I'll go alone." He sprang down the road, and madly plunged after the swift retreating crowd, one thought

only uppermost in his heart, — to save the screaming, struggling wretch he could now hear and see, as the throng tossed him up and down as they hauled him along.

It was Jim, — Jim, the hated rival, — the man who had insulted him, and who had turned traitor; but perhaps Debby had loved him, it was impossible to be quite sure; and perhaps Jim would turn back to love for his country, if he could only be kept from drinking. Then, if she had loved him before, she would surely love him anew. At any rate, for her sake he must be saved, and this blot kept from the dear name of his town. He ran, he shouted, he plunged madly on. And at last, oh, blessed relief! the sound as of rushing feet came to his ears, and the road was full of eager, hurrying men swift to follow his brave leadership, and the onslaught for Jim's liberty had begun in earnest.

But the maddened crowd, seeing here a rescue-force growing quite formidable, suddenly executed a sharp detour, and deserting their original plan of carrying their victim to a quieter and better-adapted place of vengeance, now plunged down to the river bank with only one thought, — to give the Tory such a ducking that if he escaped with his miserable life, it would be his luck. Fast on their heels came

the smaller company of rescuers. And now, down the road followed the fathers of the town in all degrees of haste, with determination and stern resolve, yet basing all their hopes on Abner and his slender force.

"Quickt Divide the company! Half keep in the rear, and close up; the others come with me/" cried Abner under his breath, the men slipping easily into the position of followers. None too soon. The men holding Jim were — one, two, three—just sending him off, when a mighty onslaught of blows, only from the fists, it is true — but who knows anything harder than the Provincial fist that understood how to hit, and when ? Down they rained, from Abner's little company in front, and from Abner's small crowd in the rear, like sledge-hammers, crowding, pushing, and thrusting the surrounded men into a snug knot where they could not use their arms to advantage. " Leave him go !" roared Abner, his blood well up, and feeling the eyes of all the town fathers upon him, " or we'll mash you to the powder you deserve to be, for bringing disgrace upon this town."

To right and to left the men were knocked and jostled, till there was small hope of telling friend from foe as they struggled and kicked and fought. When the confusion and smoke of the encounter

cleared off, no man could say exactly how it had all taken place. Some were lying on the ground, where they had been flattened and worsted, and all were looking at Butterfield bearing away down the road the Tory Jim, such a goodly crowd supporting, as made it useless to think of any successful intervention. Besides, here were now the fathers of the town closing in on their rear at the river brink with such solemn and determined intentions as made themselves known at once; and the crestfallen crowd oozed off, as many as were fortunate enough to do so, the rest being taken into custody as ringleaders of a mob who would put in jeopardy the good name of the old town, to be dealt with as might seem best after a council.

"Mother," cried Abner, his brown-face aflame, and his honest blue eyes seeking hers somewhat anxiously, the truth must be told, as he dreaded her reply, "here's Jim," dragging him within the kitchen door. "You can go now," to the men who had accompanied them to the Butterfield farm; "he's all right here," as they turned away.

"Don't dare to bring that man here," cried Mrs. Butterfield, her arms akimbo; "this house can't hold me and a traitor."

"Mother,'" said Abner. remonstrating, and, thrust-

ing Jim, pale-faced and shrinking, back of him, he spread out his hands entreatingly, "think what you would do to refuse him shelter at this time. He's been treated sorely, and there's no telling what the crowd will do to him if he's caught before they cool down."

"He better be torn limb from limb," cried Mother Butterfield savagely, standing erect in the middle of her kitchen floor, her eyes blazing. "Ay, and give his bones to the winds. A man to turn against his country, and to use his foul tongue at such a time, should be thrust from every hearthstone." She took one step with threatening gesture, and looked so very dreadful that Jim slunk down to the floor, pleading feebly for mercy. " He shall go from this door this instant! " She raised her large but shapely hand in command to her son. It was no time for mild measures.

"And I say he shall not stir from this house until I deem it safe for him to do so," said Abner in a low, clear voice, every syllable cutting her like a knife. It was the first time in all his life of twenty-five years that he had ever set himself against her will. She stared at him, her arm still uplifted, gazing blankly into the eyes that fastened themselves on her face as if they were never to move. She opened her moulh

as if to speak, but no words came. And still she stood and stared.

" Say no more, mother," Abner was speaking, she felt rather than heard. " And, Jim, you better go into the other room." It was all done quietly enough now; and somehow or other Mrs. Butterfield was alone in her kitchen, and going about in a dazed way at her housework.

" I won't answer for your life if you get out of here," said Abner to Jim, the door well shut behind them. "You best go up to the loft, and stay quiet a bit." He restrained a violent desire to kick him every step of the way up the stairs. Jim turned a wild-eyed face on him. "Debby," he made out to say.

" Stop, you hound ! " roared Abner, at the end of his patience, and feeling all the reaction of doubt at the wisdom of his course; "it needs but little more from you to make me want to throw your vile carcass out to any one who would treat it as it deserves, and not raise a finger to save you."

"But I say, Debby" —

With one bound, Abner was on him, tugging like a wild beast for his overthrow; and with a twist of his brawny arm he thrust him up the stairs, bestowing as he went, the kicks he had so longed to give, then strode to the barn, saddled his horse, and not allowing

238 A LITTLE MAID OF CONCORD TOWN.

his passion to cool, he tore madly down the road, and never drew rein till he reached the Parlin cottage.

"What is it between Jim and you? " he demanded, not minding in the least that Mrs. Parlin was present, silent and cold, spinning in the corner. " I will know." His eyes blazed at her, and he repeated in an angry tone. No one had ever heard Abner Butterfield except in slow-going and quiet accents, and for a moment Debby lost herself.

" Abner —- Abner " — she cried, hurrying to him, to clasp her hands, "oh! what is it?"

He put up one hand to stay her approach, all his soul at arms against her, yet madly devoured with his great love. " It is no time to parley, Deborah," he said hoarsely, his great eyes looking her through and through. She could see the veins on his forehead swollen, and his stern compressed lips white with the effort to restrain the hot, impetuous speech. " God knows I have loved you all my life, as no man ever loved woman before, and held my peace, as I felt you couldn't love me until some little time back, and then it seemed as if God was giving me a chance. And now Jim dares to take your name on his lips. The hound!"

Debby put up one white hand to stay the passion-

ate avowal. Oh ! why should it come now, when all hope was gone? She — a traitor's daughter — to be loved by an honest man!

" But now I will speak, although it is an insult to ask you, if you ever loved him — he — a traitor. Deborah Parlin, sooner than love one with traitor blood in his veins, one should pray to die. God can forgive everything else but that; every other disgrace but that can be wiped out. Tell me you did not love him; that's what I will know now."

" I never loved him," said Debby, standing pale and cold, with her head thrown back and her nostrils quivering.

" Thank God ! " cried Abner, in a burst of joy. He seized her hand, but she pulled it away.

"Don't speak," she cried, her voice breaking. " O Abner! do not make it harder for me to bear. Speak no further, only go*"

" I will speak now, Deborah," said Abner solemnly, and with such determination that it was useless to impede his course. " I have kept silent too long, God knows, and no power on earth shall stop me now. Will you be my wife ?"

Deborah gave a low cry of pain, and with a mighty effort held herself in check enough to utter, " No —oh, no! do not ask it."

240 A LITTLE MAID OF CONCORD TOWN.

" You cannot love me, then," he flung at her through set lips.

" Do not ask me. I can never marry you. O Abner, Abner! I must not say more."

Her quivering shoulder was suddenly grasped. Both of them had forgotten the presence of the mother. She held Debby now as in a vise, and, with a voice not lifted from her ordinary one, said, " The secret must be disclosed now; but, on your soul of honor," to Abner, "you must not tell it."

" Mother — mother !" shrieked Debby, " stop — think what you are doing. Abner, do go." She seized his arm now in her anguish, and wound her pleading fingers around it. " Oh! I implore you, if you love me, to go."

" He shall hear it," commanded her mother sternly, "then he will see how useless it is to plead for your love. My daughter can never wed, Abner. No honest man would want traitor blood in his children. Her father has forsworn his country. He is a Tory! "

Abner turned, and gave one look at Debby's face, to see there the awful truth confirmed.

"Go," she cried, with face drawn and white, "tell it not, Abner. My mother has answered you. I have my cross to bear. Go, and leave me to bear it."

He obeyed, all his fire burned down. And, stunned

by the news into more than his usual quiet acceptance of fate's denials, he passed out silently. Debby waited till the door closed, and he was on his horse; then she turned to her mother, and held out her arms. " I'm tired," she said, "and we have only got each other, mother," and fell fainting to the floor.

XVII.

RAPID PREPARATIONS.

IT was no longer possible for the old town by the river of the peaceful name to remain quiet. The God of righteous war had already marked her for his own, to proclaim to waiting worlds the note of liberty. She was henceforth to move on fast to meet her destiny.

And now came the day of retribution to the Tories. Patience had become, by this time, a crime; and the three or four traitors to their country and their townsmen were duly recorded and dealt with. Each citizen was a veritable " son of liberty," and proud enough to avow himself as such, feeling equal to a whole corps of the militia, in his one beating breast and his two good arms. And the work of preparation went briskly on. The meetings at this time were on short call, and most informal. Only one spirit bound the entire assemblies; that was the spirit of liberty, nevermore to be quenched. A committee in which the neighboring towns were represented, was chosen to take care of the Tories; and all things were well under way for the final struggle.

Up in one of the front bed-chambers of the Lee mansion, burned the candles in their tall silver candlesticks, flanking the high carved mantel. Another lighted pair stood on the centre mahogany table, with its carved claw feet and its generous surface, now strewn with papers, and well drawn away from the big carved and brightly polished four-poster, with its silken tester and counterpane. The old clock in the corner ticked in ponderous tones the hour away, and the long mirror with its little gilt divisions across its glassy surface reflected back all the solid magnificence of the spacious apartment and its solitary occupant. He was a man above middle life, restless and unhappy, to judge by his face and movements.

He seated himself in his carved oaken chair, and took up his quill, dallying with it as one who has a hateful task before him. And after a few ineffectual trials in the way of a beginning, born out of an angry and perturbed mind, he threw it down; and hastening from his seat, he went to the window, drew aside the curtain, and looked out into the night. Before him spread his ample meadows, swelling away from the gentle river flowing in caressing curve around them. As far as his eye could reach, he could say with

pride, "Mine." There were the barns and outhouses, a long line, in that state of thrift that bespoke the well-to-do and important farmer, that member of the community whose bidding was law and gospel — if — ah, if! He sighed involuntarily, and let the brocaded curtain slip from his fingers, as he moved away to divert his thought. Had these townsmen of his any sense, and wisdom to discern the practical issues of life, they must see, as did he, how useless the struggle against the mighty force arraying to crush them. Why had they not followed him, and his advice? Why was he hated and execrated, a very name to despise, as the children passed by and pointed to him ? Time was when he had been wont to receive that honor given to one whose word was law and gospel to the simpler country folk, and to notice with complacence the obsequious homage of those rustics who now were setting up opinions for themselves. Fools — fools — he said to himself, an angry glow overspreading his features.

And yet, fools as they were, they had him in a tight place, those rustics had. And unless he signed that paper yonder, lying on the shining mahogany top, it would go ill with him and his. Why did not the mother country, by one summary blow, end this incipient, foolhardy rebellion, and come to the rescue of all such stanch upholders of English law as ^e and his Tory friends ? He stepped back, and thrust the curtain aside angrily, to glance out across the quiet meadows and peaceful river, as if along their outlines could be seen the advancing army that was to him the only hope of safety to his town and to the Colonies.

But the peaceful river shimmered on, undisturbed by presence of the flower of England's army; and, watching from the stately Lee mansion, he heaved a great sigh, and went back to the big table once more.

"Whereas I, Joseph Lee of Concord, Physician, on the evening of the first ultimo, did rashly and without consideration," so a large sheet of paper, lying flat before him, showed up to his angry eye, as its preamble. Well he knew the rest of it, and that document unsigned when it was called for in the morning, no one could tell the result. There was determination now, so fixed as to be unhealthy to meddle with, in all the towns around, that sympathizers with their country's foes should meet with summary treatment once for all; and he, Joseph Lee, understood, and had silently received his sentence at his outraged fellow-citizens' hands.

But he had several kmg hours yet before the morning dawn, when his signature must be placed to that hateful paper. Wild dreams of what might happen

246 A LITTLE MAID OF CONCORD TOWN.

in this reprieve flashed across his heated brain. It might be possible that the long-looked for British army, his godsend, would descend, as they were sure to some time, upon this quiet town, and compel its surrender. If it would only happen this September night! He even went to the window again, on restless feet, and peered out as if he had half a mind to believe he saw them coming to victory, and release for him. But, alas for his hopes! The morrow was to bring only disgrace for him. By its dawn the paper was to be signed, to be carried away, and read to the people who were clamoring for satisfaction.

The old clock ticked away, every beat striking into his angered and feverish brain. "Best have it over with," he cried to himself at last ; and, hurrying back, he snatched up the quill where he had flung it —" did rashly and without consideration make a private and precipitate journey from Concord to Cambridge, to inform Judge Lee"—how his eye glowed now at thought of this expedition ! — " that the country was assembling to come down (and on no other business), that he and others concerned might prepare themselves for the event, and with an avowed intention to deceive the people ; by which the parties assembling might have been exposed to the brutal rage of the soldiery, who had timely notice

to have waylaid the roads, and fired on them while unarmed and defenceless in the dark; by which imprudent conduct I might have prevented the salutary designs of my countrymen, whose intentions were only to request certain gentlemen, sworn into office on the new system of government, to resign their offices, in order to prevent the operation of that (so much detested) act of the British Parliament for regulating the government of the Massachusetts Bay; by all which I have justly drawn upon ms the displeasure of my countrymen."

He compelled himself to read it through, knowing it by heart as he did. " When I coolly reflect on my own imprudence, it fills my mind with the deepest anxiety. I deprecate the resentment of my injured country, humbly confess my errors, and implore the forgiveness of a generous and free people, solemnly daclaring that for the future I will never convey any intelligence to any of the Court party, neither directly nor indirectly; by which the designs of the people may be frustrated, in opposing the barbarous policy of an arbitrary, wicked, and corrupt administration.

CONCORD, Sept. 19, 1774."

Again he threw the quill the table length, and sprang to his feet to pace up and down the long

apartment, anger overflowing his breast, as he clinched his hands together, and swore by all that was most dear to him that he would never attach his name to that paper. And his wife came to the door, and knocked timidly, and, in the exercise of her love, daring to knock again, though she got no response. And the night wore on, and the gray dawn came up, and the morning flush followed, and still the weary and anguished man strode on, knowing that in the end he should sign it just as surely as that the sun would burst over the hill-top yonder, to tell of a new day. But just a little longer; see, he had an hour, he glanced up at the clock ticking away like an executioner, before he should be humiliated to the dust. He flung himself exhausted into his big carved chair, and leaned his head upon his breast for a second's repose. What! is this the trumpet signal of triumph echoing down the street of Concord Town ? See his countrymen, those who so lately met him with averted looks and cold disdain, now behold them trembling and sueing for mercy as the conquering train, brilliant in their gorgeous uniforms and gay trappings, sweep by. Ha — ha — now the fools know; and how they plead with him, the rich and influential Joseph Lee, to intercede with the governor and the British emissaries

for favor; for Joseph Lee, for steadfast adherence to his Majesty's cause in the Colonies, has been promised rich emoluments, and henceforth his shall be the path of royal purple and fine linen. Hear them cheer for him — those splendid fellows, the "flower of the British Army." Hear them —

" Open the door, O husband! I pray you in mercy, open the door. They have come for the paper."

He starts from his sleep, gives one baffled, angry glance at the old clock ticking away his pride and his old traditions and his liberty, seizes the quill, dashes down a trembling, hasty Joseph Lee, at the bottom of the manuscript, undoes the door, and silently thrusts the paper out to his wife, who, weeping, would have kissed his hand had he not bitterly withdrawn it and locked himself in again.

And seven days later, on Sept. 26, the whole town was " resolved into a committee of safety," and it was " voted to raise one or more companies to march at a minute's warning." The committee of correspondence was appointed, and delegates to the proposed Provincial Congress were chosen. Concord was nearly ready for the great struggle. But one thing more of great importance remained to be achieved. This was the Provincial Congress.

On this same day, the 26th, when events so fate-

ful were being prepared for by the citizens of Concord Town and the neighboring boroughs, out of the British coffee-house in Boston Town strolled Bernard Thornton, light of foot and of unmoved countenance, but with a heart ill at ease. He went steadily down King Street, crossed over the intervening space to the Common, where, threading his way among the white tents, he came to the object of his search, all as casually as if the meeting had been of chance. There he was, the very special redcoat whom the dark eye rested upon, though it gave no sign of any recognition. The soldier was pacing leisurely up and down on guard, more for the sake of the perfunctory exercise than for any real good to ensue. Thornton came to a halt, and spoke twice before the man appeared to hear.

"Oh, my good fellow! are you deaf?" cried the young British officer pleasantly. " Never a word can I get out of you. How goes the world with you, Par-lin ? Well, I hope."

The man raised a heavy-eyed face, stolid and uncommunicative, with that sort of holdfast quality sometimes called firmness, that should be termed obstinacy, and answered never a word.

" Not sorry you have seen the best way to help your countrymen, eh ? " queried the young officer.

" No, I'm not sorry," said John Parlin doggedly.

" That's right. Take my word for it, you are kinder to your townsmen than if you stayed and made one more to urge them on to a reckless folly that is inexcusable. There is a terrible reckoning to come upon them, my man. The only way to avert it is for England to rise up in her power as soon as possible, and strike one decisive and short, sharp blow. Once she does that, and the Colonies are taught wisdom; and all who have served his Majesty and the English Parliament will be rewarded with honor and riches. You, Parlin, will be in the end the benefactor of your family and your misguided townsmen."

Still no answer.

"Mister," said John Parlin, when the pause was becoming awkward, "my little gal, my Debby, knows it now, and we never'll meet again." He snapped this out mechanically, and never turned his heavy eyes from Thornton's face.

"Eh, your daughter? Have you been out to Concord to see her?" queried the young officer all in a breath, with a quick glance that would have pierced any less stolid countenance.

"My little gal, my Debby, knows it now, and we'll never meet again," repeated his Majesty's new subject, without a change of face.

" Nonsense, man. She'll be rejoiced at your good

252 A LITTLE MAID OF CONCORD TOWN.

sense, when the end comes, at any rate. You are earning money steadily, and laying it up for your family; and when it is all over, as it surely must be soon," his dark, lambent eyes gleamed, " none will be more rejoiced than this daughter of yours. Cheer up, the call to arms will be ere long. You are pining for action, as are we all."

" My Debby knows it, and we'll never meet again/' repeated John Parlin, without a change of muscle.

"Trust me to make you easy on that score," replied the young officer, not without a touch of anger ; " and hark ye, John Parlin, an unwilling subject of his Majesty does not receive, at the final reckoning, a share of the honor and the recompense."

" I'm not sorry," said John Parlin stolidly, and not turning his eyes away.

"That's well. Of such stuff are good British subjects made. I will reconnoitre, and bring you word from Concord Town. Believe me that all will be well." He stepped lightly on his way. John Parlin, in his Majesty's uniform, marched back and forth as before, with no change of countenance or manner.

That afternoon, on the old Bay Road, at the outskirts of Concord Town, a venerable man, footsore and weary, paused to ask permission to rest beside

a cottage door. He was slim and bent, and his long white hair flowed over his thin shoulders, as he leaned trembling on his staff. The children playing beside the door ran in and shouted out that a poor old beggar-man was there, and couldn't he sit down in a chair in the kitchen. This brought the good wife to the door, with pity in her eye. She was wiping up her dishes, and mechanically went on with her task, carefully polishing up the bowl in her hand on the long brown towel, as she listened to his tale of woe with a sympathizing ear, the children, with their fingers in their mouths, hovering near.

"Yes, good man, come in," she cried, holding wide the door. " Nancy, set a chair. Susan, don't get in his way so. Here, Jonas, give him your arm, ; ' to the biggest boy in the crowd.

'• You are very good," sighed the old man, as he sank into the wooden chair; "these be troublous times, and I did not know that I should find so much kindness."

"Troublous the times may be, and you may well say so," replied Dame Woodward, going back to her dishwashing with a backward glance at him; "but that's no reason why \ve shouldn't look well to the poor within our gates. I'm sorry for you. How far have you come ? "

254 A LITTLE MAID OF CONCORD TOWN.

"Quite a piece — quite a piece," said the old man feebly, nodding his head, "so far I disremember."

"You must be very tired and hungry," said Dame Woodward pityingly. " May the Lord forgive me for not thinking of it sooner!" She dashed down her towel across the pile of dishes waiting to be dried ; and, going to the buttery, she returned with a slice of corn bread. " I will make you a cup of tea," she said, hurrying to the kettle hanging on the crane.

"Thank the Lord you have tea to give me!" cried the old man, in a revived voice. " 'Twould rest my bones more than to take ten years off from them, to get an honest cup of English tea."

" English tea ! " cried the dame, nearly dropping the big blue cup and saucer, and turning a red and angry countenance upon him. " Who are you to come to Concord Town and talk of English tea ? Never a drop can you get here to wet your throat. You may search from one end of the place to the other. No, we drink nothing that is mixed by tyrants, and stamped by a wicked Parliament." She was so very angry that the old man's head went down on his breast, and he blubbered and whimpered, and gurgled that he didn't mean any offence ; but it was so long since he had tasted tea, and he was so very tired, and he hoped she would forgive him, and all that.

" Don't scold him, mother," begged Jonas; " see him shake. He's old, and he didn't know any better."

" You must excuse me, sir," said the dame, hurrying to pour an infusion from a pot by the fire into the cup, and covering it with boiling water from the kettle on the crane; "but I'm sore worked up indeed to think that you'd believe for a moment that a house in Concord Town could hold that wicked king's tea. Here, drink this, poor man, it will rest you; for it is an honest cup, brewed in the spirit of liberty."

" I am better now. I need no tea," said the old man, not offering to take the cup she held forth.

" Yes, you must drink it," said the good wife. "You are beaten with your journey." She thrust it under his nose. " You will say that it makes you well, when once it is down."

Thus pressed, the stranger had no alternative but to accept the cup, out of which he took gingerly a small swallow, and then precipitately sought the door by a series of jerks that were supposed to represent age in a hurry.

" It is excellent — excellent," he said tottering back, and wiping his mouth on his ragged sleeve; " but my stomach is weak — loss of food, dear madam — my long walk. Pardon me." He sat down, mumbling away deep in his throat things that no one un-

256 A LITTLE MAID OF CONCORD TOWN.

derstood, although the children crowded him closely not to lose a word.

" He's hungry, mother, don't you understand," said Susan, who succeeded in getting the closest to him. " Do get him something to eat, quick," with great sympathy, as she was always in that state.

" I'm sure I will give him something to stay his hunger," said her mother, somewhat mollified as she felt this might be the reason for the low condition, unable to more than taste her splendid herb tea. " Here is the best I have," bringing the corn slice.

The stranger shook his head feebly. " Could one of your little ones put the bits into my mouth ? " he asked in a faint voice.

" You poor soul, yes," cried the good dame, quite won over from her resentment; " though I wish you would take the tea, 'twould quite bring you to."

" Let me feed him — let me," cried Susan, springing for the blue plate on which reposed the slice of corn bread.

" I want to," piped Nancy, on her tiptoes.

"You can't either of you do it straight," broke in Jonas. " I shall do it myself."

Thereupon a scuffle ensued, in which the blue plate changed hands so many times that it was difficult to say to whom it really belonged, the slice of corn

bread lying unnoticed on the floor where it had flown in the melee.

" Naughty children !" cried their mother, bestowing liberal boxes from her palm on the ears that came handy, "to fight and quarrel so when we are all in such trouble, and this poor man may be dying before us." She picked up the slice, and laid it on the table, and went to the buttery to fetch another.

" This isn't good enough for company," said Susan, calmly eating it with a gusto.

" Ma, Susan's et up the corn bread," shouted Jonas, who intended to take it himself.

" You bad girl," said her mother, giving her a shake as she passed her, " and you had two whole slices for dinner. Here, Jonas, you may feed the poor old man. How you children can be so naughty I don't see, when we are all in such trouble."

" You speak of trouble so often, my good woman," quavered the old man, as he opened his mouth to receive the liberal wedge of corn-bread that Jonas applied to his lips. " Not such big pieces, please, and don't feed me fast. I'm an old man, and I can't eat very fast."

" You've got all your teeth," said Jonas, investigating the interior that received the corn-bread supply.

The stranger closed his mouth quickly; and the

corn crumbs must have gone down the wrong way, for he coughed and spluttered, until Jonas at last put down the plate in despair at ever being able to furnish another supply.

" I don't want to feed him, mother," he announced in a loud whisper to the dame; " he's awful slow and queer."

"He's very old," whispered loudly back his mother. "We must pity the infirmities of the aged, my son. See, he's nodding ; he'll go off to sleep most likely. You children can run out to play."

Jonas and the others, having gotten all the fun out of the episode likely to come, scampered off, while the aged stranger dozed and nodded. Suddenly he gave a long sigh. " I must have lost myself," he said, opening his eyes. " Oh, well-a-day! my poor limbs were all tired out. You spoke of trouble, my good woman, — he roused himself as by an effort to be conversational — " and have you seen trouble ? You seem comfortable," glancing around the cottage walls.

"Where have you been not to know the trouble and sore distress of our Colonies ? " cried the dame wrathfully. "Have you been asleep all these past years not to have discovered it. The idea of coming to Concord Town and asking me this question!" she

added in a dudgeon. " Well, since you don't seem to know, I will tell you that wicked King George has left no stone unturned by which he might oppress us. He and his wickeder parliament are determined to crush us — but they can't do it.

The old man huddled down in his chair deprecat-ingly. "You surely do not mean to oppose the king ?" he quavered in dismay.

" Oppose ? Ay, we do. We will fight him to the death. There isn't a man in Concord Town who won't do it."

" What, fight your king ? " cried the old man in horror, and spreading his hands, quivering like aspen leaves.

" Our king," exploded Dame Woodward ; " we know no king but God. The king you call ours is a despot, and has treated us like slaves. We have obeyed him, been loyal to him, and loved him — now don't talk, you're too old, — and still he crushes us to the earth. Nothing now remains for us but slavery. Fight ? You shall see how we will fight when the time comes. Bless God, it's coming soon, we pray."

" You wouldn't have your husband go to battle, would you ?" queried the old man in a thin tone of amazement.

" I wouldn't have him not go," shrilled the dame.

" And if the men can't whip the British enslavers, we women and girls will all turn out. Where have you been not to know this without asking, pray tell?" It was her turn to look amazed.

" I'm very old and poor and tired," said the stranger feebly. " I pray you to forgive me if I make mistakes;" and then he went off into another fit of mumbling. To restore him, Dame Woodward began to talk, thinking to make him forget his blunder. " No matter how sick and poor and troubled we be, we're all for fighting. Now you ought to hear Debby Parlin talk."

The old man went on mumbling, as if he heard not. But presently he begged humbly to be forgiven again. "You were speaking of one of your relatives?" he asked.

"She's no kin to me, but I wish she was. Don't you know Debby Parlin ? Why, everybody knows her. She lives down this Old Bay Road in a little cottage against the Ridge."

"You forget I do not live in this village," said the old man.

" Seem's if everybody ought to know Debby Parlin," replied Mrs. Woodward. "Well, her father's gone off, no livin' mortal knows where. The trouble we've all been in, has prob'ly flew to his head. An'

Mis' Parlin took a dretful spell by reason of him away; an' there's that Deb'rah with her sick ma, for she's terribly changed, Mis' Parlin is, an' them three children, and she's as fierce for the war to begin as any of us. Land ! I wouldn't want to fight that girl if I was a British soldier."

"You interest me very much," said the stranger, when the busy tongue came to a pause. " And you make me forget my own troubles to hear you, my good woman."

"Well, it's a sight to make a body cry, to see that girl; why, she goes out spinning, or weaving, or doing anything she can turn her hand to, and all the townsfolk have her come an' help 'em. Everybody loves Debby. Oh, dear, dear! — an' we can't help her much, cause we're all as poor as Job's turkeys, an' got our own noses to the grindstone. You ain't goin'? "

"I must get on a piece now," said the old man, getting out of his chair, and planting his staff on the floor with a thump. "Thank you kindly, my good woman, I won't forget you ever."

"You're welcome," said Dame Woodward; "let me help you," essaying to ease his tottering footsteps to the door. "I'm sure I wish I had better to give you, but it's all we've got ourselves. At any rate, it's

honest food, and it don't belong to slaves, for we're bound to be free. Don't you fail to remember that. An' I'm glad I seen you, and may the Lord help you on your way." She shouted all this after him as he tremblingly went down the road toward the centre of Concord Town.

XVIII.

f~^ OVERNOR and Commander-in-Chief Gage sat by VJT" his fireside, in the Province House, — for the day, though in early autumn, was cool, — lost in a train of perplexed and angry musing. He had that afternoon ridden out to view the blockhouses and repairs on the fortifications at Boston Neck, which, to further subdue the rebellious spirit of the colonists, he had gotten well under way. Though none of the laborers versed in such matters in the town would assist him, he had managed to erect some sort of makeshift for fortifying purposes. He intended to pursue the work rapidly, at the same time to push forward every other scheme to break the spirit of the rebels, who were now becoming openly determined to stand by their rights, and to remain "the conservators of existing institutions, they call themselves," he said sneeringly to himself; "but rebels they are, and by King George and the British Parliament and the British army, as rebels I will subdue them."

264 A LITTLE MAID OF CONCORD TOWN.

Thwarted in all he had set out to do in the way of subjugating these troublesome colonists, Thomas Gage, received by the people of Boston in their great relief at the withdrawal of the detested Hutchinson, at first with a popular show of welcome, had failed, like the other royal governors, to grasp the situation. Here he sat in the handsome home, set apart by the Colonial Legislature of 1716 for him and his predecessors, looking back on a constantly increasing complication of the difficulty he had hoped to straighten out between the king and his subjects.

In his rage at the obstinacy and foolhardiness of these rebels, he could not but acknowledge, had he been truthful, that he lost his head when he became malignant enough to send forth his proclamation against those who were determined not to buy British goods. All his efforts to fasten the charges of treason and rebellion upon the colonist leaders, in their independent interpretation of their chartered rights, had failed utterly, leaving him in a most mortifying position, constantly forced to some new scheme by which he fondly hoped to be successful.

But the Regulation Act, immediately put into operation by him when received from the English Parliament, not only made matters worse, but precipitated the crisis. The colonists must now either be slaves,

or independent men, free from the yoke of king or Parliament. There could be no middle situation, and he, sitting there, governor and commander-in-chief of the British army, knew it, as did all the world looking on.

It was in the midst of these distressing and humiliating thoughts, that a tall and slender man, in the garb of a British officer, approached the mansion, and ascended the high flight of stone steps. He was ushered through a " magnificent doorway which might have rivalled those of the palaces of Europe." Here he left his colored servant in the outer hall, with a careless glance of his dark eye, and a manner indicative of no special command; yet Pompey ducked obsequiously, and shuffled his feet back instantly, as if anxious to get well out of range of anything that might fly in their direction.

" Ha, Thornton, is that you ? " said Governor Gage, as the young man entered. " Close the door, and come here. Stay, ring for wine to be brought."

" I want none, thank you," said Thornton hastily, " and would to business as soon as possible."

"Wine you must have," replied the governor. Even a little thing like that irritated him, who seemed not able to impose obedience. " And if you cannot touch that bell yonder, why, I can do it for you."

" Pardon me," said the young officer, the color ris-

ing to his cheek, " in that case I find that I do need some wine, and permit me to ring for you."

When the wine was brought by the black servant, and the decanters and their glasses were set forth on the shining oaken table, Thornton paused, between his slow sips, to wait the pleasure of the governor. But no summons to speak coming from the governor's lips, he at last set down his glass and said, "If you will permit me, Governor Gage, I will show you why I come to you this afternoon. Really it seems to me there is cause for grave consideration if not for serious alarm, in the various matters I shall lay before you."

" Matters that I doubt not will be trifling, as are all the affairs in which these rebels are engaged," said Governor Gage, intending to be dignified and cool, but missing his object.

" Perhaps so," assented Thornton, who had regained his usual color, and taking another sip of wine with an indifferent air, as if determined now to await the governor's request before revealing his errand.

" I shall not be disturbed, Thornton, I tell you in advance, at whatever you bring me. Remember, I know these rascally poltroons well, and can be surprised by nothing. What are their leaders, but men of low birth and fortunes like this desperate Sam Adams, or, on the other hand, weak fools who aspire

to aristocracy, like this Hancock, who is really led about by this same Adams ? Bah ! " He struck the table with his palm till the glasses rang, poured out a stiff glass of grog, and tossed it off. " Out with your tale," he said briefly, and composed himself as well as he could to listen.

" I shall sadly vex you, Governor Gage, I doubt not," said Thornton respectfully, yet not without a shade of contempt in his tone, " at what I am about to say."

" Nonsense ! " ejaculated the governor. " You cannot vex me. Have I not known you well, and from what you come ? You are an English gentleman; and, mark you, Thornton, there is no finer work of God under the sun than one such." The young man bowed in gratified acknowledgment at this tribute.

" You are of kin to Sir Francis Bernard, and have lived in the midst of all his traditions of family and government, to say nothing of being taught like him at the University of Oxford, where, if anywhere, thank God for it, men are made to believe in the divine right of kings; and your word has, I must confess, as I have ever shown to you, great weight with me," the governor proceeded, with a view to the earliest propitiation of the young man before him.

"But I warn you, nevertheless, that I am about to utter what may be instrumental in breaking up

your regard for me, notwithstanding this regard is based upon my being kinsman to your friend Sir Francis."

"Not wholly, Thornton," interposed the governor hastily. "You are a young man after my own heart and mind, on your individual merits. It is for yourself that 1 have regard; your family traditions and early associations do but enrich you."

Thornton moved his chair a trifle impatiently. " Have I your permission to proceed to the business in hand ?"

" Yes; proceed at once," said the governor, compressing his lips and folding his hands.

" In the first place, I have a confession to make to you, sir," said Thornton respectfully yet firmly. " Where I once thought that these Colonists, call them rebels if you will" —

" They are rebels," interrupted the governor harshly, and bringing down his folded hand again in a way to make the glasses ring; "rebels of the deepest dye; mark you that. Proceed."

" Where I once thought that they were hopelessly contending for a principle they would never bring to the point of settlement by the sword, I now as conscientiously believe that they will fight to the death to maintain that principle."

" You lie ! " exclaimed the governor, startled out of his composure, and leaping from his chair.

" No man, be he governor or king, dares tell me that," said Thornton, getting deliberately out from his chair and facing him.

" You are right, my boy," the governor put out a quick hand, and laid it on the young man's shoulder; " I was hasty and choleric — forgive me. By my sword, I have been more tried than even you imagine. Here's my hand, I know you are a man of honor and truth. Forgive and forget, Thornton."

The young officer silently took the proffered hand, and reseated himself, as the governor did the same.

" I am at a loss how to proceed, sir," he said after a moment, when his host was pouring out another glass of wine, and drinking it to allay his perturbation ; " I am fearful I may offend again."

" Go on, I promise not to take umbrage again, at least till you are through," said Governor Gage with a short laugh. Yet he clinched his hands tightly together to hold himself in check.

"I repeat it, sir, these Colonists" (it was noticeable that all through the conversation that ensued, Thornton did not once allude to them as rebels, and Governor Gage winced many a time at the omission) "will fight when the time comes, I believe — and to a man."

2/0 A LITTLE MAID OI- COKCORD TOWN.

"Why do you thus believe? and from what do you draw your conclusions ? " demanded the governor.

"From my own personal observations, sir," said Thornton. "I have been now, you know, many months among them, in every conceivable disguise, — peddler, aged man, — in any and every way in which I could be admitted to their confidence. It is not necessary to enumerate them. You know how I have employed every moment I could be spared from my regiment, and I will conscientiously say I have been thorough in my work."

"This I believe, knowing you," the governor opened his tightly compressed lips to say.

•"I have visited many towns and Colonies, and have acquired besides the actual knowledge needed for our commanders in the way of ammunition, men, and so forth, the additional information as to the temper and spirit of the Colonists. Lately I have centred my best work in Concord Town."

" And what do you find there ?" demanded the governor eagerly, and unclasping his hands to nervously play with his wine-glass. "I venture to say that here at least you will accord me the justice of good intuitions, when I say that they will not fight when brought to the pinch. Old Concord is too near to Boston to dare the trial. She knows too much."

" On the contrary," said Thornton in a low, strained voice, " she knows so much, that she is willing to die, but she will be free. Take my word for it, sir. Be warned in time. Concord will never be conquered."

There was an awful pause. Then came a crushing sound as the wine-glass was hurled from the governor's fingers and dashed against the hearthstone.

" I will keep my word, young man," he said, his face almost purple in his attempts to restrain himself. " I am a man of honor, and never will I forget that I have promised to be silent and upbraid you not, but to let you finish in peace. Have you more to say ?"

"Yes." The young officer nodded, and communed silently how easiest to bring all the points to the best and quickest consideration of his hearer.

"You have made, I hope, some good Loyalists?" queried the governor sharply, with a keen glance, " in all these journeyings."

"Yes," said Thornton. A pained expression swept over his face, but it was gone in an instant, and he bore his usual countenance. "I have, sir. But these are all overborne by the determined spirit of their opposers. They amount to nothing as far as stemming the current of public opinion. It is all one way. Believe me, sir, I would I had a pleasant tale to tell."

"Now, by King George," cried the governor, on his feet, and clinching both hands before him, "they shall taste the sword they are so anxious to run against. Poor wretches! will nothing bring them to reason? Are they so steeped in their folly and conceit that they can see aught but ruin ahead of them ? It is time to loose the dogs of war on them, for the longer delayed, but intrenches them in their mad delusions. Go on, for I see that you have more on your mind," he commanded abruptly.

"They have begun to raise what they call companies of minute-men among the various towns," said Thornton.

"Ha, ha! and what are those, pray tell? Men who will run the minute the British army stands before them, I make no doubt," sneered Governor Gage.

"They are men who will be ready to take up arms the minute the call comes for them," said Thornton.

" Bosh!" It was impossible to throw more contempt into a single word than that now invested with the governor's derision.

The young man's face settled into a deeper gravity. t(I wish you could see it all as I, who have been amongst them, see it, sir," he said at length. "They are men, I am convinced, who do not rebel

from fancied wrongs, nor from any lack of loyalty to our king, but from a deep-seated conviction of their rights invaded, and their charters infringed."

"Hold!" cried the governor in a loud tone; "why, you are a rebel yourself," he was about to add, but recollected his promise in time.

Thornton coolly finished the words for him. " You were going to say that I was as bad a rebel as any of these — but you had not heard me through. I was telling you the state of affairs seen through their eyes, in order that you may realize that it is a matter of conscience with them, and that as such we must recognize the fact that it will be well-nigh impossible to conquer them by mere force."

" Nevertheless it shall be tried," said the governor under his breath.

" As for me," Thornton drew himself up to his full height, " I am, as you say, an English gentleman, born and bred in the belief of the divine right of kings. This is enough."

" Quite," assented Governor Gage dryly.

"Would it not be possible," the young British officer leaned forward and searched the face before him, " to use other measures to induce them to reason ? Surely, if you could but see them for yourself, you would recognize the fact that they are easily led.

It is by no means too late to try conciliation. There are many honorable ways of bringing this about, and retaining our hold upon the Colonies, and " —

But he got no farther. " Young man," thundered the governor, " you are now transcending your province. Verily, this is an unusual thing from one so young as you, to be thus in conference with the chief executive, and you must not overstep the privilege."

" I was sought," said Thornton with hauteur. "Otherwise, you are quite aware, sir, that I should never have intruded myself to your notice or your presence;" and again the expression of contempt overspread his face.

" Quite true. Being what you are, I have gladly intrusted to you this important work, and summoned you to confidential conferences. But no one is allowed to overstep the bound, nor to dictate to me, the chief executive, the best way to deal with stiff-necked and rebellious people."

" I shall not be likely to err in this direction again," said Thornton, keeping his anger down; " I have eased my mind, and spoken freely in regard to this unhappy estrangement between the mother-country and her American Colonies. I have given you what information I was sent to obtain. Now

"CONCORD WILL NEVER BE CONQUERED." 2?$

I will, with your permission, retire." He rose and stood before the governor.

" You have done well in your expeditions, I doubt not," replied Governor Gage, endeavoring to recover his usual manner, and-partially succeeding; " I shall doubtless send you again on similar ones. Meantime gather all the news you can, from whatever source, and bring me; and carry away with you, Thornton, from this interview, only my unbounded respect and affection. Your judgment only is at fault."

The young officer bowed himself out, and motioning to his colored servant, rolling his eyes in stiff dignity on the carved oaken chair, to follow him, he stalked down the street.

"Golly, massa," said Pompey, shambling after, "I hain't gotter tell tings you brung me up to the big house fer, — about Capen James and the stuff he's keerin' fer, and all the rest? Hee-hee, dis nigger's glad!"

" No, you villain! " The young lieutenant turned suddenly and let his boot fly. Over rolled the darkey, clapping his hand to his shin. He had met his Waterloo again.

XIX.

USHERING IN THE YEAR OF LIBERTY.

MIDWINTER was fairly begun, ushering in the year of liberty. It was of January, 1775. Around the old church of Concord Town there was a great stir. From the groups of men, old and young, gathered out of the whole countryside, it was easy to discover by the fragments of conversation, that an event of unusual importance was about to happen. There were exhibitions here and there of powder-horns handed about from one to the other. Now and then an old musket appeared that seemed to have done duty in the Indian raids, or in shooting bears on some lonely farm ; and great was the envy and pride on the countenances, as these articles were displayed by their owners and passed along. Those who were less fortunate, slapped their breeches pockets, and guessed they could raise enough to buy their accoutrements. Some few hung their heads, until assured that the town had promised to buy the guns for men unable to furnish them; then their spirits revived.

" Hush, here he comes." The young pastor, fair and slender, came down the road, his

Bible under his arm. His step was springing, and there was that in his air that gave courage to the waiting men and the outer fringe of people, like the blast of a trumpet; and they all filed in and took their seats in the big square pews, while he mounted the pulpit steps, convinced that the enlistment to follow the meeting, was to be a whole-souled movement.

Simon and Jabez crowded up into a front seat. There was old Daddy Fairbanks, well along in his eighties, hurrying after. " Move up, boys," he quavered, with kindling eye, and he dropped into a seat beside them; "I want to be a-settin' up high, so 's to be one o' the fust to get my name writ down."

Here was Abner Butterfield, whose right hand nervously fingered the grand'ther's musket he bore. This had been at Louisburg, and Abner meant it to tell more tales before he got through with it. And here, crowding his toes, and shoving his long figure, was the ubiquitous boy of Concord Town, standing up big and straight, ready to demand the privilege of "jining the comp'ny." They were all there, old and young, big and little, from this and the neighboring towns, drawn to the great meeting when their revered pastor was to preach, to be followed by the

raising of the minute company to defend their rights as freemen.

The long sermon has begun, from Psalm lxiii. 2. " To see thy power and thy glory, so as I have seen thee in the sanctuary." Not a word is missed. No one thinks of fatigue. Solemnly every word is taken in by the absorbed, attentive listeners. Brought up as they were to attend divine service on each Lord's Day, and feeling it a sin and a shame to begin anything without the blessing of the God of their fathers, these men and boys look upon this effort of the preacher as the only proper step to their induction into the ranks of the fighters. And they drink eagerly in every word, only drawing a long breath of delight when the regulations are to be signed, and the real enlisting is begun.

Sixty came forward, many of them being either too old or too young to go into the militia, and signed their names to the following regulations, or agreements : —

" i. We, whose names are hereunto subscribed, will, to the utmost of our power, defend his Majesty, King George the Third, his person, crown, and dignity.

" 2. We will at the same time, to the utmost of our power and abilities, defend all and every of our charter rights, liberties, and privileges; and will hold ourselves in readiness at a minute's warning with arms and ammunition thus to do.

"3. We will at all times and in all places obey our officers chosen by us, and our superior officers, in ordering and disciplining us, when and where said officers shall think proper."

Debby Parlin sat with her mates, and between Mills-cent Barrett and Perces Wood. Her tired hands, freed from toil for this brief respite, for everybody went to the meeting, and no one thought of working any more than on a Sabbath day, rested in the palms of the girls beside her. A gentle pressure, every now and then, from Miliscent's warm, sympathetic fingers, and a glance from the soft, dark eye, told how keenly the heart of her friend was bearing the sorrow fallen upon the young life. Perces held the poor, toil-marked fingers ; but she sat bolt upright, as was her wont, and stared religiously up into the minister's face. Yet Debby knew the current under the still surface, and was content.

The enlisting went on rapidly, with a promise of more names to follow, which was afterward fulfilled, one hundred joining the ranks, so that the number was divided, making two companies, one of which was called The Alarm Company.

When it was all over, and the newly enlisted men

and boys had marched off to consider ways and means for active work, Debby turned her pale face to Miliscent, and drew a long breath. " I've got something to tell you; and I want you and Perces to come out into the burying-ground, but not the other girls."

" Come on, Debby," called one of these last, as they filed out of church with that feeling that, after such an unusual event, the hours to follow till sundown should be free from work. "You can't settle down to anything. Nobody's going home yet."

"You forget I have mother; she'll be lonely," said Debby, in the quiet way that was hers now. " But I must speak to Miliscent and Perces first; don't be angry with me, girls," she added pleadingly.

" We ain't mad/' said Louisa quickly, as she looked into the pale face. "Come away," and she led off the others, who were longing to add themselves to Debby's company.

"Now, girls," up in the old hill burying-ground, Debby stopped abruptly and faced them, " I've got something on my mind, and you must help me."

Neither girl spoke. Debby was always sure to disclose everything in regular fashion, and much better if not interrupted. But she hesitated so long- now that Miliscent said, "Well?"

" I am going to search for my father," said Debby abruptly, pale and red by turns.

" Deborah Parlin !" exclaimed both girls at once. Such a thing had never been heard of in those days as a girl's going away from home, alone, and into unknown spots; and they stared at her, after that first explosion of surprise, in dumb amazement.

" I surely am," declared Debby in clear-cut, low tones. " You know, girls, it is useless to say anything, for my mind is made up."

" But you cannot go," cried Miliscent, off her guard, and not realizing that this was not the way to deal with one of Debby's make-up. " I never heard of such a thing; nobody has. Why, what could you do, Deborah Parlin ?" She folded her hands imploringly.

" I can search for my father," repeated Debby in lower tones, but ringing with determination. " Girls, do you either of you know what it is to be without a father ?" Her head sunk to her bosom, but her eyes were dry.

" You poor thing!" Miliscent threw both arms around her, and strained her to her breast. " Oh! you know how we love you, how everybody loves you, Debby. And we just long to do something for you. But to go off for your father — you don't in the least know where he is. What will become of you ? And

282 A LITTLE MAID OF CONCORD TOWN.

then we need you to make the cartridges. Oh, dear, dear! give it up, dear Debby, do." She caressed and mourned over her and pleaded, Perces standing stiff and tall and silent.

" Perces, do say something to get this idea out of her head, and not stand like a stick or a stone," at last cried Miliscent impatiently.

" I think Debby is right to go," said Perces decidedly, and not moving a muscle.

" Perces Wood ! I wonder what your father would say if he knew you encouraged Debby to leave her home and go on such a dreadfully risky piece of work," cried Miliscent angrily.

"I'm not encouraging her," declared Perces stolidly. "You wanted me to speak, and I'm going to tell the truth. I think she ought to go."

" Perces — Perces ! " cried Debby convulsively, amid a rain of tears. Seeing this, Miliscent in a dum-founded way began to pet her. But she clung to the big, stolid girl.

" You will some time be glad that I advised you," said Miliscent, standing off in a grand way, determined now to do the heroics. " Well, good-by, Deborah Parlin," and she turned her back on the two, "if you wish to desert your work on the cartridges for a useless search."

'•' Miliscent! " Debby flung herself after her. " You don't know how you are hurting me, when I think I must give up my work on the cartridges. Stop, not another word, I know God wants me to search for my father. He will take care of me. O girls, girls ! " — she had dragged Miliscent back to Perces standing still, as she spoke, and she now laid a hand on the arm of each girl, — "I must find my father, or I shall die." Every bit of color had fled from her face; and her hood, falling back, disclosed her thin cheeks with the hollows under the blue eyes. " Think what it is to see each day go by and get no tidings from him. I must bring him back."

" You seem to feel that he's alive, Debby," said Miliscent, catching her breath at the misery of the young face before her. " He's probably dead, dear, long before this, or he would have come home. So there is no use in your risking your life, as you surely will, I feel, in going on such a wild errand."

Debby turned and looked at her, but did not release her hold on the arm. What'would the girls do if they knew that her father was a Tory! She almost felt like a traitor, to be accepting their affection and confidence.

"If he were dead," she said solemnly, "I would not mourn, but take it as the will of God. I must bring back mv ^ther."

"I see there is no use in talking," said Miliscent with a break in her voice, " and that you are going. Forgive me for what I said." The tears gushed from her eyes, and she fell on Debby's neck with many sobs.

" You didn't mean—you cannot know," said Debby, " unless you had it to bear yourself, what it is to live through — O Miliscent 1 O Perces! if you will only help me in this one thing."

They hung on her words, one tearful and sympathetic, the other stolid and with dry eyes.

" Just go as often as you can, without neglecting the cartridges, to see mother" — Debby's lips trembled — " and the children. They've learned many nice ways since Mrs. Butterfield took them for a visit; and they're handy about the house, so she won't miss me much about the work. But she's lonely in her mind, and you know she never goes out; and oh! I'm so worried about her." And the white face was overcast by a cloud. Perces spoke up.

"Don't you worry. I'm a-going down there to stay. You know I'm so slow I'm no good on the cartridges."

"Perces!" it was now Debby's turn to be astonished. As for Miliscent she sank down on one of the graves, and clung to the tombstone in amazement.

a §
- -I?

"Mother doesn't need me," Perces was saying steadily. "She's got Betsy Higgins there now ; she's had to give up her farm, you know, and father told her to come to our house. And I'm really no good on the cartridges; so I'll just go and see after your ma, Debby, and you can go off easy in your mind," she added, with the air of a woman of forty, who was accustomed to settle big matters every day.

Miliscent peeped behind the tombstone and gazed at her. Debby had seized her hands, " O you Perces, you good Perces !" and was laughing and crying at one and the same time.

"Perhaps your mother won't let you go, Debby," said Miliscent, feeling as if the whole world were upside down, and she had no bearings at all.

" She will; she knows it — of course I told her first," cried Debby breathlessly. " O you good Perces ! "

" Then I must give up, and let you go," said Miliscent with a sigh, getting up and shaking the damp mould from her blue stuff gown. " And, Debby, since you are really going, I promise to help you every single bit I can while you are gone. I can't go to stay all the time at your house," — with a pang at the thought of Perces's happiness, — for we've such loads of children; and then grandfather and grandmother expect me over there every day — and there are the

cartridges. But every minute 1 can spare, I'll be down to see your mother. O Debby!"

She fell on her neck again, but this time without tears; and at last, as the sun sank down behind the hill, they parted, and went their several ways.

" Mother," said Perces Wood, going straight up to the matron's side when they were alone in the big kitchen, " Debby Parlin is going away to find her father, and I am going down to stay with her mother. I knew you'd let me. And don't let us tell any one."

Mrs. Wood looked up at her daughter. "Well, you can go," she said slowly, after a while.

"I knew you'd let me," said Perces in a matter-of-fact way; "and so I told Debby this afternoon."

"But as for not telling any one, we shall inform your father, of course," -said Mrs. Wood, feeling for the moment younger than her daughter, and not caring to show in the presence of so much composure how startled she was at this news of Debby's plans. Evidently the times were days of development for the girls, who, if they couldn't fight, could show their pluck in other ways. She went silently about the old kitchen with many conflicting emotions within her. And Perces, as if such things were of daily settling, put up the supper dishes on the dresser with her usual precision and slow care.

The next morning she put on her hood and big shawl and went out, hearing Betsy Higgins say, '•La, where's she a-streakin' it to now, I wonder," with the freedom of the New England homestead, where all were on a footing of equality. But Betsy got no reply, Perces felt quite sure, as no one but herself knew her expedition, her mother allowing it without asking why.

The girl kept on her slow and steady way, till the two miles between the Wood mansion and her destination were traversed. Then she turned in at the Butterfield farmyard, and rapped at the big green door.

" My senses, it's Perces Wood!" exclaimed Mrs. Butterfield, as if announcing it to an imaginary company. " Your pa out in the waggin, or your ma most likely?" craning her neck.

"No," said Perces; " I came on foot and alone. I want to see Abner, Mrs. Butterfield."

" La, well, you do ?" said Abner's mother, much puzzled. Perces never was a girl to run after the boys; but here she was now, sure enough. And Mrs. Butterfield began to draw lively conclusions of the motives that had induced rich Mr. Wood's daughter to travel those long two miles, and a com-placent smile overspread her big features 'at the

thought of so much appreciation of her son. " Though I always knew he could pick and choose through the hull town. But, la me 1 I wouldn't have him really marry any one but Debby, bless her heart! Ab-//<?r / " she screamed at the foot of the stairs leading up to the corn-chamber, while Perces waited on the door-stone.

" You ain't goin' in in that rig," she remonstrated, as Abner came down the stairs in response to the summons ; u it's the Wood girl, an' she wants to see you. Do go an' slick up a bit — I'll keep her talkin'."

But Abner pushed past her, and was already at the door. " Did you want to see me 1 " There were dark hollows under his heavy eyes. Mrs. Butterfield followed heavily after.

" I want to see Abner alone," said Perces, quite composed, and with no circumlocutory effort.

" This way, then." Abner was about to fling wide the keeping-room door; but remembering with a pang the night that Debby had given therein her confidence touching Tory Lee, he closed it hastily. " You can tell me out here," he said ; and they stepped beneath the large oak just on the edge of the house-place, Mrs. Butterfield, as on that other occasion, left in thwarted curipsity—this time, however, with the satisfaction born of the fact that she could command a good view

from the kitchen window of all that went on under the oak.

" It don't look like love-making," she soliloquized, as she peered out —" and of all beings, Perces Wood, who's as stiddy as a clock. But then you can't ever tell about these girls — an' no wonder they are crazy about my Abner; an' these quiet ones are the most dangerous, I reckon. Well, she sha'n't get him away from Debby. She'll have me to tackle first."

Outside, Perces was saying in a matter-of-fact way, and looking straight in the young man's face, " Debby Parlin is going to look for her father. I thought I'd tell you, but no one else is to know. Good-day;" and she trudged down the path, and out the gateway.

"Well, if ever I see anything more sing'lar in all my born days; she hain't had time to say a dozen words skeercely, and gone, an' he a-standin' there as if struck dumb." Mrs. Butterfield hurried to the door. " Abater f" she called. " What did she want ? "

Abner started, and passed his hand over his forehead. " Oh! you heard Perces say that she must tell me alone, mother."

Then Mrs. Butterfield's thoughts deserted their first charge and flew, as they ever must, to the impending dangers. " Did Mr. Wood send her ?" she demanded

hoarsely. " It's something about the Britishers coming, I know."

" Nothing of the sort," denied Abner shortly, turning on his heel, and wishing the war only would commence, to give his .torturing thoughts something to dwell on that could lead him into action.

XX.

A SEARCH THROUGH BOSTON TOWN.

ALOW knock sounded on the green door of the Parlin cottage that evening. Debby took up the candle, and went out into the little entry. As she lifted the latch a sudden gust of wind blew the door wide, and extinguished the light.

" Don't be scared," said a voice.

" Oh ! is that you, Jim ? " said Debby.

" Yes; but don't be scared. I say, Debby, I've come to tell you something before I'm off. Can you trust me to shut that door and step outside a minute ? "

Debby closed the door back of her, and followed Jim to a little distance from the cottage, where he paused. There was no moon ; but the sky above was studded with brilliants, and the air, despite the season, was soft and balmy.

" What is it ?" asked Debby patiently. " If you have anything to tell me, Jim, say it at once, or I shall go back to the house."

Jim seemed to find great difficulty in beginning.

He cleared his throat several times, and at last blurted out in sheer desperation. " I'm awfully sorry I treated you so, Debby, but " —

" If that is all you have come to say, you might well have remained at home," said Debby in scornful dignity, and moving off toward the cottage.

"Well, it ain't," cried Jim hastily; "but I wanted to get that off my mind first. I'm powerful sorry, Debby; but I had to, for fear you'd tell on us, and spoil the job. Don't you believe I'm sorry ?"

" Let that pass," said Debby, arresting her footsteps at the suggestion of some other piece of information weighing on Jim's mind. What if he should know anything of her father ? flashed through her mind, always on the alert for chance news of the absent one.

" I was run into Ab Butterfield's house the day they seized me at the Common to tar and feather and duck me," said Jim suddenly in a burst. " He saved me ; blast him, I'd rather 'a' been saved by any one else than Ab. I've been hid away since; and, as it ain't healthy for me to be seen around these parts, I've streaked it over here at night to see you, for I don't want you to think altogether bad of me, Debby. I'm in Boston Town, where there's lots o' Tories to keep me comp'ny. Now, before I go back, I'm goin' to set your mind at rest somewhat about your father. Don't you worry a mite about him; he's prob'ly joined the Reg'lars."

A low cry broke from Debby's lips. " O Jim! anything but that!" moaned the girl, clasping her hands, and gazing up to the myriad lights above, with anguished eyes. " If you told me that he was dead, and up in yonder sky, I would not mourn ; but to take up arms against his country, O my God! my God! "

Jim trembled like an aspen leaf to hear her; and he managed to say, " Don't mind it so, Debby, lots o' good men are Loyalists; " drawing near as he did so, with the vain hope of comfort.

It was at this instant that a tall, square-shouldered figure stepped upon the soft greensward behind the big elm just within the Parlin enclosure. Abner But-terfield had mastered his fear that Debby would be displeased at his intrusion upon the grief and shame overwhelming her at her father's treachery to his country, and had followed the instincts of his heart bounding toward her at Perces's disclosure ; and here he was, to give her what comfort he could. When he caught sight of Jim, standing with her in the evening shadow, in an apparently confidential attitude of complete understanding, he could not believe his eyes. He had not seen Jim since he had slipped off one night, weeks before, from the Eutterfield homestead.

294 A LITTLE MAID OF CONCORD TOWN.

But a second view, and Jim's voice, now sympathetic and confident, left him no room for hope. Stung to the quick, he started back, and strode off into the night.

" Speak not to me of good men who are Tories," cried Debby in passionate accents. " There can be no forgiveness for a traitor. O father, father! "

Jim twisted uneasily from one foot to another. " I'll tell you the man who put him up to it," at last he said, determined to make a clean breast of the whole matter. " It was the same one who made me see things as they be. He was a peddler, but an awful smart fellow, and he opened my eyes."

Debby's white face was upturned to the glowing heavens ; her lips moved, but no words came.

"Well, some day maybe you'll see it, when the tussle is over, and the British have whipped us out o' our boots, as they're bound to do. Then your father's being a Tory, is what'll save you, Debby Parlin."

She did not even hear him, but in agonized accents was begging piteously for some clew to her father's whereabouts.

" I d'no any more'n the dead where he is," declared Jim desperately ; " on my soul I wish I could help you. 'Twas a good many weeks back I run across him suddint like. An' he told me he was goin' to join the

Reg'lars. I hain't seen him since. It'll be your salvation if he does; an' you ought to know it, Debby Parlin."

With a low cry of despair, she went swiftly into the cottage, and up to her little room under the eaves, where she flung herself on her knees with only God to comfort.

It was morning in Boston Town. The unrest pervading all classes was visible to any chance observer, who met every few steps of his way the British soldier, insolent with gun and bayonet; the youth of the town wild with repressed indignation ; the grave and determined Patriot; and the ardent Loyalist, bitter and outspoken. The Common, white with the encamped army of the invaders, was alert with military activity, having within its borders the Fourth, Fifth, Thirty-eighth and Forty-fifth Regiments, together with twenty-two pieces of cannon, and three companies of artillery.

" And over all the open green,

Where grazed of late the harmless kine, The cannon's deepening ruts are seen,

The war-horse stamps, the bayonets shine."

Within the limits of the town, the Tory party, endeavoring to secure followers, and driven, many of them, from their homes in the countryside by indig-

nant fellow-citizens, was rapidly taking refuge, and swelling the tide of bitterness against the Patriots, toward whom there was now nothing but open abuse by the tongue of the most virulent sort.

While the British coffee-house on King Street, opposite the Custom House, was the resort of the high Tories and the British officers, the Green Dragon Tavern on Green Dragon Lane was the meeting-ground of the Patriots. It was "in front a two-story building with a pitch roof, but of greater elevation in the rear ; and over the entrance an iron rod projected, and upon it was crouched the copper dragon which was the tavern's sign." Here, among others, assembled Paul Revere, with a band of thirty men, mostly mechanics, who volunteered to keep watch of the movements of the British, and did so during 1774-

'775-

As Governor Gage felt his power over the people daily lessening to the precincts of Boston and Salem, then the seat of government, he confined himself in his futile rage and chagrin to the completion of the fortifications on the Neck, and raising the general standard of the British army in quality and accoutrements, and thus getting ready for decisive action in the matter of subjugating the rebels. Accordingly the British vessels continued to discharge their relays

in the harbor of "the flower of the English army," till the old staid town began to literally bloom into color, as the men, gay with their scarlet and gold and military trappings, marched hither and yon along her streets. The barracks were full to overflowing, and all things seemed ripe for the downfall of the Patriots. But despite the fact that there was within her borders all royal authority,—the king's governor, the king's judges, and the king's army, — all of these combined had not been able to make the courts to sit, nor the jurors to serve, while the people steadfastly refused to obey. The Massachusetts Assembly, being repulsed by Governor Gage at the Salem court-house, had been equal to the emergency; and going off to Concord Town, had continued the Provincial Congress, electing their own officers, and showing themselves capable of taking care of the interests committed to them, and in full accord with the Continental Congress at Philadelphia. The minute-men were forming in the various country towns, while the ranks of the militia were rapidly filling up. "Forward for liberty!" and "Down with oppression!" were the watchwords. "We will stand by our chartered rights! " was the ultimatum of the people; and when the people make a stand, it is useless for a king to speak. A young girl in a blue stuff gown, and hood

drawn well over her face, and a packet on her arm, was wending her way along the roadway, entering the town on this spring morning. It was easy to see that she was from the country, not so much by the free spring of her foot that bespoke the field and the meadow, as by a certain innocent grace of each movement, and the modesty of her bearing. She addressed no one to inquire the way; yet a keen observer could have told that this was first time she had trod this thoroughfare, and that hitherto she had been a stranger to the town. Yet there was no uncertainty in her demeanor, nor aught of perplexity, as she went calmly on her way, apparently not noticing many curious glances cast upon her from the passers-by. At last, when well within the borders of the town, she halted, and drew from her packet a small paper.

" I would better ask the way to Dame Barker's house," she said to herself, "than to waste time in trying to find it. I will inquire of the next person I meet, if the face warrants it."

But the next persons were two British soldiers, who stared at her in a way to bring the pink color to her cheeks as she haughtily passed by; they endeavored to look within her hood, and playfully challenged her with their muskets, calling her '"Pretty Rebel" mean-

while. But Debby bit her lips together, and decided to go on her way by the guidance of her own mind and intuitions. With a bosom swelling with the indignities pressed upon her, and upon all other Patriots, she passed on, careless of the direction her steps were leading her, until she looked up. She was on King Street, and beneath the windows of the British coffee-house.

A party of young British officers was descending the steps. Back of them stood some florid-faced, older men, who had evidently been but shortly detached from the card-table and the punch-bowl. She paused involuntarily, her feet refusing to carry her farther, as her eye rested on the foremost figure of a tall and slender young man. In this instant of time his piercing dark eyes had met hers; and despite his gorgeous uniform, gay in scarlet and gold, that set off his dark, refined face and tall, slender figure, she knew she was looking at "the peddler." In the next, he was talking and laughing with the bevy, his back to her, while he pointed up King Street, directing the attention of his comrades thither as the direction they should take.

"Stay a bit," called one of the florid-faced Englishmen on the steps; "there's a deucedly pretty little rebel," pointing to the young girl. " Come

back, Thornton and Herford, and you other fellows," as they were moving off. " Don't turn your backs on the little beauty."

Thus summoned, the men glanced back, particularly one of their number, who had seen for himself. " Come on," said Thornton sternly, "Harlow is deep in his cups. Don't sink so low as to listen to him."

"Verily, she is a beauty," said the one who had noticed her first, and taking a few steps toward Debby's side, who still stood as if paralyzed, with heart beating fast in her bosom. Oh! if the men would only go away, and let her ask this young British soldier who had it in his power to tell her where her father was!

" Fair maiden, where do you come from ? " queried the young man who had turned back, now putting himself directly in Debby's way; the older men on the steps thrust their hands in their pockets and smiled to see the encounter, some going down to the pavement to get a nearer view of the pretty stranger.

Thornton wheeled suddenly. "This is dastardly!" he exclaimed, without a glance at the girl. " Are ye Englishmen?" he cried, his eyes blazing. "Well would it be for our country if she could call you all by any other name."

Young Herford by his side sprang into the circle.

"Shame on you for Englishmen!" he exclaimed, his hot blood in his boyish cheeks; "let the maiden go, and molest her not by idle talk."

Debby had by this time regained her composure; and she stood pale, but dignified as an angry goddess, viewing them all with clear, undaunted eyes, till they quailed, and with a foolish laugh backed off up the steps, averring that Thornton with his deuced scruples was carrying matters with too high a hand for their liking.

"Whoever you may be," said Thornton to Debby, looking full at her, but with a glance that betrayed no knowledge of ever having seen her before, " I would warn you that it is unsafe for a maiden who is a stranger to go unattended upon the streets of Boston Town at this troubled time. I pray you, take my advice, and return to your home."

Debby turned a white face to him, and was on the point of crying through ashen lips, " My father, can you tell me aught of him ?" when Thornton, touching his cap, and bowing to her reverentially, drew off Herford most abruptly, leaving her no other course than to retrace her steps, which she did as in a dream, when some one abruptly stopped her way. She looked up, and saw Abner Eutterfield.

" Deborah," he said, speaking hurriedly, the color

302 A LITTLE MAID OF CONCORD TOWN.

coming over his brown cheek, " you ought not to be here alone. This is King Street, where daily and nightly tumult is likely to occur if anywhere. Come, let me take you to a quieter place, where I can help you maybe," he added awkwardly.

Debby lifted a calm face to his heated one, as if with mind lost to her own need. " Do not be afraid for me, Abner," she said. " You know why I am here. I have come to look for father. Oh! I may meet him now at any moment."

"Where are you going to stay?" asked Abner, essaying to lead her off.

She fell into step by his side, like a docile child, and went on steadily. "At Dame Hannah Barker's. She is a kinswoman of my mother's, you know. She wrote me in response to my letter, and said I could stay there while I searched for father. Is it far from here, think you, Abner ?" She took out the paper again from her packet, and gave it to him, bending anxiously over it as he perused it.

"At the farther end of the town, I think," said Abner, wrinkling his brows in perplexity. " Come this way, Debby; I will find it for you."

In all his distress over her, his mad rage at Jim, and the fate that had enveloped her with the friendliness and sympathy of the miserable wretch, it was

heaven to be walking by her side, to note the sad droop of her sweet face and the touching confidence with which she now resigned all care of the expedition to him. They went on silently for some moments, Debby scanning eagerly the face of every passer-by, particularly if King George's uniform covered the pedestrian. Suddenly they heard a great commotion and the rattle of muskets, with loud shouts and jeers. Abner instantly sought to turn Debby down a quieter thoroughfare; but there was no opportunity, before a negro man, running at full speed, chased by taunting British soldiers handling their bayonets suggestively, dashed into them, nearly knocking them prostrate. " Save me —▬▬▬▬▬— save me!" and falling on his knees he clasped Abner around his long legs. It was Pompey.

Abner swung his legs free, and put himself between the grovelling negro and the soldiers, who now seeing double game in a couple of rustics added to the fun of frightening the darkey, manipulated their bayonets in a way calculated to bring out much amusement.

" Put up your weapons," said Abner quietly, as Debby lifted her face and looked at them calmly, while one hand soothed Pompey's woolly head, that in the last weeks had taken on a frostier hue.

304 A LITTLE MAID OF CONCORD TOWN.

"We are peaceable citizens, and law-abiding, and as such shall have protection of this town."

"This nigger insulted us," shouted one of the soldiers, pricking the negro's leg with his bayonet, which made him roll over on the ground in an agony of apprehension, so that it exposed his eyes, and he saw Abner's face for the first time. Debby he had not noticed, save that she was a woman, and not likely to be of much help in saving him. The astonishment and delight that seized him was now so great that it overpressed the pain and fright. "O Massa Ab-ner! " he exclaimed, in a delirium of joy, and jumped up and precipitated himself into Butterfield's arms; "you done sabe ole Pomp!"

"Is he your nigger?" enquired the man who had played his bayonet on Pompey, and falling back a little.

"He is my servant," said Abner sternly, "and whoever touches him will have me to answer to."

" He's a lying, thieving nigger," spoke up a soldier, who found little pleasure in having the game disturbed, and was casting about for some excuse for their persecution.

"You lie yousef," shouted Pompey, raising his head, quite re-enforced by Abner's protection, since in him he had recovered his long-mourned master.

" Shut your black mouth! " threatened the Regular, advancing on him, bayonet well poised.

"Kick his shin — that fetches a nigger," advised another.

"Oh, no — no — no!" roared Pompey, far gone in his dreadful fright, and whirling around Abner, whom he grasped with both hands, so that the two revolved rapidly, until Butterfield thrust his newly recovered servant determinedly back of him, and endeavored to address the soldiery.

"Listen," said Debby, laying her cool hand on the frantic arm of the negro. " No one shall hurt you. Don't you know me, Pompey? I am Deborah Parlin."

Pompey turned an instant, rolled his eyes till there seemed nothing but the whites displayed, and gasped without speech. Meantime the hubbub brought to the spot another squad of redcoats, who had turned at the noise on their way to their barracks.

"What's the trouble?" cried their officer, levelling his musket at the young countryman. " Sir, I think you will have to come with me to the guard-room," without waiting for an answer, " for creating a disturbance in the streets."

" I think not, sir," replied Debby in clear tones, and regarding him fearlessly, "when you come to hear the cause of this noise. It is " —

306 A LITTLE MAID OF CONCORD TOWN.

" A mere fracas of words," hastily set in the soldier who had pricked Pompey with his bayonet. " Corporal, nothing to speak of; these country people don't understand the ways of the town, and addressed us in a manne̶r̶ ̶b̶e̶c̶o̶m̶i̶n̶g̶ ̶t̶h̶e̶ British soldier to receive. But let it pass, —

it was but a trifle."

"That is not the truth," said Debby in a clear voice, and not taking her blue eyes from the round red face of the corporal; " we were quietly proceeding on our way, when these soldiers," pointing to them, "who were ill-treating the servant of my friend, embroiled us in abuse and confusion."

"Who is this nigger?" demanded the corporal fiercely with an oath, for the first time perceiving the grovelling Pompey.

" My servant, sir," said Abner sturdily.

The corporal's color ran high on his cheek. Dearly would he have loved to punish these independent rustics who dared to thus face him. But realizing what he in his turn would be obliged to face when the story should come out in the guard-room that he had permitted any abuse of the property of American citizens, — as clearly from their attitude, it could be proved that the soldiery had interfered with their servant, — he hesitated in a surly fashion.

" I tell you, Corporal, it's but a trifle, and they know

no better," exclaimed the British soldier who had been chief spokesman.

" You keep your place, Jones," angrily commanded the corporal, " and be less lively with your tongue. To your quarters, men;" and he flourished his musket and swore roundly until the heavy tramp died off down the street. " Now, you miserable Yankees, disperse and go your way with your nigger; and hark ye ! if I catch you kicking up any more tumults, I'll deal with you as you deserve."

" We shall not be ordered off from Boston streets, as long as we are not disobeying the law, by you or any other person," declared Abner sturdily, his big brown hands working hard.

The corporal's face was livid with passion, and he made as though he would run Abner through with his bayonet; but thinking better of it, " We'll bear with you now," he cried, "because we're sure to have you all in our hands sooner or later, to do what we like with," — with a parting oath.

308 A LITTLE MAID OF CONCORD TOWN.

XXI.

HOME TO CONCORD TOWN.

" r INHERE is no time to lose now, Debby," said

-L Abner hurriedly; "some of these drunken fellows may return; we best make haste to Mistress Barker's. Get up, Pompey; you shall tell me later how you came to run away, and to fall into such a plight."

"████, massa, I tell you now," cried Pompey, as they hurried on ; " 'twas de debbil shore done took me. An' he got such a long leg, he have, an' he let it fly at my shin — oh, whee ! " The negro stopped to rub his leg now in exquisite distress at the remembrance. "Only get me safe home to yer ma, an' I axes nothing but to die."

"Come along," cried Abner, impatiently striding on, "or we'll leave you to be taken again, ███████████████."

Thus warned, Pompey scuttled after the two; and devious wanderings, not necessary to detail here, at last brought the three to the Barker homestead. It was a little many-gabled house, with its doors

and garden palings painted green, and a wide space before neighboring yards.

Here Debby was drawn into shelter; and Abner, imploring motherly Mrs. Barker, a wholesome-looking woman of fifty, to look well to her kinswoman, and not to let her venture alone upon the streets, took Pompey in charge, and started off home for Concord Town.

" Though why I promised, as shouldn't, to go with her every time she puts her face out-o'-doors, I don't know," said the discomfited woman to herself, when Abner's back was turned. " Cousin Debby looks verily like a child accustomed to have her own way — an' me, la, I never could make a cat obey me. Dear, dear! well, I hope she'll find her father; I hope these pesky Britishers will leave us alone. These be dret-ful times, the Lord knows, an' me a lone woman, with no one to look after me."

Dreary and heart-breaking for Debby were the days that followed. At first good Mrs. Barker made a show of attendance upon her young cousin that presently dwindled away to nothing ; and Debby would patiently tie on her hood and fold her big shawl around her morning after morning, and make the search alone. She never knew how near she came to the object of her sad wanderings. Once, while

nearing the Province House, she paused and looked up at the splendid big brick mansion, well set back on its beautiful lawn, and guarded by a stately oak on either side of the gateway. All her strength at this moment seemed to desert her, and she leaned heavily against the fence with its ornamented posts; her tired eyes drooped to the ground. A wild desire to risk everything and rush to its forbidding portals, and throw herself on the mercy of Governor Gage's wife, who was American born, for a moment seized and overbore her serene, undaunted spirit. Surely she would, she must, help her to find her father. And then the girl bitterly reflected that it was the last thing that the wife of the commander of the British could do, — secure the dismissal from the British ranks of soldiery, of a man who had been won to them.

" O God in heaven!" cried poor Debby, overcome with grief and bitterness, "help me, for there is none on earth who can."

A soldier on duty before the Province House looked at her sharply, and in an instant stepped behind the angle of the mansion, his heart beating as high as that under the maiden's bodice. Who can tell what the father suffered now ? or how near he came to deserting his post? Death, and disgrace to his name, must ensue; and how could this help Debby?

He watched her every movement, and the droop of her sad face, though no expression other than that intense gaze was on his countenance. And when at last she turned off, and went on her patient way, he cursed God in his heart, and prayed to die.

In all this weary search, the only thing that comforted Debby was the fact that she could find out many things that would not be possible for one of her countrymen to gain. No one would suspect a young woman, so absorbed in her own personal matters, of trying to acquire any knowledge that might be of benefit to the oppressed people. And so it chanced that Debby gained many valuable bits of information that she hid in her heart to reveal to her townspeople on her return. Her return? She was slowly coming to face the fact that she could delay it but a little longer; she must go back, and with a heavier load to carry than the burden she bore away, for then she had allowed herself to be buoyed up by hope.

Revolving these thoughts one day, and feeling faint and ill at the prospect, she turned a sudden corner, and came, without a hint of warning, upon the young British officer Thornton. There was no chance of his evading her, for they met face to face. With a countenance as pale as her own, he fixed

upon her his keen dark eyes, and lifted his cap gravely, again bowing low and reverentially.

" Oh, sir! whoever you are," cried Debby, clasping her hands, " undo your wicked work, and help me to get back my father to the love of his country and his home!"

The young officer continued to look at her, but did not speak.

"It is useless to attempt to deny it," said Debby in a torrent; "you were disguised, and you came to our town to steal away the hearts of my countrymen. Is this the part of honorable warfare that Englishmen should play upon a defenceless and well-nigh crushed people ?"

He could not turn whiter, for his pale face was ghastly now. But he looked at her steadily.

"God is on our side," said Debby, her bosom panting, and her pale face and eyes alight. " He will avenge. You need not think, sir, that you will go unpunished for your deed."

"I do not for an instant think this," said Thornton in a low voice, clear and well modulated. " Believe, Miss Parlin, in this word of mine."

Her hand, that had been involuntarily raised in warning, fell to her side, and it was now her turn to gaze at him open mouthed.

"My punishment is not for the future; it is here and now," he said, his eyes piercing her through and through.

" Oh, sir!" cried Debby joyfully, the pink color coming to her pale cheek, and clasping her hands in gratitude, " now may God forgive me for my harsh words; you can give me back my father — and pardon me for forgetting to thank you for saving my poor life."

The young officer put up a protesting hand. " I cannot help you to recover your father. He is in the British army. No power on earth but his own desertion can free him. You must not be seen talking with me. May that God whom you serve, keep you !" He was gone in an instant, whither Debby knew not. She staggered on a few steps, paused weakly, and gathered up all her soul to reach her kinswoman's door. But the reaction had been too great; and with only one thought, "This must be death," she sank to the ground.

A crowd collected, and kind hands picked her up. "Where to?" they queried. "She's from the country, sure."

It was near the Salter homestead, at what is in this day the corner of Winter and Washington Streets ; and a gentlewoman looked out of the win-

dow. It was Mrs. Stedman, then a resident of the house.

"Run," she said, to her domestic, a Mrs. Gibson, whose husband belonged to the British army, "and see what the tumult is in the street. Perhaps some woman is sick or in trouble."

Betsy Gibson threw her apron over her head and ran out, and presently came beneath the window and screamed, "It's a young country girl, and they've nowhere to carry her."

Mrs. Stedman deserted her embroidery, and got out of her high-backed chair, and casting a glance in the tall mirror discovered there that she was a comely spectacle. She passed out and over the broad stairway, and picking up her flowered morning-gown over her stuffed petticoat, she descended with dignity to the thoroughfare. The crowd made way for her respectfully. There was poor Debby, propped against the tree with white face and closed eyes. Her hood had fallen off, and her sunny hair floated away from her marble face. Her poor hands were folded, and she looked indeed dead. But the practised eye of Mrs. Stedman saw a faint movement of the blue kerchief that denoted life. "Lift her up," she said with the air of authority, "and take her into my house; and do some of you run for Dr.

Church," pointing to his residence but a short distance away.

The same kind hands that had raised Debby now bore her to the hospitable mansion; and there, on a big couch, with Betsy running for hot water and the simple restoratives of the matron, they all awaited breathlessly the arrival of the good doctor, who was to bleed the patient into sensibility and a new lease of life.

But Debby was saved this experiment. The worthy doctor was off on his horse, with saddle-bags of medicines and surgical instruments, miles into the country; and so Debby came unassisted, except by such attentions as could be shown her by the good matron and her frightened domestic, back into life again. And she sat up on the big couch, and tried to tell enough of her history to satisfy the curiosity of both, Betsy especially plying her with eager questions.

"Concord? I have heard that it is a goodly town," said Mistress Stedman reflectively.

But the girl could not speak. Big tears rolled over her white face, and she put up no resisting hand.

"Take yourself off, Betty," commanded Mistress Stedman, when she saw this; "she is too ill for idle questions."

"I am well enough to go on my way now, madam,"

said Debby, essaying to get to her feet. The furniture seemed to sway about her, and the brocaded curtains to swing from their fastenings. " I must get back to my kinswoman's."

" And who is she ?" demanded Mistress Stedman.

"Dame Hannah Barker," said Debby faintly succumbing to the inevitable, and sinking back again, closed her eyes.

Mistress Stedman went out speedily, and nearly overturned Mrs. Gibson, who was applying her ear to the crack of the door.

"What are you doing here, Betsy?" cried her mistress sharply.

"A-polishin' up the latch," said Betsy, beginning now to rub the end of her check apron smartly over the brass trimmings of the door. "I see it needed it dreadful bad the other day."

" Nonsense 1 do you put on your shawl and hood, and find the house of one Dame Hannah Barker. And let no grass grow under your feet. Tell her that her kinswoman — oh, dear me! J didn't get her name, and she is too far gone again to trouble her more — is ill in this house. And be sure not to bring her back, if she is a fussy or unwholesome person, Betsy; for I'd rather take the care of this young girl myself than to be over-burdened with a meddle-

some creature." With this warning repeated to the iast, Mistress Stedman saw her domestic depart.

"Betsy is a good creature in the main," she said, watching the rotund form disappear, "though Heaven knows I sigh for the day when we shall be in quiet peace, and the power to adjust our households to our liking. Though I ought to be thankful that I can obtain even the wife of a British soldier. British soldiers! " her comely cheek took on a rosy red, and her bright eyes snapped beneath her matron's cap; " forsooth, what right have they to be quartered on us in desecration of our town and our liberties ! "

The ribbons of her cap trembled in indignation as she hastened back to Debby, glad that she had for the time some distracting element to draw away her thoughts from the ever-present distress and humiliation. And loving all household practices, and especially that of nursing, she speedily made all things as comfortable around the sick girl as possible, giving a sigh of relief when Betsy came back and alone.

Evidently Dame Hannah Barker was not anxious to intrude herself on the personality of the big mansion. She held herself as good as anybody, but preferred to take no chances at comparison. And since Debby was apparently in the best of hands, judging

from the wholesome appearance of the domestic, and the good sense and kind heartedness of the sender, she decided, as nothing was said about her coming, to stay at home.

"I don't know but Deb'rah has got herself into trouble with the Britishers, and madded some on 'em, she's so bent on her pa. An' I'm a lone woman and a relict, with no one to look after me." She glanced around her tidy house with its accumulations of years of hard work by herself arid her spouse, whose black silk silhouette, and also portions of his hair wrought into an endless chain of flowers, reposed on the high mantel-piece, and she shivered in dread.

"You tell her I'll maybe walk up to-morrow an' see how she's a-gettin' on. If she ain't no better, your missis had better send out to Concord for her folks."

Instead of which, Mistress Stedman, within a few days, sent a letter, of which the following is a transcription : —

DEAR MADAM, —

I take my pen in hand to inform you that your daughter Deborah is in my house with a disorder that is not of great moment, but which nesesitates her being under good nursing. She is a good girl, and I mind that she seems to be

well brought up, and to have a lively consideration for the feelings of others, which is not always possessed by the young people of our age. She was with 3. kinswoman, a Dame Barker of this town, a commonplace creature enough, I should judge, having never met her, and with no soul to apreciate your daughter. It behooves me therefore to beg of you, my dear madam, the satisfaction of a reply, to say that you are agreeable to this care that I will exercise for your daughter, and to add that I will send her home at the earliest moment that you insist upon, although I hope to retain her, being strangely attached to her. Yours to command,

BATHSHEBA STEDMAN.

For the first time in many months Mrs. Parlin awoke from her state of bitter indifference. She frightened the children, who had brought her the big letter written on blue paper and sealed with immense red wafers, by saying, "You mind the house; " and throwing her shawl over her head, without waiting for a hood or a bonnet, she almost ran to the road.

"Oh, oh, she's gone crazy again! " screamed Johnny, as she disappeared; and running out of the door, he plunged across the greensward between their cottage and the Felton yellow house.

Doris screamed after him, "Don't you bring old Miss Felton, or we shall all be crazy," she said.

((I'm goin' to beg Mr. Septimius to go after her/ shouted Johnny, "and bring her back." But Mr. Septimius was not to be found, being apparently off exploring the silent haunts of nature on the hilltop, that wooed him daily; and Johnny, blubbering and wringing his hands, returned to the cottage, harassed by the steps of Aunt Keziah, bearing aloft her herb-pot.

"Come in, come in!" cried Doris, pulling him well within the green door and turning down the button. "Don't bawl so; she can't get at us."

"I don't know about that," said Johnny through his tears; "she's a witch, and witches can go anywheres."

Doris shook mightily at this; but it was necessary for some one to be brave, so she said, " Pshaw, there ain't witches now! and I'll set the kettle biling, and scald her if she comes in. There, see! she's gone home."

Debby was at this instant saying to good Mistress Stedman, "I am strong now; I must go home."

And looking in her face, the kind matron knew there was no longer an excuse to keep her back. But she sighed, "I find it in my heart to detain you, child," she said; "for you verily have grown into my love."

Debby for answer kneeled on the low ottoman at

the feet of her kind friend. " You have been so good to me," she said brokenly, putting her young hands on the gay-flowered lap.

Mistress Stedman threw aside her embroidery, and gathered the girl up to her breast. "You do not need to tell me your trouble, Deborah; it is enough to me that you are in distress of mind. Oh, if I could only help you! But, alas, child, how many hearts are sore and torn in these cruel days, and there is none to render assistance !"

"God sent you to my aid," said Debby, pushing back the terrible sorrow that must be borne alone. How could she tell that her father was a soldier in the British army ? And yet she felt meanly indeed, and sore at heart, to be accepting sympathy and aid when, as a traitor's daughter, she deserved to be thrust without the door.

"Yes; I must go home, my dear Mistress Stedman," she said brokenly, and in a shame-faced manner. " I shall pray for you every day of my life to the good God. He will reward you, though I cannot."

Mistress Stedman pressed a kiss on the soft, round cheek, regaining a little of its wonted color, and the tears filled her eyes. "There may be much woe ahead for us both, Deborah," she said; "God knows. Whatever comes, we will hold close to each other."

And that afternoon Abner Butterfield, who had been summoned by the mother love, awakened and hungry for her daughter by the written words of another woman, drove up in his big green wagon to the Salter homestead, and said, " Deborah, your mother has sent for you, with kindly words of thankfulness to the one who has befriended you."

The young man was too much shocked at Debby's changed appearance to keep his countenance.

"She is quite strong now," said Mistress Stedman cheerfully. "I could wish that she might have my nursing a bit longer, but it may not be," she added sorrowfully, all her heart going out to the girl.

She stood on the steps of the hospitable mansion and watched them depart. "It is easy to see that the honest fellow devours her with his eyes, and that his heart is wholly hers. But that little flower of a maiden, despite her rustic gown and speech, is worthy to grace a high station, and I pray God that she be not sacrificed. If she could only remain with me, I could fit her for her evident destiny." She sighed, and turned back with irritation to her embroidery.

XXII. "i AM A TRAITOR'S DAUGHTER!"

THE keeping-room of the Wood mansion was astir with patriotism, the walls echoing and re-echoing to the fearless utterances of the fathers of the town, met in deliberative council, informal, and at short notice. They had sat there for an hour or more discussing various ways and means at this juncture, of helping toward some decisive crisis, the complications in which they and their unfortunate countrymen were entangled. Suddenly Mrs. Wood's pale, earnest face was put within the doorway. "Father," she said, "Deborah Par 1 in has something to say to you and to the others."

"Let the child wait," said Mr. Wood quickly, to whom Debby seemed but a little one in pinafores along with his Perces. And he went on with his talk with Brother Hosmer.

"Indeed, I think, father, it would be well to see .Deborah before you decide thus," Mrs. Wood ventured to say.

"I agree with you, Mrs. Wood," said Mr. Hey-wood; "for since Deborah gave us so much information of matters in Boston that she learned in her visit there, I for one feel her to be an uncommonly sensible young person. Perchance she may have come into possession of some news of great value."

"If that is so, I would have her called in at once,' 1 said Mr. Wood, relenting; and he laid down the paper upon which he had been laboriously lining and interlining various paragraphs, sighing, however, as he did so.

Deborah came in, paler than was her wont, but otherwise not changed in appearance or manner, except for a certain gravity that overlaid her old sprightliness, and became her greatly.

"Thank you for letting me come," she said simply; "I will tell my story quickly."

"What is it, Deborah child?" cried Mr. Wood eagerly, leaning his ponderous body forward to catch every word; "some news of the enemy?"

"Have they advanced? are they coming?" cried one excitable individual, springing from his chair, and beginning to look for his gun, which he had set up in the corner on entering.

"Nay," said Deborah; "it is not of the enemy I come to speak to-day. I know naught of them."

" It ill befits thee then, child, to interrupt us at our conference," said Mr. Wood in cold reproof. " Another time, Deborah, we will hear thee, if thou desirest to speak; but go thou away now."

" Nay, nay, dear Mr. Wood, do not send me away till I have told thee all," cried Debby, in a voice of so much anguish that every one started to see her face changed to one torn with sorrow and shame. " I have struggled with myself so long in order to make my heart and mind willing to come — oh, do not send me away until you hear my story!"

"The child has something on her mind, and it would be the best and easiest way to let her free herself," said Mr. James Barrett, now a colonel. "Come, Debby girl, what is it?" he asked kindly.

Debby controlled a violent desire to turn and rush from the room; instead, she took one step until she stood within the circle of watchful faces, and stood by the big mahogany centre-table. "My father is a Tory, and a soldier in the British army."

The entire circle stood upon their feet. " It is not possible!" thundered Mr. Wood. "In the British army? Girl, you are dreaming!"

"As God lives," said Debby, "my father is in the British army. You should know this, though I have struggled with myself to make it seem right to keep

326 A LITTLE MAID OF CONCORD TOWN.

it from you." And then she told her story: How he had been led away; of her mother's illness and changed condition; and of her decision to fold the sin and shame in her own breast; of her search for her father in Boston Town; of the inevitable and hopeless result; and lastly, of her battle with herself to keep from laying the secret bare.

It was all told; and still the circle stood as one man, unwilling or unable to believe that John Parlin. whom they all believed dead, had turned traitor to his country, and was even now bearing arms against her.

"It is a sorry tale," observed Colonel Barrett; "and it distresses me greatly." He looked strangely moved, and glanced at his fellow-townsmen. They were all affected to silence by the sudden surprise. Debby, having told her story, stood pale and motionless in the centre of the group.

"But, Debby, child," Mr. Wood found his kind heart coming to the rescue, and his good sense as well, "there surely is no fault to be laid to your door, and no stain."

"You forget," said Debby, standing now with proud scorn, and uplifted eyes where before they had drooped in shame, "I am a traitor's daughter; there is his blood in my veins. Every one must know

"*I AM A TRAITOR'S DAUGHTER!*" $2?

it, and the very ground will cry out when I go abroad. All the people will despise me, as well they may, —• a traitor's daughter !"

" Debby, child, are you mad?" cried Mr. Wood, seizing her arm. "No such shame can be laid to your door. Shame is the result of sin. Your love for your country is as pure and true as ours."

"Ah," cried Debby with sudden fire, "but you can do something to prove your love. You can save this town; you are men, and you can make your names so that they will ring with your country's praises. What can a poor weak girl do but die in shame at her father's treachery and her own weakness? "

" What do you want to do, Deborah ?" asked Mr. Hosmer in pity, and more for the purpose of humoring her mood than for any answer she might make.

"Anything where there is danger — that is needed. Make me a spy. I am trained by what I have learned in Boston Town, and able also to use my powers. I can learn many things that may be of use to this town and to my country. Oh ! I long to do something to prove that I have, as you just said, a love for my country as pure and true as yours."

"My poor child!" Mr. Wood took one of the cold hands in his big palms; "do not fret yourself at your

328 A LITTLE MAID OF CONCORD TOWN.

lack of opportunity. Deborah, the time is coming to you, I verily believe, when in this town you may be able to prove your bravery and your devotion. It is coming for us all I believe also," he added solemnly. "And we who are standing here, each man of us, feels it in his soul, I venture to assert." They all silently bowed their heads. "Meantime hearken, Deborah. Whoever bears such a cross as do you, and patiently serves out each day with the work allotted to you, holding firm and high the love of country, such an one is a Patriot. Bless you, my dear child; say no more,. only go your way in content, and worry your poor heart no longer."

But great was the consternation in Concord Town when it became known that John Parlin was not only a traitor, but in the active service of his Majesty, actually belonging to the regular troops. It seemed at first as if all his old friends (and who of them had not been glad and proud to claim honest John as friend and fellow-citizen?) could not curse his name and fame with too loud and deep objurgation. What to them was now his former fair name but so much added reason to hold up his infamy to the world of neighbors and fellow-townsmen ! And Debby was right. The innocent must suffer with the guilty; and although she had their love and their pity, many there

were who raised only feeble doubts when it was hinted that they "guessed Parlin's family got a good price for his serving as a redcoat," or " the Parlin girl doesn't seem to mind her father's bein' a Tory," when she went with the children to the old meeting-house as usual on the Sabbath day. And she bore many cold looks and averted faces from people who were embittered by privation and distress, and fears of coming evil of darker portent.

So the days came and went, and the red cloud of war was arising and illumining the sky. The ranks of the minute-men were filling up rapidly. There was the noise of the drum-beat and of the fife in the air, to awaken the echoes from farmyard and meadow. Men began to voice themselves still more boldly, and to work with ill-concealed delight at the preparations for the coining struggle. And the girls, working in Milis-cent's house, with Debby in their midst, labored fast and furiously now at the cartridges, each little instrument of death destined to help forward the war that now began to be talked of as what must surely come.

The girls were lovely to Debby, encircling her, after the first horror of the thing had passed, with their loyal devotion, and striving in every way to make her forget. On Miliscent seemed to rest the special privilege and responsibility of soothing the over-

wrought sensitiveness that shuddered even when no suggestion of or allusion to the painful story was thought of. She often kept Debby at her house over night after the work of making the cartridges was done for the day, and by every means in her power sought to alleviate the sore distress that had fallen upon her dearly loved friend.

"Miliscent," said Debby one night, — the two girls had said their prayers and kissed each other goodnight, but lingered a while at the window, in the pale moonlight flooding the farm land,— "just think how very long we have been getting ready for what is coming in this town — the list of the big days, when for years and years Concord Town has spoken out for freedom and her country's rights, and that you and I have kept. I read mine over every day."

"Yes," said Miliscent. getti-ng up from the floor where she had been kneeling, her head on the window-sill, to go over to the high shelf and take down a long white paper, tied with one of her few treasured bits of ribbon. "It is blue, because it is true," she said coming back with it in her hand.

"That is the ribbon you had given you when you went to Cambridge; I remember it," said Debby; "your grandmother gave it to you for your hair."

"Yes," said Milliscent, "Grandmother Barrett did;

but I had rather tie up my Concord Town days with it, so I saved it, and put it on here." • "I didn't have any ribbon," said Debby with a sigh; " I tied mine up with a linen string, and it was white, and part of mother's setting out, and she spun it with her own hand."

"Well, that is better than mine, and white is for purity," said Miliscent comforting her; "and I should never have thought of writing them all down if it hadn't been for you, Debby dear. I saw it first in your room. But you had a red bit on yours too, the last time I saw it."

Debby hesitated. "Yes; I put it there since father " —

"Don't speak it," said Miliscent, laying her hand on her friend's mouth; "just keep it in your heart, and never say the words. Well, red is for courage, Debby, as well as for blood. And you can show yours, dear. I do believe there is some splendid thing coming for you to do for your country." Mi-liscent's eyes glowed and her bosom heaved.

" Father has become a man of blood, and taken up arms against his country, and I must never forget it," said Debby steadily; "although you and the girls are all kind to try to make me, Miliscent. And, oh! thank you for believing that something will

be given for me to do that can help this town to be free."

"And now let's talk of the great days of Concord Town," said Miliscent cheerily. "See, Debby, as long ago as October, 1767, how we began to oppose the Stamp Act ! Look, I put it down with tremendous letters, see! and I blotted it as well," she added mournfully. "I never shall forget my distress; and I tried salt on it, and vinegar and everything, for you know I couldn't get another piece of paper. Grandfather had given this to me with especial charge to keep it nice, for it was all he could spare."

"Well, then, December, 1767, is the next date that I put down," said Debby, losing her sorrowful thoughts for a moment.

"That's just it. I copied from yours, you know," said Miliscent—"when the selectmen sent in the report they had made, and the town voted ' to encourage industry, economy, frugality, and manufactures at home and abroad, and to prevent purchasing so much as we have done of foreign commodities.'

"And then Sept. 22, 1768, grandfather was chosen a delegate to the Boston convention," said Miliscent in pride; but remembering Debby's father, she quickly passed on to the next event in big letters, headed town meeting, Jan. n, 1773.

"I wanted to copy this every word," she said. "I heard grandfather read 'em ; he had the committee at his house ever so many times, and grandmother and I used to hear them talking it over. But they are all on the town records, so I only put town meeting down, and let it go at that. And the next one is " —

"Jan. 20, 1774," said Debby, "about the exporting of tea, you know, and that Perces Wood's father signed, don't you know." She laid her head in deep distress upon her folded arms on the window-sill. These other girls, with their beautiful and holy memories, what a heritage they had! and she — a traitor's child !

"Debby," said Miliscent tenderly, her soft arms around her neck, and her loving voice in her ear, "we will put this up, if it makes you feel badly. Come, it's getting late, dear, and we ought to go to bed."

"I shall always meet something that brings me face to face with the fact that I am a traitor's daughter," said Debby in a bitter tone, and raising her head; "no, go on, Miliscent; — so I read over and over my list every day, and it strengthens me to work for the future. Go on, dear/' she added more gently.

"Then the non-consumption covenant, June 27,

334 A I-ITTLE MAID OF CONCORD TOWN.

1774," said Miliscent. "Just think, more than three hundred men signed that, Debby. I know your father must have been among them, for he was always so good and patriotic. May Heaven deal with those who led him astray, instead of counting it sin laid to his charge.

"And then in August how many dates there are," she hastened to add, "of town and county conventions. See, Debby, ever so many ! "

"And all along after," said Debby, "thick and fast. But the Provincial Congress is the best of all, and the Committee of Safety day, and the Minute-Men day, and the day the cannon were bought and brought."

"And the Liberty Pole day," cried Miliscent in great excitement, "and" —

" Girls ! girls ! go to bed! " called Mrs. Barrett.

"And the Enlistment day," whispered Miliscent, as she hung up her precious list, — she had left out the Tory day, and the meetings on the Common for consultation and action on their cases,— "and all the rest. O Debby! Concord Town has got to do some splendid work now, after being such a long time getting ready. And you and I, depend upon it, will have a little piece of the work for our hands."

They kissed each other again, and climbed into the four poster. Miliscent was soon asleep, her breath falling lightly upon the air; but Debby lay with the moonlight flooding her, a prey to wretched and hopeless thoughts, stretching down to the years in which she could never forget that she was a traitor's daughter.

XXIII.

"THE REG'LARS ARE COMING !"

IT was the i8th of April. The Provincial Committee of Safety was meeting up town as it had met three times before during the month. The minute companies were out for their military exercise, while hitherto peaceful citizens might be seen wending their way along, their guns over their shoulders. Even the Sabbath day saw some of them thus accoutred. But nature was at peace. Soft was the air and mild the season. The open winter had brought forward an early spring, her youthful arms full of promising vegetation. "The winter grain had grown several inches out of the ground," and "the fruit-trees were in blossom."

"I saw a robin down by Mill Brook," said Doris coming in, in great excitement, " and I ain't going to wear this old hood any more," casting it on the floor.

"Huh! that's nothing — one old robin; I saw two robins last February," declared Johnny, who had

never ceased boasting of it. "Great big ones, with my own eyes, Doris Parlin."

Doris didn't care, since the robins had come to her, and evidently to stay, how many he had seen. She continued to remark that she wasn't going to wear her hood any more, and she was hot with that dreadful thick dress on, and couldn't she take it off.

"And go squealing round with the earache," put in Johnny, resenting the lack of interest over his robins.

"Stop it! I don't squeal half as much as you do," retorted Doris, her usually stolid face red with anger.

"I don't squeal; it's only girls that scream and cry. Say that again, and I'll slap you."

"Children, children, don't quarrel!" said Debby, spinning over in the corner. " How can you, when no one knows how soon we shall be in a dreadful war? Do let us all live in peace with each other."

"No one can live in peace with Johnny," said Doris, relapsing into her matter-of-fact way; "he's worse'n the Britishers. He did scream when he cut his thumb, and then he went behind the wood-pile and cried and cried."

Johnny sprang after her, beating the air with his fists, but Debby got between the two. "O children, just think! who knows how long we shall have our

338 A LITTLE MAID OF CONCORD TOWN.

home or each other? and here you are wasting these precious moments in bickering."

"I won't let the Reg'lars get in," declared Johnny, veering off to the never-tiresome topic,—the dread of a raid of British soldiery after the stores. " When they see me, I guess they'll run, and let our home alone."

"You know nothing about what you are talking of." She shook her head sadly, yet there was a fire in her blue eye. "Well, go to your work, and pray God you may be brave children when the time comes."

"I'm going to make a little garden when I'm through with my work, and plant my seeds Mrs. But-terfield gave me," said Doris, trying not to be crushed at sister Debby's rebuke.

"I'll help you," said Johnny magnanimously; "at any rate, I will to-morrow. Wait until to-morrow, Doris, then we'll fix it out under the big elm."

" All right," said Doris amicably; " to-morrow morning just as soon as I get the dishes washed up, then we'll begin it."

The candles were extinguished early in the Parlin cottage; and Debby, soothed by the soft air that played through the little window, and worn out by her toil of a tedious day, fell into slumber. She was wandering in the old days, when the talk of coming trouble with the king and Parliament could not vex the soul of a light-hearted maiden, scarcely more than a child. Her little world of girls and their favored swains in old Concord Town was again gay and happy. How she had laughed at Abner Butterfield, holding him up to the ridicule of the girls for his big hands and awkward ways, and then laughing more yet to see how he took it to heart when she smiled on Jim and the other young men in a way she never remembered being able to help. Miliscent and she were off gathering flowers, or following the course of the river in its woodside meanderings, and yes, there was Per-ces and her other mates, and life was sunny, and she was joyous once more, for her world of dreams never hinted of a father's dishonor. And now Miliscent was ahead, and had discovered a lovely flower spot, and was calling her. " I'm coming, Miliscent!" cried Debby in answer, and she sprang up in bed, a smile on her dewy face.

"THE REG'LARS ARE COMING!" shouted a voice, as a horseman clattered by, the hoofs of the animal striking deep into the road with every spring. In a flash Debby was on her feet, throwing her shawl over her shoulders, and rushing to the window. It was Dr. Samuel Prescott, she could tell by his voice, if she could not see in the dim light his figure, as he bent to his horse's mane, urging him to top speed.

"THE REG'LARS ARE COMING!" back peals his cry, echoing through all the open meadows, across the road guarded by the Mill Brook and the silence of Walden Pond beyond. " THE REG'LARS ARE COMING !"

Debby hurried on her clothes with hands that knew no quaking. The past had dropped from her like a cloud, and she recognized that for the daughter of the traitor had now dawned a day of opportunity. Slipping down stairs lightly, her shoes in her hand, not to awaken the children, she said softly, "Mother, did you hear it? It's come. The Reg'lars are on the way 1"

"Yes," said Mrs. Parlin stonily; "I heard."

"Mother," — the girl crept in the bedroom, and laid her cheek down against the thin white one; Doris slept, a round body of blissful composure, on the other side of the big four-poster; the baby was cuddled in the trundle-bed; and Debby whispered low against the ear that did not appear to notice or to care,—"I'm going to give the alarm too."

" Do 1" cried her mother fiercely. " I would that I could. And hark ye, Debby, bear yourself this day, whatever comes, as if you knew naught of traitors or traitor's blood in your veins. You are my daughter too; remember that. And my blood, loyal and true, will leap to rescue you from your shame. Would

to God I could go too, and could work and fight." She covered her face with her thin hands, and shook with tearless sobs.

"Mother, mother!" cried Debby, thrilling at her words, "you will wake the children. See, I'm going now; give me my blessing, for I may not return, but take you at your word."

" I bless you," said Mrs. Parlin putting both hands solemnly on the sunny head; "only show yourself worthy of my blood, and may God keep you!"

" Mother, you will take the children and go over the Ridge to Aunt Sophia's," said Debby; "it's safer there. Take over the silver buckles and the pewter ; they are all done up in the checked apron, you know. The Reg'lars may be down over this road. Good-by, mother."

" Good-by, my child."

It all took but a few moments, and Debby was out in the soft light of the morning twilight. Even now it gave promise of the "ever glorious morning" with which the patriot Adams ushered in the dawn of that memorable day. Without so much as a glance at the scenes burned into her memory, Debby sped on, giving her young voice to the morning air, as she shrilled out clear and high, " The Reg'lars are coming! The Reg'lars are coming!"

It brought Septimius and Aunt Keziah to the windows of the yellow farmhouse. " O Mr. Felton," she cried, "do come and help!" Aunt Keziah grunted something inaudible at a distance; but Septimius flushed deeply, and closed his shutter hastily. " I want not to mingle in scenes of blood," he said to himself as Debby sped on.

Seeming not to touch the ground, the girl ran, making here and there a detour from the main road, down which she knew Dr. Prescott had aroused the inhabitants; and into many a lonely farmhouse she rushed to spread the news and arouse the minute-men, calling and shrilling it out as she hasted on and on, oblivious to fatigue, and scarce knowing that she was in the body. And now the church-bell clanged out on the edge of three o'clock.

At last, in the full flush of the morning splendor, and fresh from the massacre at Lexington, there marched over the Old Bay Road, sent out to Concord Town, eight hundred strong, the grenadiers, light infantry, and marines, the "flower of the British army."

Passing the jest along, The jubilant host march on, and Concord Town, by her river of peace, was waiting to receive them.

At this moment Debby, having done what she could by way of summons, now had a sudden pang at thought of mother and the children; and she retraced her steps to rush into the little old kitchen. The children were crying, and hanging to Mrs. Par-lin's skirts, who had clasped her baby in her arms, and now stood quite bewildered in the middle of the floor.

"We can't get her out," sobbed Johnny; "we've pulled and hauled, and she won't stir a step."

"Come, mother/' said Debby soothingly; -'we are going to Aunt Sophia's, you know. Here, take my hand. Johnny, you can carry the apron bundle." She could hear the dull echo of tramp, tramp, and her fancy at least brought her the rattle of the swords and musketry, with a sickening dread for her little family about her. " Hurry, there is no time to lose. Dear mother, come."

" It's my home," cried the distracted woman stubbornly; "no British soldier shall drive me out of it," while the children roared harder than ever, and the baby in sympathy put up its lip and whimpered.

Tramp, tramp! it was clearly denned now; yes, there was the dreadful rattling noise, and voices of command, and a confused babel of sounds as of a large advancing body.

"Mother," said Debby, "your daughter kneels to you." She sank down, still clinging to her mother's hand. " In a few moments it will be too late. Come mother, dear mother! we must save the children, if we care not for ourselves."

At the word "children" a shiver passed ov«r the frame of Mrs. Parlin. She glanced around at her small brood, and gathered the baby closer into her breast. "You are right, Debby," she said; "I will go to Sophia's."

Debby sprang up, put Johnny, grasping the blue-checked apron bundle containing the silver buckles, some precious bits of linen, and other household stuff, in front, marshalled Doris, and still grasping her mother's hand, she opened the old green door.

A glance down the road, a wild throbbing at the heart, an attempt to thrust the mother, who is closely following, back into the house — too late! the advance guard of British soldiers, only a few rods before the army, rushed up to her, and charged their bayonets almost into her face. Johnny stared, wide-eyed and dazzled by the scarlet uniforms ablaze with gilt, stunned into silence. As for Doris, she was too frightened to open her mouth. Mrs. Parlin dropped to the threshold, and strained her baby to her breast.

u What would you do with us ? " demanded Debby with flashing eyes, and drawing herself to her full height. "Do you send a full army," glancing at the glittering host, "to a quiet, peaceful town to attack defenceless women and children? " in withering scorn. "You see our defenders," she pointed to Doris and Johnny and the baby, who peeped out from under his mother's arm.

"Egad! but you are a bold little rebel, and need to be taken over to King George for treatment. However, I'll let you off with a kiss for my pains, and a mouthful of breakfast, pretty one." He advanced to her as he spoke with that easy familiarity that betokens the conqueror. But Debby held him with a clear blue eye, and he stopped in a shame-faced way that he hoped none of his comrades saw. "As sure as there is a God in heaven," said the girl, lifting her slender hand, and pointing to the sunlight reflecting the Ridge in its golden beauty, "a curse will fall on you this day, if you touch one hair of our heads. Go search our house for food, if you wish. You will find it bare enough. God alone knows how we have lived while we tried to serve him. Go, and find what you can, and see the cottage you would rob." She pushed the door wide with her scornful foot, and viewed them all, and the advancing host, with absolute composure.

346 A LITTLE MAID OF CONCORD TOWN.

"Let the girl alone," commanded the leader, coming up, and learning the cause of the uproar, " Have we not all large work enough before us this day without wasting our precious moments. Before nightfall we'll have every rascally rebel in this town under our feet. March on, my men." He swung his sword, and stepped off down the road, as confident a specimen of manhood as one could hope to see. And after him went the glittering ranks of red and gold, every man smiling into the faces of his comrades. Oh, what a feast of varied pleasures should be theirs when once this proud old town had fallen into their hands!

Debby stood rooted to the spot, and gazed after them. It was not until the last line had disappeared in the curve of the wayfaring, that she stirred. Her eyes had looked upon "the peddler" as a British officer, tall and handsome in his resplendent uniform. In that dreadful moment, when her whole soul was calling upon a righteous God for vengeance on him, there shot to her from his piercing dark eye as he passed, a glance of suffering, appealing and swift. It went through her like a knife.

"Come, mother," she said, touching her arm; but the mother did not move, and Debby, with a nameless dread at her heart, leaned over to see that she

had fainted, it was now the work of a few moments to resuscitate her as best she could, with Doris, whose dumb admiration changed to fright and anger, clinging to her, impeding every movement. At last Mrs. Parlin opened her eyes. " O daughter! " with a long-drawn sigh, "have they gone?"

" Yes, mother."

"And taken nothing? "

"Yes."

'•Are your grandfather's silver buckles safe?"

"They are here in the bundle."

" Get the silver pieces in the stocking leg in the chimney closet."

" You forget, mother," said Debby in a low voice so the children might not hear, "that we have spent those lately."

"True," cried Mrs. Parlin with returning passion, and she sprang to her feet with sudden energy. "O Debby! let us go. They will come back here. Shut the door fast, though there is small hope that house or home will be left for us if we ever do get back. Now let us be gone to your Aunt Sophia's."

"Are you able to walk there, mother?" asked Debby, gazing at her fearfully.

"Yes, yes; only let us get out of this dreadful place," cried the mother with feverish energy. She

fairly thrust Debby off the flat door-stone; and herself, with the baby at her bosom, rapidly led the way up to the Ridge by the trail their feet had often worn.

Debby shut the old green door, and took one long look around on all things. "Come, Doris," she said, grasping her fat hand.

Old Aunt Keziah peered out at them from her side window when they were well within the trail. "I can't get Seppy to go; no, I can't, an' more's the pity; for our house'll be burnt round our heads, an' he doesn't care."

Rose Garfield and Mr. Felton stood by the old well in the Felton dooryard. Debby vouchsafed only a contemptuous glance at the pensive, silent man, like an indifferent spectator at his country's peril, as she sped on.

Shortly the dense wood was reached, then the plateau was passed. Debby could hear the shouts and confusion of the town beneath, as it was wafted to her tortured ears, and her heart leaped in her bosom at what she believed was the beginning of the slaughter to come to the old town; though that it could result in anything but victory for Concord, the girl never once allowed herself to imagine. Drenched in blood she seemed to see all things, in

S s

a confused and awful dream; but out of it, somehow, some time, God was to interpose and save his people. And fired by all these thoughts, and her terrible anxiety to be up at Colonel Barrett's, where she felt sure she could help, Debby put forth every effort to urge the footsteps of the little party to the utmost speed. On the wings of the wind, Mrs. Parlin needed no urging. Her slender feet scarcely touched the ground; and Debby, impeded by stout little Doris, had hard work to keep up with the mother.

At last the red roof of Aunt Brown's little story-and-a-half house was seen, and redoubling all their energies, the four were soon at the kitchen-door and begging for admittance; for it was heavily barred, and everything pulled down before the windows, so that they could not see within.

"Oh, she's fled; Sophia has fled!" mourned Mrs. Parlin, sinking down exhausted on the step.

"I don't think so," said Debby. "She is scared like, she is so feeble; and the boys, of course, are off with the minute company. Aunt Sophia! Aunt Sophia ! " she called, and rapped on the little window-panes.

A shuffling noise was heard within, the heavy oaken bar was withdrawn, and Aunt Sophia's pale, haggard face appeared.

"O Lyddy!" she fell on her sister's neck a moment, then drew her into the kitchen — " and you poor children. Oh, the Lord has forsaken us!" and throwing her apron over her head, great sobs shook her thin, spare frame.

"Take care of mother," said Debby, swiftly consigning them all to Aunt Sophia. " You'll be sorry, aunt, before night that you said those words, for God is our helper." Then she set a kiss on her mother's lips, and ran off, not heeding, —

"Debby, Deborah Parlin! Why, where is the girl going, Lyddy? " from her aunt's lips.

As swiftly as a young fawn, knowing no such word as fatigue, she sped, skirting the road, till she reached the confines of the burying-ground hill, where she concealed herself from view, and silently watched the preparations for the on-coming struggle. The Regulars had paused to reconnoitre before proceeding farther on their way to secure the military stores at the homestead of Colonel James Barrett and their other hiding-places in the old town.

The houses in the vicinity were shut and barred in the poor way that was all they could command for protection, and the women and children huddled within them for safety. Excited knots of townspeople might be seen on the Milldam, — citizens, militia,

minute-men, — trying to protect all such Provincial stores that the hasty alarm had not allowed time to remove to a place of safety.

A part of Captain Brown's company had paraded at daybreak. The minute-men and militia were also on duty on the Common getting their ammunition from the court-house, and marching down to see if the Regulars were really coming in over the Old Bay Road; while a party of the minute company from Lincoln, who had been aroused by the calls of Samuel Prescott, were also early on the ground, making in all something like one hundred men armed enough to fight. When, behold ! about seven of the clock, the glittering forces of England's trained soldiery, fresh from the massacre at Lexington, advanced in all their military splendor over the winding thoroughfare, with faces set toward Concord Town.

" Let us stand our ground! " cried young Parson Emerson, who had been busy going about among the men to stimulate and to exhort; "and if we die, let us die right here ! "

Eleazar Brooks of Lincoln was reconnoitring from the hill, when some one cried, " Let us go and meet them " — " No; " he called sternly, " it will not do for us to begin the war; " and they waited on the northern slope of the burying-ground hill till, one hun-

352 A LITTLE MAID OF CONCORD TOWN.

dred and fifty strong, they obeyed the command to march to the Old North Bridge and —

Hardest of all to wait, To say coolly, one by one, "We will never fire a single shot Unless first fired upon."

The British army, in the flower of its youth and beauty, halted; the grenadiers were posted on the Common, while six companies of light infantry were stationed on the hill. Debby, from her place of concealment, could see all this, and keep unobserved herself. Gorgeous in their gay uniforms and shining arms, with high spirits, they chaffed each other, and passed the word of badinage along their glittering ranks! What a pity! Could not some intervening power keep these simple, misguided farmers from further show of resistance? Really it was in the conquering hearts to pity the poor fools who were to fall such easy game before the British guns.

And amongst the glittering ranks of soldiers she spied two central figures of importance on the old hill burying-ground. One of them had a field-glass, and the other was talking earnestly, both helped by the previous intelligence as to topography of the town and the location of the military stores, from the Tories and the English spies. Debby thrilled at

sight of them, although she did not know that her eyes were looking at Major Pitcairn and Colonel Smith. It seemed to her that in their keeping was the destiny of the town, as they examined and consulted over all the points and indications of the situation. It was through that field-glass perhaps that lay the clews to the indefensibility of her poor, oppressed people.

But even in that dreadful moment her heart did not falter. With a prayer, unuttered it is true, but just as surely winging its way to the God of nations, she glanced around the old hill burying-ground, eloquent with the quiet dead, whose lives had been passed in toil, in oppression, in anguish and dread, but never in a loss of the simple and rugged faith of their fathers, and the steadfast hope of the help to come from the mighty God whom they served.

And thrusting her fingers in her ears to shut out the ominous signs of the portending struggle, and longing to close her eyes as well, she plunged unobserved down the back of the hillside, and made all possible speed toward the Barrett homestead.

It being of the utmost importance to the British io gain control of the two bridges — the Old South and the Old North — that crossed the river and

guarded the main avenues of the town, the struggle had now begun for their possession. Hoping to keep the militia and minute-men thus at bay, Colonel Smith therefore remained in the town centre, while he sent six companies of light infantry to hold the North Bridge, and then to set about the work of capturing the stores. Out of these six companies three were to guard the bridge; the other three were ordered to Colonel James Barrett's home to destroy the military stores. The Tenth Regiment was stationed at the South Bridge, while Smith and Pitcairn, with the grenadiers, held the centre of the old town, pillaging what ammunition and provisions they could capture. Excellently well planned, with plenty of soldiers, and apparently a clear field before them.

As Debby ran lightly on, already were they set about their work. The noise of it shocked that quiet spring morning, and reached her as she fled. On she rushed over by-path, and through nook and field and forest, scarcely daring to breathe freely until she stood in the Barrett kitchen, in the midst of the stout hearts and busy hands swiftly concealing the property of the town and the Province, left as a sacred charge to the shelter of their household.

XXIV.

SEARCHING FOR THE STORES.

WHERE'S Miliscent?" cried Debby, bursting into the "muster-room."

Stephen, the son, had been posted off to Price Place at the juncture of the roads, to warn the Stow and Harvard minute-men not to come down the Barrett Mill Road, as this would make a meeting certain with the British soldiers, momentarily now expected at the old homestead.

" She's been helping her father get her mother and the children off to a place of safety," answered Grandmother Barrett, pale and determined, but with a light in her eyes no one had seen there before. It was as if a positive delight now took the place of watchful outlook for impending evil, and her step was as free as a girl's. "To the woods back of the house, more'n likely. Then, when they're fixed, he's going to join his company, and Miliscent's coming here." She spoke as if all this were only every-day preparations. One must rub one's eyes and believe

himself to be dreaming, to think of a terrible struggle perhaps already begun, but two short miles away, in a war for liberty against oppression.

" Here, Debby, run up and put those balls in a barrel of feathers you will find up in the garret," she said, pointing to the ammunition in the corner on the floor. " Sink 'em well down at the bottom, and pile the feathers lightly over them."

"The cartridges — oh, where are they?" cried Debby, bundling the balls rapidly into her blue-checked apron.

" James took off the last load yesterday afternoon," said grandmother. "Thank the Lord, they will be doing their blessed work before long," she added grimly.

"Oh, yes, thank the Lord!" Debby's brain was in a whirl; but she blessed Him, as she staggered over the attic stairs and did as commanded. Then, just as she was running down again, her eye spied a big hair trunk under some boxes.

" I remember Miliscent said once, when we were up here putting away the butternuts, that there were silver pieces in it, and papers that must be saved if any harm threatened the house. I'll look within."

She got the boxes off, and freed the trunk for observation, and, throwing up the lid—yes, there were rolls and packages of yellowed papers tied with linen

strings, and down in the corner was a stout bag that rattled its contents when shaken. Here doubtless were the silver pieces. There was no time to lose in investigation; and hastily closing the trunk, Debby thrust the papers and the bag down under the feathers also — then rushed over the stairs.

" We may be only women and girls," said grandmother, "but I guess we can outwit our tyrants. Here, Debby, run with this, and turn up the furrow back of the house with the spade, and drop it in. Mr. Barrett has ploughed the ground up this morning, and sunk the muskets and balls and other things. Stay, child," her busy hand dropped, and her strong face grew a shade paler, "I forgot; there are some papers and a bag of silver pieces in" —

"The old hair trunk in the garret?" interrupted Debby. "I hid those in the barrel of feathers too, along with the balls."

"Now bless you for a sharp-witted girl," breathed Grandmother Barrett thankfully. " Save the pewter platter, then; we may need it for bullets yet. Run, Debby, child. Oh, if we can but get through before they come!"

None too soon. Just a breathing-space, and down the Mill Road came the redcoats. Some were whistling with the fun of the expedition, and laughing and

358 A LITTLE MAID OF CONCORD TOWN.

chatting. It was a most informal raiding-party, intent on two objects; and these were the destruction of the military stores, and the capture of that rebellious subject, Colonel James Barrett, to send over to England.

On they came, right merrily, and swarmed over the Barrett meadow and field and house-place, and presently they were within the old house.

Stephen, hurrying home, fell into their clutches, and they dragged him into the kitchen. "You are my prisoner," thundered the emissary of King George, the officer in command, as the soldiers hauled Stephen into their midst. "I have orders to carry you to England."

" Those orders were for my husband, Colonel James Barrett," cried Grandmother Barrett spiritedly. "This is my son Stephen. Touch not one hair of that young man's head, or his blood be upon you. You were ordered to take Colonel James. Take him if you can find him. Loose my son. and let him go this instant."

" My orders are to take Colonel James Barrett at all hazards," said the officer in some confusion, falling back. "Take your hands off from the young man's person, but keep an eye to his movements," which the soldiers obeyed, their arms falling to their sides sullenly.

"Well, now, my men, to work! We've no time to lose. Let the search begin. Thornton, see that it is carried on thoroughly. Let nothing escape you."

This to a younger officer, a man about six or seven and twenty, tall and slender, though firmly built, and having a pair of keen dark eyes in his pale, refined face. Debby. pressing up back of Mrs. Barrett, with Miliscent, who had just run over, followed the direction of his command. At last she saw him face to face, where he could not escape her. It was the peddler spy, the tempter of her father, the young British officer come to finish his deadly work.

In spite of the peril of their position, — the swarm of redcoats, grounding their muskets on the floor and filling the house with their boisterous mirth, and only Grandmother Barrett, the serving-woman, Miliscent, and herself to defend the home, — Debby opened her mouth to utter the torrent of denunciations that her bosom could not contain.

In a twinkling the young officer said, " Captain Parsons, while you search without, my men shall go above stairs; " and with the word of command, before Debby could utter one syllable, he and the squad following him had left the apartment.

"Are you mad, Debby?" said Miliscent in a whis-

per, and seizing her arm. " I saw you; you could not contain yourself."

" It was he," gasped Debby, her hand at her heart. " The villain — the tempter — the British spy ! Oh, why did I not have a chance to let him see that the Concord maiden is not afraid of him and his wickedness ?"

" You must not, you shall not attempt it again," cried Miliscent, as Captain Parsons was saying, " Madam, do you expect us to be detained here in this way ? The stores are in this house, and it will be vastly better for you to tell us where. You will then be let off easily, and probably the order for the capture of Colonel James will be revoked."

"You will receive no help from me, sir," replied Mrs. Barrett spiritedly. " Not to save a life will one of us lisp a syllable. And as for the capture of Colonel James, take him if you can find him. He is in God's hands, and he will deliver him from you."

With a brace of round oaths the officer gave the word, and the search began; and soon in the cellar, the kitchen, the barn, and the sheds, the Regulars were running in and out, in full spirit with the work, and confident that each instant the coveted articles would come to light.

Stephen all this time was between two soldiers, to prevent any interference on his part. He clinched his fist, and was about to pitch in then and there; but reflecting that such a movement on his part would only bring destruction upon the house and its inmates, he gulped down his mortification and anger, only mollified by the thought of the warning he had carried to the minute-men of the neighboring towns, who were now probably safe with their comrades at the Old North Bridge.

"I'm going up to listen at the foot of the garret stairs," said Miliscent. " They are up there now ; I hear them. We must save those things."

Debby crept up after her, the beating of their young hearts seeming to proclaim their approach.

" There's a beggarly old Yankee trunk. Rip it open with your sword."

But the lid was thrown wide without that trouble, as the girls, with bated breath, crouching at the foot of the stairs, well knew.

" Ha ! Grandfather's precious papers, safe — and the silver pieces safe; that is,' so far." A storm of oaths followed the noise of that search.

"The old beds — a ctffse on these rascally rebels! Where have they hid the stuff? " roared another voice. "Tear open the beds! Confusion to them! We'll

fire the house over their heads. Then the rats will tell rather than roast."

" Hold I" It was the voice of their commander. "Behave like Englishmen and gentlemen in this house, and respect the rights of others, or, by my sword, you'll find it the worse for you. I'll run you through."

Debby held her breath in stunned silence.

"Oh, how good he is!" whispered Miliscent gratefully into her ear.

This stung her. " Good!" she spurned the thought, and turned on her with flashing eyes.

"Hush, hush!" implored Miliscent; "hear what they are saying."

"Rebels have no rights against our king," one soldier ventured to grumble out. The others stared at his temerity.

"You have only your orders to obey," said the officer sternly; "and they are to search this house quietly, without violence or personal harm to the occupants. Another word from you, my man, and you will find yourself in the guard-room on your return to Boston."

Milly raised her slender hands and her beautiful dark eyes in thankfulness to heaven. Debby gripped her with speechless passion.

The garret had now become a scene of wild confusion. The dragging of heavy articles about continued for some time, as the search went on. At last oaths and angry exclamations of disappointment followed.

" The barrel yonder of feathers!" screamed one soldier at length, when all else had failed to disclose the coveted stores.

Miliscent wound her arms around Debby, and the two gazed in anguish in each other's faces.

"There is no good to be obtained by our waiting longer," said the officer. " Go below, men ! "

One soldier hung back, and rushed to the barrel, thrusting his hand into the feathers.

" You fool you! plough up those feathers, will you," jeered the rest. ;< What do you expect to get there for your pains ? " sang out one man. " Another goose, perhaps, to match you. " A roar of laughter greeted this sally, a rattle of bayonets on the floor in applause, and a chorus of jeers, the victim of it all turning back from the barrel with a red face and discomfited manner.

"Fly, Debby," warned Miliscent; "they are coming down!"

Debby, torn with conflicting emotions, the uppermost one being anger at Miliscent's gratitude to the

364 A LITTLE MAID OF CONCORD TOWN.

British officer, dashed after her, her blue stuff gown catching on a long nail by the side of the doorway leading up the attic stairs. She pulled at it to tear herself free, but cloth was made honestly in those days, and it would not yield. They were close upon her; she was surrounded by armed men, the muskets were at her head, the bayonets as well; and helpless and alone, Miliscent, supposing herself followed by Debby, having reached grandmother's side by this time, she was in the centre of a baffled crowd of soldiery, whose angry eyes gave her no good reason to expect any mercy.

As many of the men as were near him were thrust aside impetuously. "Allow me," said the young officer, as deferentially as though she were a great lady and he her guest. And in an instant he had released Debby's gown, and with one quick movement, his fingers closing on her arm, he had put her behind him. It was impossible to describe Debby's feelings at the touch of his hated hand, so gentle and deferential, yet with a grip that was like steel. She trembled with passion.

" Ah!" she cried, " I would rather die than be saved by you;" and she shook herself free, and looked him full in the piercing eyes.

" The saucy rebel! " cried one of the soldiers.

advancing on her. " You shall pay for this, girl, and find out what it is to defy English authority," clamored another threateningly.

"Silence!" thundered their commander, drawing his sword; "the maiden is sore distressed. Are you men, with mothers and sisters, that you would add to her suffering? March below!"

Debby essayed to speak; but the rattle of their arms and their heavy tread, as they filed by her, with flashing eyes and glances that boded no good, drowned all her attempts. She was only conscious, as the noise decreased, that the tall figure of the British officer was before her, and that they were alone.

"May heaven forgive me for what I have done," he said in a low tone. " Miss Parlin, it could not be undone. I must warn you now that your father is here to-day with our men."

She had no time to utter even a low cry of anguish, for his hand gripped her arm again. " Forgive me," he said, " but I cannot again hold back my soldiers if they hear you. Your father was forced to come. Do not turn against him. Believe me, he will do no harm to his townsmen," he added significantly. " I will save you and your people from every annoyance, and pray God we shall return quietly to Boston."

"And I," said Debby deliberately, in a low, clear voice, "pray God that I may die before sinking to the shame of a rescue from the slayer of my father's honor."

He drew back with a swift expression of suffering in his piercing dark eyes, bowed silently, and motioned for her to proceed before him to the rooms below. Debby swept off, holding her head high on her slender neck, gained the "muster-room," swarming with soldiery, heard him say to Captain Parsons, "We could find nothing, although our search has been exhaustive."

" Hark ye ! " exclaimed Captain Parsons sharply, as Grandmother Barrett uttered a " Heaven be praised!" "your gratitude is short-lived. While we have possession of the whole town, as we presently shall, the matter of a few stores is of trifling importance. Now give us something to eat," looking into the sullen and disappointed faces of his men, " for verily we need it sorely."

"Yes, give us something to eat," they clamored.

"We are commanded to feed our enemies," said Mrs. Barrett with dignity. So she gave orders to Miliscent, to Debby, and to the serving-woman, to set forth the doughnuts and the big pans of milk, the boiled meat and the bread and ham and the

pies, on the mahogany centre-table. " Draw up, and eat your fill," she said when all was ready, with the air of a queen dispensing royal favors.

"Truly the old lady has grit in her," observed one soldier to his comrade, as they took their portions of food to a quiet corner.

"I like those two pretty maidens, and I'll have a bout with them," said the comrade who had remained below stairs with Captain Parsons's company, and fixing his eyes on the two girls, obeying, but with panting bosoms and flashing eyes, the commands of grandmother to set the food on the table.

"Better not; I think that the flaxen hair and blue eyes is the identical maiden we encountered at the cottage some three miles from here, before we reached the town."

" The veriest nonsense!" exclaimed the other, munching his bread and beef with a gusto; "that little maid is saying her prayers with chattering teeth in her home chimney. Fancy her running up here into our muskets. Ha, ha, ha! "

"You may laugh if you like," said the other doggedly; "but I'll take my oath she is one and the same. She'd have slain me with her eyes, and flown at us tooth and nail, if we had not turned away and left her poor miserable little house in safety. The

temper of this one is just the same. Let these girls alone, and stir them not up by any notice. Our orders are not for such work."

"Nevertheless, I shall try my luck with that fair rebel," persisted the first soldier stubbornly, "and get a word and a kiss."

"And your head cracked for your pains." Another comrade drew near. "You should have been upstairs with us to have seen Lieutenant Thornton. Confusion to him; we were about to teach that same saucy little rebel to respect the English army, but he interposed."

" Did he so ? " cried the other men.

"And hark ye — we must move carefully with him around," dropping his voice; "he's the devil and all, as you know, when he's roused."

"The aristocrat!" grumbled the soldiers under their breath, prefixing the title with an oath.

Captain Parsons was throwing some pieces of gold into Dame Barrett's lap. "We are not robbers; we pay for what we eat," he said.

"We take not the price of blood," she replied with spirit, tossing them back; but he left them where they fell.

" Now collect the gun-carriages, and we will fire them," was his order.

One of the sergeants interrupted. "We have hard work before us, Captain; we must have some spirit to drink. This house must hold a lot of the stuff, or at least some cider; and this Yankee drink is not bad, you know."

"Not a drop!" commanded the captain sternly, and drawing his sword. " Hard work we have before us, ay, and bloody as well, before the sun goes down. We will do it as Englishmen, and not as drunken fools. Hark! the firing has commenced. March! my men, and wipe out the rascally rebels !"

The scattered redcoats formed into glittering ranks. Angry though they were at the failure to secure the coveted stores, yet they preserved their good temper at the prospect of the victory that should lay the whole town in one conquest at their feet. Military stores and everything else would, before nightfall, be theirs. They could afford to bear little annoyances now. They beat a hasty retreat, the two comrades who had discussed the charms of Debby and Miliscent gave them a parting glance of admiration, the audacious one kissing his fingers toward Debby's pretty face, despite her anger, which amused him greatly.

The firing indeed had begun at the bridge, although as the detachment left the house, and started on a

370 A LITTLE MAID OF CONCORD TOWN.

quick step down the Barrett Mill Road, they did not then know their destination, where they should get into the battle they were so eager to help forward.

Debby seized Miliscent with her strong young hands, and drew her off to the little entry. Stephen had rushed off the minute the soldiers turned their backs, and was already half across the fields, on his way to the conflict. Mrs. Barrett had sunk to her knees in prayer, while the serving-woman was pottering about the remnants of the food, with a " Lord have mercy on us, how those British do eat! " and mumbling a spasmodic and scanty petition to Heaven as.the report of each volley at the bridge smote her ear.

"I've got a gun, and I'm going!" cried Debby in a hoarse tone. "Kiss me good-by, Miliscent, and — and"-

" You are mad ! " cried Miliscent, her dark eyes dilating in terror. "You are a girl. It is improper ! "

"I shall go." Debby's spirit flashed high. "It is no more improper than for us to make the cartridges."

XXV.

THE "SHOT HEARD ROUND THE WORLD."

MEANTIME, during all this search for the military stores at Colonel James Barrett's, the grenadiers and marines under Smith and Pitcairn were alert and determined at the same work in the centre of the old town. But the distress and privation and suffering the citizens had gone through with had sharpened their wits, and the larger portion of the oubiic stores were now concealed in such places where they were practically safe; the remainder must be defended by the tact and the cleverness of the besieged inhabitants. Despite all their efforts, however, about sixty barrels of flour were burst open; the trunnions of three cannon were knocked off; carriage-wheels were burned; and wooden trenchers and spoons, and hundreds of pounds of balls, found a resting-place in the millpond and the wells of the vicinity. The flames overcoming the liberty pole on the hill had been started, firing the hearts of the townspeople into fresh anger, but not dismay, when a British officer

372 A LITTLE MAID OF CONCORD TOWN.

stalked up to Captain Timothy Wheeler. " Open your barn," was the order, short and sharp. The barn was opened by Captain Wheeler with a " Certainly, sir," that charmed by its ready acquiescence in the inevitable ; and there was a stock of Provincial flour, together with some belonging to himself, now revealed to the devastating hand of the enemy.

Captain Wheeler put his hand on a barrel. "I am a miller, sir. Yonder stands my mill. I get my living by it. In the winter I grind a great deal of grain, and get it ready for market in the spring. This is my flour;" touching another barrel, "this is my wheat;" and pointing to another cask, "this is my rye."

"In that case," said the officer with a longing glance around, "I must leave it untouched. We do not injure private property."

The tumult was now great. The soldiers, maddened by the pillage they had succeeded in effecting, but more by what they had missed, rushed hither and thither, without strict military discipline or order, only intent on destroying as much of the public property as possible. The Province treasurer, who boarded during the sessions of Congress at the tavern of Ephraim Jones, left in his care the chest containing money and important enclosures. At this time Captain Jones was a prisoner, with five bayonets

"fixed and pointing at him." But wanting some refreshment at the bar, the guard of five soldiers released him for this purpose, and then searched his house, as were all houses searched, if the soldiery were so disposed; and there they discovered the chest. But Hannah Barns, a member of the family, spoke up, "This is my room, and contains my property." They parleyed and bickered; but she stood her ground sturdily, and forced them to retire.

"The court-house is on fire! Quick! the top of the house is filled with powder; and if you do not put the fire out, you will all be killed ! " screamed Mrs. Martha Moulton, who lived near, and who, with a servant of Dr. Minott across the way, was endeavoring to extinguish the flames. On this the British soldiers in the vicinity turned to and gave them assistance.

Into the houses rushed the soldiery, now hungry and defiant. The whole town was in an uproar, and swarmed with redcoats; while the defenceless citizens, too old to fight, and the women and children, with the able-bodied men who were set to guard the public stores, were the sole defenders of the town.

Over at the South Bridge, meanwhile, Captain Mun-dey Pole, of the Tenth British Regiment, and his squad, set up a special search at the house of Eph-

374 A LITTLE MAID OF CONCORD TOWN.

raim Wood. His distinguished patriotism and his public office in the town made him a shining mark, and they hoped to secure him. But he was " engaged in directing the important events of the day, and assisting to remove the stores; " and thus, being from home, he escaped.

All this time the minute-men and military companies from the adjoining towns were assembling, until now there were in the neighborhood of two hundred and fifty men.

Joseph Hosmer, acting adjutant, " formed the soldiers as they arrived, singly or in squads, the minute companies on the right, and the militia on the left facing the town." He then, observing an unusual smoke arising from the centre of the village, went to the officers and citizens in consultation on the high ground near by, and inquired earnestly, "Will you let them burn the town down?" and they "resolved to march into the middle of the town to defend their homes, or die in the attempt, and at the same time they resolved not to fire unless first fired upon."

Colonel Barrett has given orders to march; Major Buttrick has led the men in double file to the spot, — the birthplace of liberty and the triumph of the American cause; the Acton minute-men with Captain Davis at their head, and the Concord minute company under Captain Brown, get into position in

THE OLD NORTH BRIDGE.
King George's troops stood where The Minute Man marks the
the monument was erected. position of the Provinci
And the river rolled between.
front; and the quiet river of peace slips gently by at their feet.

Over on the east side, the rustic bridge between, the British are tearing up the planks. Major But-trick, in a loud tone, orders them to desist. A few shots are discharged into the river, probably as "alarm guns;" and then a single gun, in the hands of a British soldier, speeds a ball that strikes Luther Blanchard of the Acton company and Jonas Brown of the Concord company, both minute-men. Now follows a volley from the British. Isaac Davis and Abner Hosmer, both of Acton, fall dead. Brave Major Buttrick leaps from the ground, and cries,—

"Fire, fellow-soldiers! for God's sake, fire!" and the embattled farmers, so long held back, respond with "the shot heard round the world."

It was at this instant, "between ten and eleven o'clock," that the three companies under Captain Parsons were on the double-quick step from the search for the military stores at Colonel James Barrett's, that Stephen was rushing across the fields, and Debby was securing the "grand'ther's musket" she had taken pains to have ready against the time of need. Oh, wonder of wonders! the British, leaving their dead and wounded, are running by the bridge! the scarlet uniforms in a mad confusion and rout,

closely pursued by the embattled farmers with stern, set faces, and firing as they go at the flying foe, intent on getting over the great field to stop the enemy at Merriam's Corner. All military order now is broken up. Henceforth it is to be each man fighting for freedom, and each man defending himself on the retreat.

Debby, skirting the thicket at the foot of the Ridge, and concealed by the thick growth of young pines and scrub oak, unmindful of the heavy musket she carries, looks about with watchful eyes. Ha I here runs a hated redcoat, and then a squad of the flying enemy. Now God defend her good right arm and give her clear sight; but without warning the foremost man turns suddenly, leaves the thoroughfare, and plunges into the "heart of her covert," disturbing her aim, while the rest rush on. She pauses, her fingers on the trigger. He has laid down his gun, and is tearing off his coat to thrust it from him with mad gesture, tossing out his long arms to heaven. She shuts her eyes. "O God! I cannot kill him thus defenceless;" and waits, praying for strength to do it when he sees her, and it is an equal fight. He turns, seizes his gun from the earth, and meets her eyes. " Father!" she screams.

"I haven't fired a shot," he said hoarsely. "I was in the thickest of the fight at the bridge ; but although I prayed to die, every ball passed me by. Hinder me not; I am John Parlin of Concord Town once more, and God give this gun power over the tyrant."

She was at his knees, sobbing and clasping them with her arms. " O father, father! " she moaned, "forgive me for the wicked thoughts against you."

He lifted her from the damp spring mould. "Kiss me, child," he said solemnly, "and say, 'Father, I know you love your country now."

She said the words after him between her tears, and laid her head on his bosom, soothing his bronzed cheek and hair with her hand.

"Put away your gun, Debby," he said, "or give it to some man to use upon the enemy." He seemed to guess at her reason for carrying it, and it brought the hot blood to her cheek to see that he divined it. "Your father will do your work now. One more kiss now, daughter; for this day will be my last on earth, something tells me, and it is better so."

"Father!" she screamed after him, and fell senseless on the red coat he had spurned.

John Parlin strode over the Ridge his feet knew so well; and deadly was every ball he sent at the flying redcoats on the Old Bay Road beneath, harassed and

spent, not knowing where, behind stone wall or tree, in thicket or covert, the invisible enemy were intrenched. With feverish haste he pressed on, loading and firing, and loading again, leaving all along the thoroughfare the dead foe to mark his swift, unerring aim. He only paused a moment when he reached his cottage, and raised his head to look at it, half expecting to find it burned to the ground. There it stood; but the memory of the happy days passed within, and the wreck of the sweet confidence, changed to bitterness and wrath, burned into his soul as he thought of his wife. " She will know that I am true to my country now." He did not dare to trust himself to even look within the small-paned window for the sight of her face for which he longed, despite the abiding scorn and shame he had seen there in many stolen visits in silent remorse, but plunged on to the fight beyond.

They were hotly at work when he came up at Merriam's Corner. The king's troops, vainly endeavoring to keep together and retreat in good order, became surrounded at this point, where the old Bedford road ran into the main thoroughfare, by the Provincials. These made a spirited attack, led on by a tall, square-shouldered, sinewy minute-man, who was in the thickest of the fray. At too short range

sometimes to use his trusty musket, he then employed his fists, that, like sledge-hammers, brought down their man every time. His blue eyes shone; and his hair, tossed back from his brow, disclosed a long sabre cut that had trickled blood all down his homespun clothes. But he knew it not, and felt nothing but exultation running high in his veins, as he endeavored to keep the British from massing together to a successful resistance.

"That's right. At it, Abner! " shouted John Par-lin from the hilltop, and dashing down to his assistance with a yell. The enemy, made desperate by concealed foes, and thinking it the cry of a party of re-enforcements, lost heart in the mad confusion of the moment; and the bloody encounter that ensued, in which the Provincials, surrounding them on all sides, easily picked off their men, resulted in a complete rout of the foe, in which not a farmer was injured.

Abner, at that cry, glanced for a moment in its direction, saw that it was Debby's father, and dealt his blow that felled the scarlet coat before him to the dust, then gathered up his soul with a new gladness as he fought on.

It was an awful struggle. The British moved off, to be caught up by balls from invisible opponents.

380 A LITTLE MAID OF CONCORD TOWN.

laid low in the dust, and trampled, perchance, by mad, on-rushing feet. Into the very teeth of muskets, run out over the stone walls, some plunged to their death, as the farmers dashed ahead to wait for the foe, hurrying on their retreat ; then the assailants would dash ahead to repeat this process, till the brilliant troops were sadly decimated, and reduced to a straggling, chaotic company in flight for their lives. Abner and John Parlin kept together, bound by more than the common tie of love of country. It rejoiced the stalwart young farmer to see that wherever the danger was the greatest and the conflict the thickest, Debby's father was there, his passionate face upturned, his head bare, and in his shirt-sleeves, fiercely waging such an onslaught that the redcoats, at sight of him, ran in dismay. "When it is all over," flashed through Abner's mind in the horrid tumult, " if I live, how I can gladden Debby's heart by the recital, and how proud he will be; " for that such invincible strength could be conquered seemed past belief. The next instant a flashing sword descended on the bare head before him. It was in the hand of an officer, who came up unseen, as Parlin was fighting the soldiers in front of him; and to Ab-ner's horrified vision it seemed to cleave the body from crown to toe. The officer then turned, and ran

to the woods. Abner dealt fury and destruction to all in his path, and ran to kneel and take the poor maimed head of Debby's father upon his breast.

"Tell her and my wife " — as he sighed his life out against the young man's heart, amid the tramp of the departing enemy, leaving them alone on the highway — "that I " — and his eyes glazed.

"All shall be told," said Abner, careless of the danger he was in as he knelt there. "For love of country you die," he added, as the breath left the body. He dragged John Parlin gently to the roadside, and broke off a branch of pine, covering with it the poor, still face, bathed in blood; then he ran off, mad to avenge Debby's father.

Skulking behind every protecting bush and shrub and tree and stone wall, ducking at every step, crept a negro, alternately clasping his trembling black hands and mumbling in fright, and raising a head where the wool had whitened fast, to peer about the spot like a frightened rabbit. It was at the foot of the Ridge, and just a short remove from the Parlin cottage. When Pompey saw where he was (for Pompey it was) he breathed the first sigh of relief for many an hour. "_____, ef I can't creep in yere and rest a bit; I'm all tired to def; an' Massa Abner he give me gun, an' tell me to fight, but I done los it long ago."

Pompey scratched his wool helplessly, unable to satisfy himself why he hadn't fought, or where the gun was now. He only knew he had been caught up, as it were, on the tide of the rushing throng that had swept him like a dark leaf on the swift current down the Old Bay Road, until too scared to attempt a return, he only sought shelter till the hot conflict should be over.

"Pompey," said a voice he wanted least of any in the world to hear. He instinctively ducked, and clapped both black hands over his shins.

"It is I who am at your mercy now," said he who had been the peddler, now the young British officer. He was lying prone upon the ground, at such a short distance removed that the trembling negro must have discovered him before but for the panic into which he was plunged. " Take my gun," he tapped it with his long fingers, — how well Pompey remembered those fingers,— "and, Pompey, take good aim," as the darkey, shaking like a leaf, received the weapon. "Look at me; you are to shoot me through the head — through the head, remember."

"Oh, _____, massa!" exclaimed Pompey, tumbling back in terror; "I couldn't go fer to murder you;" the gun executing nimble movements : . Ms quaking fingers.

" You will do the _____ you _____ exercise more _____ _____, and kill yourself as well," observed the young officer. "Now, listen. I am an enemy of your country, whom it is not only lawful, but it would be a praiseworthy action on your part, to kill. I beseech you, therefore, Pompey, to despatch me at once. I assure you I have no wish to live, and would thank anybody for putting me out of existence," he added bitterly.

" Maybe you ain't much hurt, massa," said Pompey, dropping the gun at a safe distance from the long fingers, and still with a thought for his shins he knelt down in a heap at the young officer's side.

"Ah, Pompey, I am afraid not; 'tis but a trifle in the side here. Never mind the blood; it needs not to be quenched. Listen. I wronged you too. Forgive every kick."

Pompey's shins quivered, and he wriggled them under him. " I fergib ye, massa," he said humbly.

" Can you remember a message, do you think?" suddenly asked the young officer, with a piercing gleam of his dark eyes.

"I specs I kin, ef 'tisn't too long, massa."

"Say after me: MissParlin."

"Is that Miss Debby or her ma?" queried Pompey suddenly.

" Miss Deborah, you black rascal. Don't interrupt; you are to say: Miss Par 1 in."

"You are to say Miss Parlin," repeated Pompey like a parrot.

" No, no," cried the young officer impatiently, and trying to raise himself to his elbow.

"No, no," said the negro, with violent efforts to do it all just right this time.

The young officer sank back, his face growing whiter, and closed his eyes.

"He goin* to die fer shore," groaned Pompey; "then what become o' dis darkey? Maybe de Britishers will tink I killed him. Wake up, massa, don't go an' leave Pompey."

He fairly shook the lithe figure, in his terror.

"Will you tell Miss Deborah Parlin that I never fired a shot at her countrymen, and that I did what I could to undo the wrong I had done? " demanded the young officer, suddenly opening his eyes, and dismissing all hopes of teaching the lesson by repetition.

", I will, massa," promised Pompey, nearly tumbling backward at the sudden resuscitation.

A rushing noise. Stragglers from the enemy, left behind in the flight for safety, now plunged over the road, some of them skirting their thicket. Not knowing who or what they were, but fearing the worst fcr

the negro if discovered, the young officer quickly commanded him to fly into the denser covert.

Pompey's teeth shook in their sockets. ", massa," and his eyes showed little but their margins, "dey'll kill you fer shore! I'll carry you into Miss Debby's." And before Lieutenant Thornton could utter a protest, fright lent such sudden strength that the darkey lifted the young officer in his long arms, pushed open the door with a desperate foot, no longer trembling and uncertain, and laid him on the floor, then softly closed the door and fled.

my life once, yes, twice; give me leave to save yours."

"Thanks be to God if you will let me die," he cried.

"No, we do not so with our enemies," she said gently, her hands moving swiftly over the wound; and bidding a basin of water and a towel to be brought her, she tenderly bathed the blood away till the terror of it grew less.

"Oh, my , you pretty dear ! " cried both Mrs. Butterfield and Pompey as they came noisily in. The farmers, when they saw somebody come with help, hurried off. Debby looked up gratefully. " How good of you," she breathed. "Now you can tell me what to do for this poor man."

Mrs. Butterfield, despite the strain of mercy in her disposition, which was large, could not come up to an expression of delight as she saw the redcoat. When she found that he was a lieutenant of the king's troops, she sniffed out, "Well, I sh'd think 'twas pretty poor taste to come in here, after all you've done to us."

" Madam, I can assure you it was against my will that I came." said Thornton dryly.

" I brung him," said Pompey. " The pesky redcoats

were coming down de road ; an' he tole me to run an' save myself, an' I wasn't goin' to leabe him."

"The redcoats wouldn't have hurt him," said Mother Butterfield grimly, and rolling up her sleeves with an inflow of satisfaction impossible for such a born nurse to conceal.

"I didn't know whether 'twas all redcoats, an' he didn't know but 'twas de minute folks," grumbled Pompey in a discomfited fashion. ', Mis' Butterfield! 'twas one or turrer, an' de Lord hissef couldn't tell; dey's been so mixed up all day."

"Well, they ain't mixed up any longer," declared Mother Butterfield with energy; " and we beat you, young man, whoever you be," nodding to him on the floor.

"I thank the Lord you did," he said, not taking his eyes from Debby.

Mrs. Butterfield dropped everything, then trotted to Debby. "The first thing to be done," and she lifted her like a child and carried her to the sofa, " is to put you here. That man there has gone clean crazy. Pompey an' me will look after him."

"Instead, you may say he has come to a clear mind," said Thornton addressing her, but still looking at Debby. "Now, my good woman, I do not

doubt that you are the best nurse in the world; but if there is a physician in this village, I must see him. Pompey, run your fingers in this pocket." He moved as well as he could, even this effort making his bloodless face whiter yet; and Pompey obeying, though with great awkwardness, at last succeeded in bringing forth a wrought leather purse heavily bound with silver. "Open it," commanded the young lieutenant.

A shower of gold pieces fell to the old kitchen-floor. Pompey's eyes protruded. " Oh, golly, massa! " Mrs. Butterfield endeavored to look indifferent, and as if gold were nothing in her eyes; but the effort could not be called a success. "Take two of those," said Thornton, " and go with all speed to the village, and bring your physician here with some men and a wagon."

"There are dead and dying all around us," said Mrs. Butterfield sharply, at the thought of her nursing faculty gone to waste; "and it ain't likely that Dr. Minott can leave 'em, 'specially when our own townsmen will suffer by it."

"You speak with sense, madam," observed Thornton coolly, "nevertheless, Pompey has his orders. See how quick you can be," to the darkey, who closed his broad thumb over the two pieces of gold, and hurried off. " And now will you be good enough to feel

in this other pocket for me, and get a pencil and a small packet of papers you will find there?"

Mrs, Butterfield got down on her fat knees with a long sigh; and suppressing many more, she finally put the articles into the long fingers, taking special note how exquisite were the skin and nails, in the interval that consumed some time before she regained her perpendicular.

The young British officer turned with great difficulty on his side, and began to write, covering page after page of the paper he took from the packet.

Debby motioned to the matron. "Put a pillow under his head, and prop up his back, do, dear Mrs. Butterfield."

He shot her a grateful glance, although her speech was low, and continued to write, even through Mrs. Butterfield's fussy manipulation of the pillows.

"Have the kindness, my dear madam," he said, folding up the paper, and putting it within the packet, "to return these articles to my pocket. And if anything should happen to me, remember to send the packet to the address on its cover." He looked at Debby as he spoke.

"All shall be done as you wish," she said.

And good Dr. Minott came, but not for the gold, for he did not see it. Long before Pompey got to the

town centre he had lost both pieces, through much turning and returning of them in his thick, awkward fingers. He scrabbled around for them in a fright in the roadside thicket where they had fallen, and at last, in a deadly terror that the young British officer would die before he got back, he left them, and fled precipitately to Dr. Minott's, where he told such a harrowing tale of need for his services that £he good doctor started at once in his gig, with the darkey by his side, for the Parlin cottage. He came none too soon. Death and he had a battle, fierce as any that was waged that day. In the end the doctor was to win, though he knew it not that night.

It was a soft, warm day in early June. Far in the distance seemed now the day when —

"On the rude bridge that arched the flood, Their flag to April's breeze unfurled, Here once th' embattled farmers stood, And fired the shot heard round the world," —

a shot that proclaimed Freedom to be born on Concord plains, by the side of her river of peace.

The wild-flowers had gone long ago; the old robins were flying about careless of their little families that were taking care of themselves by this time; the

earth was fragrant with its sweet increase. The soldier-farmers, vigilant and wary with musket and bayonet for any chance warning, were drilling with renewed zeal; for their victory over the British troops had made them a shining mark for fresh attacks, and never, since that birthday of liberty on their riverside, had they slept on guard. Bitter need would be their portion, they realized, for many w'eary months, and maybe years — sore the privation as the war drew its length. And so they tilled and planted, toiling, as never before, to sustain Me, and the victory so hardly won.

Debby threw wide her window, and looked without. The little birds sang to her their sweetest; she never heeded, although her heart was at peace. Just above, on the Ridge, lay her father at rest. Her mother and herself would have it so, when the fathers of the town begged that he might lie with those others, who had served their day and generation well, in the old hill burying-ground. For his sin had been more than wiped out by his mighty valor on the day of crisis, when he had been terrible for the enemy to look upon, and his good strokes had helped to "hold the town."

"Nay," said Mrs. Parlin, "let him be at home now, where he longed to be. It is his right; and

within sight of the cottage windows shall be his bed of rest."

And so they had brought him hither, after the great victory — brought him from the roadside, all gashed and gory; and nothing that could be done or said for a hero was lacking as they laid him away in his winding-sheet. And good Parson Emerson preached the funeral sermon; and Miliscent and Perces and the other mates of Debby planted the periwinkle above the mound, and watered it with their tears, and brought flowers, and tended the resting-place ceaselessly. And Debby welcomed a glad and peaceful joy stealing into every tired sense. And the mother each day felt the way back to the recovered heart of her young happy wifehood. Had she not John back again, crowned a hero in the eyes of his townsmen, and through with the strain and stress of life? He was hers to worship now, and not do wrong to God or man by so doing. And she could sit beside him on the Ridge ; and he knew all her heart, with no veil or shadow between them. And each dawn was a landmark on the way back to the strength she knew would all be needed in the weary, terrible months and years before her countrymen.

"John, I must live up to you, dear," she would whisper above the grave. "I will be strong so that

I may help forward what you died to get, and not be unworthy of your name."

And the little birds, swaying in the pine branches above her head, cooed and trilled, and made sweet love to their mates.

The other grave on the Ridge was sweet, too, in the cool shade of the benignant forest, under the flowers that Miliscent and Debby planted with gentle hands and pitying tears for the mother over the sea, who had lovingly yearned for her boy to keep good and true and pure. Better perhaps was it that young Herford should rest here safely, where he fell by the hand of Septimius Felton on that day of conflict, than for a longer life to be his, whose light-hearted, boyish spirit was ill-fitted to cope with the sterner issues of life.

And Mother Butterfield, to whom Dr. Minott had consigned the sick British officer when he was able to be moved to the Butterfield farm, was happy and radiant. Added to the Concord victory, was it not the cap-sheaf that she be installed chief nurse, where all her faculties could have free play? And through all his ravings, when the brain fever was at its height, she was placid and benignant.

One day, however, she shut the door hastily. " If Abner heard him now," she said under her breath,

"he might find it in his heart to reproach me for bringing him back to life. Debby is but a girl, and young, pretty things are won by gold. I would he had kept to his British training, and his love to the king, then she'd spurn him like the dust beneath her feet. But now — oh, alack, alack!"

But Abner had heard, albeit she was now so careful, though he gave no sign. And he kept his patient tongue quiet, and hid the tale he had refrained from speaking to the girl, till she had chance to do honor to her father without interruption, and to recover her peaceful heart. When he brought, as hasten he did with it that night after the battle, the grand story of John Parlin's death, he longed to fold her in his arms, with a new story of the great love he bore her. But all was confusion in the Parlin cottage, owing to the pr:sance of the stranger supposed to be dying; and he could get no speech alone with Debby, and her great eyes in the white little face seemed to implore him to be let alone to find peace. So he read them. And since that time he had tried to content himself with doing for her what he could, and biding his time, meaning soon to speak. And now — must it always be a time of renunciation with him? he cried alone in his agony in the forest, where he plunged after hearing the ravings of the young British officer. First, oh,

so long ago,—for he had loved Debby even a little maid in pinafores, — he had given her up in his mind to Jim and the other fellows of their set, who were handsome and cleverer than he; and now, when at last he had a right to show his heart, fate had thrown among them this stranger. Good? yes, Abner knew in his soul that the man was good and pure, and willing to renounce what he saw was an unrighteous cause. And last of all, for to Abner's thinking this would weigh more in Debby's mind than the gold, this redcoat officer had been born and bred in an English home of aristocracy, educated in a British university, and had about him that nameless quality that fascinates the world of men as well as of women.

" My flower! my Debby ! the only woman in the world! shall I speak now ? The queen's palace is not too good for you. Poor fool am I ! " He flung his sinewy, brown arms to heaven, looked at them, and laughed bitterly. " I would not speak now if I knew she would look at me in pity, for she ought to take what God has provided for her. It is her right."

On the ground, in the depth of the forest where he had wandered, he flung himself on his face, for the first time in his life allowing the hours to slip by over his neglected work. When he came back to the

farm he was the same quiet Abner, going in and out, but with more helpful solicitude for Thornton's recovery than before.

"Poor boy! if he only knew," sighed his, mother; and she racked her brain to get him his favorite dishes to eat, and to show him all possible attentions.

And sometimes, when the ravings were very bad, they would have to send for Debby. And it was Abner who went for her in the big green wagon. And she would lay her cool, soft hand on the poor wasted brow, and her tears would fall for the mother or sister in the distant English home, who ought to be in her place, and Abner would rush out to go all over again with the agony and temptation he thought he had conquered. And at last the fever turned; and now, on this soft, warm day in early June, although the young British officer had lingered, the time had arrived when it was no longer seemly to do so.

There were footsteps without, slow, but decided. Mrs. Parlin, with a peaceful smile beneath her white cap, looked up from her spinning. When she saw that it was Thornton (no one called him now "the young British officer," knowing well that the American cause had won him to its side), she smiled. It was one of the strongest reasons for Abner's belief

398 A LITTLE MAID OF CONCORD TOWN.

that Providence willed it for Thornton's love to prevail with Debby, that her mother had long ago bestowed upon the young man that love and sympathy that his Jieart craved. Good Mrs. Butterfield might toil and slave, be up nights on the anxious watch, potter over gruels and other helpful messes for day and night in and out; but let Mrs. Parlin come into the sick-room, and sit there in her white cap, her hands folded in her lap, and smile at him, and say, "You poor boy," and Thornton, ungrateful wretch, grimaced in Mother Butterfield's face at the gruels and the medicines, and lay serene and happy so long as he could see Debby's mother.

Why did she so ? Ah, her John was a hero, enshrined in the heart of the town, and safe, forever at rest. Perhaps, had it not been for the work of this misguided young man, the glory of that eventful day would have been less for the farmer-soldier, slow of purpose and action. And the Englishman but did his duty, he believed; and he was won to the American cause by her Deborah. Should she not devote that brilliant life and gold to the service of her suffering countrymen? Debby might yet be a great lady in the Colonies, and worthy her father's name.

She smiled on Thornton, and bade him be seated. He came close to the spinning-wheel, and held her

with his intense eyes. "I have your permission to speak?" he asked feverishly.

'•'Yes." She knew he was weak and still sick, and words should be few. " I will call Debby; " and after she had done so she hastened to John's grave, glad that their daughter was to meet her sweet, victorious womanhood.

It was the same room — the keeping-room — into which he had been laid, and where Debby had knelt to him, tending his wound, to which he had now brought the heart that had so long been hers, to put it at her feet. She stood before him, her clear blue eyes raised to his, and her sweet face still pale. But the mouth was firm in its curves.

"I am glad you are better," she said gently. "Do not stand; you are still weak."

"Instead, I would kneel at your feet from henceforth," he said feebly. "Miss Parlin, I need not many words to tell you why I come to you to-day. My ravings have spoken my heart; good Mrs. Butter-field has confessed it."

She put up her brown hand, thin and shapely, but his great will mastered her to silence.

"No; I must speak. For my crime against your father " —

"Speak not of that," she interrupted him; "our

400 A LITTLE MAW OF CONCORD TOWN.

hearts are at rest. And I have a crime against you, nay, many, that I wish you to forgive." The kerchief on her bosom rose and fell with her quick breathing. "I was unjust and cruel when you did what you thought your duty, and I would that you forgave me."

He could not speak, yet he would not so much as trust himself to touch her hand. His iron will must master every impulse until his tale of love had been told.

"Ah, you cannot forgive me!" said Debby sadly.

He turned on her then, and burst forth, his plans of speech all scattered, "Cannot forgive?" his great eyes burned into hers with a devotion that stirred her very heart and soul to its depths, his thin white face worked with the passion that knows not the need of words. "Deborah, come to me, if you can. Have pity, and come." He flung wide his arms. "All — all I have and am is yours, and the Cause you love."

One instant, — not hesitation for the fame and the gold, the brilliant career of a leading lady in the Colonies, nor the pride of the handsome scion of an old English family won to her and to her cause, but only to consult her woman's heart how gently to strike the blow.

"I will throw myself on your mercy," her lips

were tremulous now, "so that you may see that God will not let me take your love. My heart has been another's for long, long years; and oh! have pity on me, for I am like you,— he loves me not." She stood there, in her womanly shame, the pink glow over her face, her appealing eyes raised to his face.

He had time to gather himself up; and he cried hoarsely, " Now may God have mercy on me, and help me to do his will." He reverently bent and touched her brow with his lips.

The next day he sailed from Boston Harbor. Close to his heart lay the writing on the packet, in which he had transferred, in case of his expected death, his English estate to the little Maid of Concord Town, to be recorded in proper shape as soon as his foot touched his native soil. No wife nor children should be his, he had sworn in his empty heart; and the struggling Colonies that she had lived for, ay, was living for yet, should some time be the richer for his sojourn among them.

The grave on the Ridge was soft in the moonlight. Debby laid her heated face against it. "Father," she mourned, " comfort my mother for her sore disappointment. I cannot bear to look in her eyes. O Abner!"

It was as if she called him, yet she had spoken never a word; for there he stood, as she raised her

head, standing on the other side of the grave, tall and still.

Debby sprang to her feet. " Abner! " she gasped, laying her hand on her beating heart, " when did you come ? "

He did not seem to hear. He only stretched his hands out to her. And the little Maid of Concord Town went within them, and laid her head upon his breast.

"His parting words to me were, 'She loves you,'" he said at last, when words began to be spoken between them. " O Debby! what have you given up for me?"

She drew away a bit to look into his steady brown eyes, —

"Instead, I have gained all, for my heart came to life in Concord Town, Abner," she said, her blue eyes shining into his.

THE END

APPENDIX. I.

THE framed manuscript copy of this letter, to which the scissors are appended, hangs in the Public Library at Concord.

BRONXVILLB, N. Y., March 24, 1875.

CHARLES THOMPSON, ESQ. ;

Dear Sir, — About one hundred and one years ago, Dr. Warren sent a young man, his nephew by marriage, Joseph Swain, son of Rev. Joseph Swain, of Wenham, to Concord, to take charge of the rebel armory. After repairing the guns generally in use, he attempted to make some new ones. For this purpose he returned to Salem, to the edge-tool factory of Mrs. Proctor, where he had previously had charge, and secured such tools as were to be had; and among them this anvil, which I now, through you, present to the town of Concord. On this anvil the first gun-barrel was welded in Concord.

Colonel James Barrett and his son James had, during the French war, furnished, through the commissary department in Boston, oatmeal and some other provisions. This continued on until near 1774. It was a common occurrence for a young staff officer to come to Concord on this business, and, while waiting a reply, would amuse himself by talking loyalty with James Barrett's oldest daughter, Meliscent, to hear her rebel replies. He asked her what they would do if it should become necessary for the Colonies to resist, as there was not a person who even knew how

APPENDIX.

to make cartridges. She replied that they would use their powder-horns and bullets, just as they shot bears. "That," says the young man, " would be too barbarous; give me a piece of pine, and I will show you how." After whittling the stick to the proper form, he took these scissors, which I now present to the town of Concord, and cut the paper for the pattern cartridge.

The sequel shows how apt a scholar she was, for all the cartridges were made under her superintendence by the young ladies of Concord; her only male assistant was her younger brother, the late Major James Barrett, who drove the last load of cartridges from the house after the British came in sight on the igih of April, 1775. After the war, Joseph Swain returned to Concord, and married Meliscent Barrett, and took these relics to Halifax, Vt., where I came in possession of them.

Yours,

JAMES P. SWAIN.

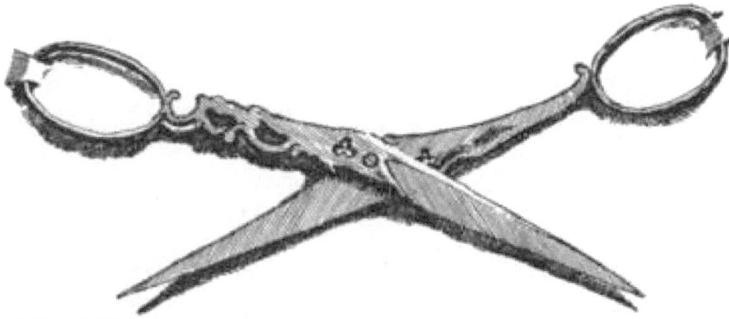

MELISCENT BARRETT'S SCISSORS. (Now in the Public Library, Concord.)

NOTE. — The name " Miliscent" is spelled in various ways in different documents and genealogical records. The author has chosen the one given above. " Meriam " was the old way of spelling this family name, now written " Merriam."

Made in United States
Troutdale, OR
07/10/2025

32813258R00084